Road Trip
with a
Rogue

BY KATE BATEMAN

HER MAJESTY'S REBELS

Second Duke's the Charm
How to Fall for a Scoundrel
Road Trip with a Rogue

RUTHLESS RIVALS

A Reckless Match
A Daring Pursuit
A Wicked Game

BOW STREET BACHELORS

This Earl of Mine
To Catch an Earl
The Princess and the Rogue

Road Trip
with a
Rogue

KATE BATEMAN

St. Martin's Paperbacks

First published in the United States by St. Martin's Paperbacks, an imprint of St. Martin's Publishing Group.

EU Representative: Macmillan Publishers Ireland Ltd., 1st Floor, The Liffey Trust Centre, 117-126 Sheriff Street Upper, Dublin 1, DO1 YC43, Ireland.

ROAD TRIP WITH A ROGUE

Copyright © 2025 by Kate Bateman.

All rights reserved.

For information, address St. Martin's Publishing Group, 120 Broadway, New York, NY 10271.

www.stmartins.com

ISBN: 978-1-250-90738-7

Our books may be purchased in bulk for specialty retail/wholesale, literacy, corporate/premium, educational, and subscription box use. Please contact MacmillanSpecialMarkets@macmillan.com.

Printed in the United States of America

St. Martin's Paperbacks edition / August 2025

10 9 8 7 6 5 4 3 2 1

For Carrie, who loves the word *defenestration*.
Here you go, Bob.

*The road was a ribbon of moonlight over the purple
moor,
And the highwayman came riding—
Riding—riding—
The highwayman came riding, up to the old inn-door.*

. . .

*"One kiss, my bonny sweetheart, I'm after a prize
to-night,
But I shall be back with the yellow gold before the
morning light;
Yet, if they press me sharply, and harry me through
the day,
Then look for me by moonlight,
Watch for me by moonlight,
I'll come to thee by moonlight, though hell should
bar the way."*

—ALFRED NOYES,
"THE HIGHWAYMAN"

Chapter One

Hampstead Heath, London, April 1817.

Daisy Hamilton had been looking forward to her first highway robbery, but someone had beaten her to it. Several someones, in fact.

Bloody Hell.

The three men blocking the moonlit road had clearly identified this wood-lined stretch as the perfect place for an ambush—just as she had—but while their decision to hold up this particular coach was presumably random, the crest painted on the door singled it out as her specific target.

She had the worst luck.

Daisy slid silently from her horse, tied the reins to a branch, and crept forward for a better view, careful to stay within the cover of the trees.

A broken log had been dragged across the lane to force the coach to stop, and the burly coachman up on the box was cursing as he tried to control the plunging horses. Two highwaymen had positioned themselves in the middle of the track with pistols drawn, while the third had circled around to the rear of the carriage.

"Stand and deliver!" the foremost robber bellowed.

The coachman paid him no heed. The horses reared, pawing the air, as he fought with the reins. When he finally managed to control them, he shouted, "Move aside, damn you!"

Daisy raised her brows at his tone. He sounded more annoyed than intimidated. Perhaps he'd encountered thieves on this route before? Or perhaps he was an ex-soldier, a veteran, no stranger to threats of violence. Even so, his bravado was unwise, considering the odds of three to one.

She doubted he'd be getting any help from inside the coach. Spoiled eighteen-year-old heiress Violet Brand and nineteen-year-old Peregrine Hughes were eloping—a process Daisy had been engaged to stop. Being set upon by highwaymen could hardly have featured in their plans. Violet was probably having a fit of the vapors in there, and a pampered youth like Peregrine had probably never fired a pistol in his life.

Daisy's lips twitched in dark amusement. The idiots *deserved* to be robbed. Who went out into the world so unprepared? She felt naked without at least two blades on her person at any given time. Even in a ballroom.

Still, she cursed her own hubris for telling Ellie and Tess that she could catch the runaways on her own. Her fellow investigators would have been most welcome right now, since she was obviously going to have to intervene in this farcical scene.

She was bloody well going to double her fee when she sent Violet's father the bill from King & Co.

Daisy cocked her pistol, waiting to see what the highwaymen would do next, when the driver of the coach suddenly lurched to the side and grabbed something near his feet. He straightened, a huge blunderbuss in his hands, and fired at the nearest robber just as the man gave a shout of alarm.

The explosion was blinding, and she ducked instinctively as the man's companion returned fire, shattering the quiet of the night.

Bloody Hell!

She blinked as her vision cleared. The first robber lay lifeless on the ground, his horse galloping away down the road. The second man was struggling to reload his pistol as his own mount bucked and reared, and the brave coachman had been hit; he was clutching his arm and groaning in pain, slumped sideways on the seat.

"You shot Ned, ye bastard!" The rider who'd been behind the coach galloped forward with a shout. He aimed his pistol at the coachman's back to deliver a fatal shot, and Daisy didn't stop to think. She leveled her own weapon and fired.

Her ball struck the rider, and his shot went wide, splintering the side of the carriage. He tumbled from his horse in a blur of limbs and dark clothing, hitting the ground with a sickening thump, but there was no time to check if he was dead.

The last man abandoned his attempt to reload and leapt from his horse, stumbling toward the gun that his fallen companion had dropped. If he reached it, the coachman was dead.

Daisy threw down her own spent pistol, pulled a knife from the sheath at the back of her belt, and stepped out into the road.

"Don't touch it!" she commanded, lowering the register of her voice to sound more masculine.

The man in the road froze, surprised by the appearance

of an unexpected third party from the bushes. Daisy raised the blade so it glinted threateningly in the moonlight, glad of the tricorn hat hiding her face and the scarf she'd pulled up over her nose and chin. She was dressed as a male—high boots, breeches, and an enveloping greatcoat—but with her wobbly voice and short stature she doubted she cut a particularly menacing figure.

Her opponent clearly came to the same conclusion. He made a scoffing sound.

"Stand aside, lad. This ain't no business o' yours."

"I disagree. I can't let you to hold up this coach."

He snorted. "You're barely old enough to shave. Go on, now. This is our patch."

Daisy shrugged. "Don't make me hurt you."

The man gave an ugly laugh. "As if you could, whelp." He started toward the gun again.

"Stop!" Daisy growled. "I've killed with this knife before. I'll do it again."

The man stilled, weighing the truth of her words. She was lying, of course. She'd never killed anyone, with any weapon—unless the man she'd just shot by the coach was dead. Her stomach lurched at the thought, but she forced her hand not to shake.

"Move away, slowly," she ordered.

The man pulled back, but just as she started to relax, his friend by the coach regained consciousness. He groaned and writhed, kicking his heels in the mud, and in the brief moment her attention was diverted, the other man seized his chance.

He lunged for the pistol.

Daisy threw her knife just as he fired. She dived to the side as the ball whizzed past her ear, horribly close, and in her confused state she thought she heard *two* shots, one from in front of her, and one from behind.

That made no sense. She rolled over in the grass, her heart pounding furiously, then pushed up onto her elbows to see if she'd hit her target.

She had. The man was lying flat on the ground, her knife embedded in his shoulder. But why wasn't he moving? The wound she'd inflicted shouldn't have been fatal. She'd only meant to make him drop the gun. Was he pretending to be dead to lure her closer?

Fully expecting a trick, she pushed to her feet and staggered toward him, staying low. But his chest was still, not rising and falling, and she gasped in horror as she got close enough to see his glassy eyes staring up at the sky.

He was dead, shot in the neck. A dark puddle of blood was already filling the muddy rut below him.

A wave of nausea rose in her throat. She tugged down the scarf covering her face, clapped her hand over her mouth, and swung away, trying to make sense of what had just happened. Had the driver on the box fired a second weapon? It seemed unlikely. He was still cursing and trying to bind his injured arm.

She turned to the man on the ground by the carriage. Had he pulled another pistol and tried to shoot her, only to miss and accidentally hit his colleague?

No. He'd lost consciousness again, and there was no gun on the ground near him.

Daisy shook her head, feeling dizzy. Her heart was beating so quickly she could feel it in her throat, and she sucked in a deep lungful of the cold night air to steady herself.

A noise came from the carriage, and she belatedly remembered the existence of the two passengers. Dear Lord, they must be frightened out of their wits! She took a step toward the vehicle, ready to reassure them, but her attention caught on the glint of a pistol protruding from the darkened window, held in a large, gloved male hand.

She stopped, surprised. Had Peregrine managed to load and fire one of the carriage pistols? Had *he* been the one to kill the third man?

The door handle turned. She opened her mouth to thank him for his unexpected help, but the words died in her throat as the panel swung open and a tall, dark figure that was definitely *not* Peregrine Hughes stepped down into the road.

Daisy's stomach dropped, and a wave of horrified disbelief swept over her as she took in the man dressed entirely in black, save for a pristine white evening shirt and cravat.

Oh, shit.

Shit. Shit. Shit.

Dark hair, broad shoulders, straight nose. Eyes as black as Hades, and full, mocking lips. She knew that face; its cruel beauty was engraved into her heart.

Lucien Vaughan. Marquis of Exton.

Daisy shook her head. *No, not the marquis anymore.* His father had died, sometime last year. He was the duke now. The Duke of Cranford.

Standing in the road.

What in God's name was he doing here?

She was about to ask him that very question when a twig snapped behind her. Startled, she started to turn, instinctively reaching for her second knife, sheathed on the inside of her wrist, but before she could reach it a thick arm wrapped around her shoulder and came across her throat in a chokehold.

She gasped and tried to free herself, kicking and wriggling like an eel, but the pressure of the arm only increased. The man behind her squeezed, lifting her off the ground, pressing his fingers into the side of her neck, and she opened her eyes wide, trying to fight off the encroaching darkness.

Bloody Hell. What a stupid way to die.

And in front of Vaughan too. How utterly humiliating.

She had no hope that *he* would save her. He was a villain, despite his glittering military career. He'd save his own skin at the expense of hers.

Daisy kicked weakly against her assailant, but all the strength had left her limbs and a dark wave of fatalistic humor seized her. The last thing she saw before the darkness swallowed her was Lucien Vaughan's sinfully handsome face.

It had a pleasing kind of symmetry, she supposed. He'd haunted her dreams for years. Perhaps, if he watched her die, she'd haunt his.

She bloody well hoped so.

Chapter Two

Lucien William Devereaux Vaughan, the twelfth Duke of Cranford, glanced down at the unconscious woman in the road, then back up at his faithful—if somewhat overenthusiastic—valet.

"You didn't need to strangle her, Finch," he said coolly. "You could have just held her arms to restrain her."

Lucien frowned as he crouched down beside her and tried to still the uncharacteristic pounding of his heart. Few things managed to increase his heart rate anymore, but the female before him had always managed it, even against his will.

Daisy Hamilton. He'd recognized her the moment he'd heard her voice.

She was still breathing; she'd come round in a moment or two. He'd seen Finch use that same move countless times to incapacitate an enemy, and he knew precisely the amount of pressure to employ, but that knowledge didn't seem to prevent Lucien from worrying, apparently.

Finch gave an unapologetic shrug and dipped his chin

to indicate the lethal-looking knife that had fallen from her hand.

"You saw what she did to that bastard before you put a hole in 'im." He gestured toward the body lying in the road with her knife embedded in its arm. "I didn't think it wise to underestimate her."

Lucien grunted in reluctant agreement, even as his gaze roamed over her features as if he'd been starved of the sight of her. Her wild mop of curly brown hair was the same as ever, unsuccessfully restrained by a black ribbon at the back of her neck. Her skin was pale in the moonlight, her eyebrows dark, but he could see the sprinkle of freckles that peppered her nose, and the lush perfection of her lips.

His body heated. He'd kissed those lips. Five years ago, now. And God, if it hadn't been one of the best and worst nights of his life.

He was glad her eyes were closed. Something strange always happened to him whenever their eyes met: he experienced a tightening in his chest, an instant rush of desire that turned his cock to iron. It was infuriating. No other woman had ever had the same effect.

She'd been pretty at eighteen, before he'd left for war. An impetuous wide-eyed beauty just shimmering on the edge of womanhood. Now, at twenty-three, she was enough to stop a man's heart.

He'd glimpsed her a few times, briefly, at various social functions since he'd been back in England, but he'd never allowed himself to approach her. Like an alcoholic who knew he couldn't be trusted to look at a tumbler of whisky without needing a sip—and then the whole bottle—he'd stayed far away from her. He simply hadn't needed the aggravation.

Had he occasionally imagined her beneath him while he was fucking a dark-haired courtesan? Yes. Had he once accidentally breathed her name while debauching his mistress? Yes again.

But those were perfectly acceptable substitutions. The *only* safe scenarios in which he would allow himself to think of Daisy Hamilton.

She was not for him. Not back then, and certainly not now.

Thanks to her brothers, he knew she worked as some sort of private investigator, but he'd resisted the urge to learn more. She was his curse, not his salvation, and he'd been right to let her go. It had been for the best. Noble, even. But regret still scorched his veins as he remembered his deliberately cruel rejection of her.

If the horrified look she'd given him just before she lost consciousness was any indication, she'd neither forgotten, nor forgiven, that particular episode either.

Bloody Hell.

What in God's name was she doing *here*?

Cursing himself for a fool, he gave in to the temptation to touch her. At least he was wearing gloves. His leather-covered thumb stroked her cheek as he cupped the back of her head, gently cradling her skull, while his other hand tugged impatiently at the handkerchief tied at her throat to allow her to breathe.

He suppressed a dark laugh. Daisy being unconscious was the only way he'd ever get the chance to undress her.

His heart gave a relieved thump as she stirred. He released her and leaned back on his haunches, trying not to loom, as her eyelids fluttered and she took a deep gulp of air. Her eyes opened, and for a brief minute the world fell away as she stared up at him in complete incomprehension. She looked dreamy, delightfully confused.

He knew the exact moment she recognized him: her lips parted in a gasp and she reached for her knife.

Finch, thankfully, had removed it, because Lucien was certain she would have stabbed him in the heart without a second thought.

"You!" Her voice was a croak, but full of loathing. "What are you doing here?"

Lucien schooled his face into the expression of bored indifference he'd perfected over the years. "I could ask you the same thing, *Dorothea*."

She scowled at his deliberate use of her full name—she'd always despised it—and he bit back a smile. God, he'd forgotten how much he loved teasing her. It had always been his favorite guilty pleasure.

"It's Daisy," she said, pushing herself to a seated position. "And I asked first."

He rose and stepped back, not trusting himself near her now that she was fully conscious.

"A man can travel in his own carriage, can't he? What are *you* up to, dressed like that, and interrupting a highway robbery? Are you mad? Does your father know the danger you're getting yourself into?"

"I don't suppose he'd care."

"He certainly would, if his only daughter turns up dead by the roadside dressed as a stable boy," he said. "And what about your brothers? I can't imagine they'd approve of such idiocy. God, I ought to spank you for being such a fool."

A splash of red stained her cheeks as she glared up at him. "Don't you touch me. What I do is none of your business."

She started to stand. He put his hand down automatically to help her, but she batted it away. "Get off. I'm fine."

"You're not," he retorted. "And you became my business when you showed up here, ruining my night."

"I just saved your life, you ungrateful beast!" She glanced behind her at the bodies lying in the road and shuddered. "If I hadn't stepped in you would have been shot."

He raised his brows. "You think so?"

She frowned, clearly realizing that her help might have been unnecessary. Despite the fact that Geordie, his coachman, had been wounded, he and Finch had been more than capable of dealing with the interruption.

"Why did you intervene?" he pressed. "You certainly didn't know it was me in there."

"Of course not," she said bitterly. "If I'd known it was *you*, I'd have ridden in the opposite direction. I thought the coach belonged to someone else."

"Who?"

"It doesn't matter. Where are my knives?" She tried to move past him, but he blocked her with an easy sidestep. She scowled as she encountered the expanse of his chest, but didn't come close enough to touch him. Wise girl.

"Finch has them."

He nodded to Finch, who'd reclaimed her second blade from the corpse's shoulder and was busy dragging the bodies to the side of the road with his usual brisk efficiency.

She held out her hand, palm upward. "Give them back."

Finch glanced at him for permission, but Lucien shook his head. "Not just yet." He turned to the box, keeping her in his peripheral vision as he did so. He didn't trust her not to try to run while his attention was elsewhere. His hand itched to grab her wrist to detain her, but he resisted.

"How badly are you hit, Geordie?"

His old army mate gave a grunt of annoyance. "Bastard got me near the elbow. I've bound it up, but the ball's lodged in there. It's going to need to come out."

Lucien nodded. "Move over, then. Finch can drive us to the nearest inn. Where are we exactly?"

"Just to the north of Hampstead Heath," Daisy supplied, irritation clear in her tone. "Barnet's about four miles that way."

He glanced down at her. She really was incredibly small. Barely up to his shoulder. It was a miracle Finch hadn't done any permanent damage to that pretty neck of hers. The thought made him a little queasy.

"Good. In that case, why don't you get in the carriage while we move that log?"

Her recoil was almost comical. "What? No. I'm not going anywhere with you."

He sent her a cynical look. "You are if I say you are."

"My horse is just over there." She gestured vaguely into the woods. "I'll be off as soon as your man returns my knives."

"You think I'm going to leave you here, alone, in the middle of the night?"

"I do indeed."

"So you can get yourself raped, killed, or worse, while making your way back to London? I don't think so."

"I don't see what could be worse than being raped or killed."

"That's because you haven't lived through a war. There's worse. Far worse. Believe me."

She let out a low growl of frustration. "You can't force me to go with you."

He smiled, showing his teeth. "I think I can." He deliberately let his eyes roam over her body and enjoyed the angry flush that rose to her cheeks. "You weigh less than a wet rat. You can either get in that coach by yourself, or I'll pick you up and put you in there."

Her eyes widened in outrage, and amusement flashed through him at her impotent fury. Her gaze flicked down to his hands as she clearly imagined them on her body, and a jolt of arousal clenched his belly. He ignored it.

"Fine. But let me go get my pistol and my horse."

She was as transparent as a window. "No. I'll get them. I'm not having you galloping off on your own."

"I got here on my own," she ground out. "And if I have my knives and my pistol, I'll be perfectly capable of dealing with whatever comes my way."

"The same way you dealt with Finch?" he mocked.

She narrowed her eyes. "I was distracted."

"And overpowered," he said, just to rub it in. "And then unconscious. A less noble man would have taken advantage."

"Noble!" she scoffed. "That's not a word I'd ever use to describe you."

"No? You're alive and unmolested. You should be glad I'm such a saint. I didn't even search you while you were insensible."

She looked ready to slap him, and he bit back a laugh. "In any case, I owe it to your brothers not to let you endanger yourself any more tonight. Or to let you terrorize anyone else on the King's Highway, for that matter."

The comment clearly reminded her of the man she'd shot. She turned and walked the few paces to where he lay on the grassy verge, then bent and cautiously pressed her fingers to his neck, checking for a pulse. She let out a relieved sigh when he moved and moaned.

She glanced back over her shoulder. "He's not dead."

"Want me to finish him off?" Lucien drawled, just to be provoking. It was clear she was suffering an horrific amount of guilt at the fact that she'd shot the bastard.

"What? No! Of course not."

"Why not? He would have killed you without a second thought."

"That's not the point. Killing him would make me just as bad as him."

Lucien shrugged, enjoying playing devil's advocate. "I've killed so many men I've lost count. One more won't make any difference."

She sent him a look of utter loathing.

"He'll hang for highway robbery anyway, if he's caught by the authorities."

"I'm not leaving him here to die," she said fiercely.

"Well, he's bloody well not coming in my carriage. My charity only extends to rescuing damsels in distress—no matter how ungrateful and undeserving they are."

She glared at him, as if she could burn him to ash with the heat of her eyes alone, and he let out a put-upon sigh. "Fine. Finch can bandage him up and we'll send someone back for him when we get to an inn. Does that please your majesty?"

"I suppose that's acceptable."

He gestured back toward the carriage. "Get in."

Clearly realizing she'd been outmaneuvered, at least for now, she tugged open the door and climbed up the step.

A primitive flash of satisfaction swept through him at having her in his clutches, but Lucien ignored it. Careful to keep one eye on the coach, in case she tried to slip out the opposite side door—as Finch had done to ambush her earlier—he helped drag the log out of the road, tied her horse to the back of the carriage, and slipped her pistol into his jacket pocket from where he found it in the under-growth.

Finch tied a tourniquet around the surviving brigand's thigh; the man wouldn't bleed to death before help arrived, but Lucien hoped he'd forever walk with a limp. It was the least the bastard deserved.

He glanced back over at the coach and shook his head. Daisy Hamilton was the last person he'd expected to encounter tonight, and a part of him was irritated with fate for shoving her into his path yet again.

A larger, less rational, part of him was disturbingly glad to have her back in his orbit. She'd always been a thorn in his side, but he must be a glutton for punishment because the prospect of being close to her, of sparring with her again, was one he was anticipating with an unholy amount of glee.

She was sitting inside, arms crossed defensively across her chest, when he stepped in and tossed the hat she'd lost in the melee onto her lap. She caught it, but didn't thank him as he lowered himself onto the seat across from her.

Finch climbed up onto the box next to Geordie, and the carriage jolted as he urged the horses forward.

She did not look pleased to be alone with him in an enclosed space, and Lucien suppressed a dark smile. That made two of them. But for entirely different reasons.

He crossed his own arms, mirroring her pose, and stretched his legs out toward her so she was forced to draw her feet back to avoid contact.

"So, explain why you're loitering in the woods at midnight," he demanded. "A duke's daughter shouldn't need to resort to robbery. What's this all about?"

Chapter Three

Daisy's heart pounded against her breastbone as she stared at her unwelcome companion. A lamp set in the wall illuminated the interior, and the warm glow highlighted his dark features with disturbing clarity.

Her throat hurt from where his man had strangled her, but she could only have been unconscious for a few seconds. Vaughan probably hadn't had time to find the knife she'd slipped into her boot. That was some small comfort. She hated feeling at a disadvantage, especially with him.

He was even more intimidating in such close proximity. His body seemed to take up most of the velvet seat, and her stomach somersaulted as his masculine scent enveloped her. It was dark and delicious, like a sandalwood-scented forest, and a sudden memory caught her like a punch to the chest: of him pressed against her, his fingers in her hair, his lips at her throat.

She closed her eyes and took a deep breath through her mouth to banish the image.

When he moved, she flinched instinctively, raising her hand as if to parry a blow, and his brows lifted in amusement.

"So defensive."

She scowled. He obviously didn't see her as any kind of threat. "I can do that same chokehold, you know. Devlin taught it to me. It's not all about superior size and weight. You just need to apply the right amount of pressure in exactly the right place."

The corner of his lips quirked. "You think you could take *me* with it?"

Her skin heated at the thought of putting her hands on him, of feeling his broad back pressed hard against her chest, but she shook her head.

"Only if I managed to catch you by surprise. You're stronger and heavier. If you decide to overpower me, there's not much I can do about it, without my knives. Although I'd hope to give you a black eye and a bloody nose for your trouble, at least. I have no qualms about fighting dirty."

His dark eyes studied her, as if she were some bizarre oddity, and she fought not to squirm.

"I'm not going to attack you, Hamilton. I prefer more subtle ways to get what I want."

That was hardly reassuring.

"So, why are you here?" he repeated.

Daisy sighed. There was no reason not to tell him, she supposed. "It's a case I'm working on for King and Company. We've been hired to stop the elopement of a young lady and return her to the bosom of her family." She frowned. "She was supposed to have been in *this* carriage. With a golden lion on the door."

His chin dipped and he drummed his black-gloved fingers on his knee. "A case of mistaken identity, then. My ducal crest includes a golden lion."

Daisy shrugged. "When we get to Barnet I'll ask if

they've already passed by. If not, I'll wait for them and force them to return."

"You'd ruin the happiness of two people desperately in love?" His tone was deeply cynical.

"Her family doesn't approve. She's an heiress—Violet Brand. Her father doesn't want the scandal of an elopement. He thinks the man she's chosen is a fortune hunter."

Vaughan looked supremely disinterested. "What if they're already ahead of you? I assume if they're eloping, they're heading for the Scottish border. Gretna Green, most likely. You can't possibly ride your horse all that way."

Daisy slumped in her seat—something that was far easier to do when wearing breeches than a skirt. "I don't intend to. Even if they've already passed Barnet, I'm sure I can overtake them before the next staging post."

His mouth curved. "You plan to force them back at pistol-point, do you?"

"If they won't cooperate. Or I'll think of a way to sabotage their carriage."

"And they call *me* a heartless monster," he snorted.

She glared at him. "They call you a heartless monster because you killed a man in cold blood before you even left for war."

Her harsh words fell between them like a shock of icy water, and she cursed her impetuous tongue. She held her breath, expecting a vicious, cutting response, but while his jaw hardened, he merely shrugged.

"That's true enough."

She waited for him to elaborate, to explain the circumstances that had caused the rumors to swirl about him all those years ago, but he seemed in no mood to relieve her curiosity.

In truth, she hadn't expected him to. He'd always been content to let the gossips say what they liked about him. If anything, he'd seemed to enjoy cultivating his dark and dangerous reputation.

He rested his arm along the back of the padded seat and let his gaze roam over her. Daisy forced herself not to fidget under his intense regard, even though her skin prickled uncomfortably.

She raised her chin. Let him look. She wasn't the naive debutante who'd thrown herself at him five years ago. She was older, wiser, and considerably more cynical. He'd taught her a painful, but valuable, lesson: love was for children and fools.

The tone of the carriage wheels changed as they emerged from the forest and joined the cobbled street that led into Barnet, and she let out an inaudible sigh of relief. She wouldn't have to endure Vaughan's stifling presence for much longer.

When they pulled in to the first inn, a white-painted place called The Mitre, she tucked her hair up under her hat, pulled the rim down low, and left the carriage with unseemly haste.

Vaughan climbed down languidly after her, and watched as his manservant helped the wounded coachman down from the box and into the taproom. He shook his head when the hostler offered to change the horses, but Daisy took the opportunity to question the man before he returned to the stables.

"I don't suppose another carriage has come through here recently? With a golden lion on the door?"

The man scratched his bushy beard. "Happen there was one, but it didn't stop. It were going at a right lick too. Nearly hit old Nelson, there."

He pointed to an ancient-looking hound that was curled up on a mound of hay.

Daisy's spirits dropped. "How long ago was that?"

"An hour, mebbe more?" He shrugged and yawned.

Daisy cursed inwardly. She'd missed them; they must have been just ahead of Vaughan's carriage, and they probably wouldn't need to change horses until Hatfield. She'd have to ride another fifteen miles at least.

It was going to be a bloody long night.

She stalked back to Hero, her chestnut mare, glad to see that Vaughan hadn't removed her leather saddlebags, but before she could untie her from the back of the carriage he appeared out of the darkness.

"What do you think you're doing?"

"Going after Violet. She and Peregrine have already passed through."

"I thought I'd explained this. You're not going anywhere alone at this hour."

Daisy tried to calm her temper. "You have no say in anything I choose to do, *Your Grace*." She spat the title at him like a curse. "You're neither my father nor my husband."

"Thank God," he drawled.

She wondered if she could reach high enough to punch him. It wouldn't have much effect, but it would feel incredibly satisfying. "Stand aside."

He shook his head. "You always were a stubborn little thing."

She clenched her fist, and he smiled, holding up his hands in a placating gesture. "Wait! I have a proposition."

"What?"

"It's clear that you're determined to catch the runaways."

"I am."

"Then let me help you."

Daisy snorted in disbelief. "You? Help me? Why on earth would you do that? Don't expect me to believe you possess a single shred of decency."

His teeth flashed in a smile. "Oh, certainly not. I'm famed for my indecency, am I not? But I also like to be entertained, and helping you might relieve a little of my boredom."

"Was being held up by highwaymen not exciting enough?" she countered acidly.

"A mere skirmish. And besides, I'm already heading in that direction."

"Why?"

"I'm going north to visit one of my holdings, up past Harrogate."

Daisy squinted, trying to read his features in the poor light cast by the inn's lanterns. Was he lying? And if so, why? It couldn't possibly be because he wanted the pleasure of her company. He could have approached her any time in the past year to renew their acquaintance, and he hadn't bothered.

She'd ignored the bitter sting of rejection.

"If you're thinking of claiming the reward for yourself, you can think again. That money's mine."

"How much is it?"

"Five hundred pounds."

He rolled his eyes. "I wager ten times that amount every night at cards."

Daisy ground her teeth. He was probably telling the truth. He was a duke, for heaven's sake, at least as rich as her own father. Five hundred pounds might be a fortune to her, vital to ensuring her continued independence, but it was pocket change for him. She remembered

Devlin once telling her he'd made a fortune on the Exchange too.

"I'm not here to entertain you, Vaughan. I'm here to do my job." She bit her lip and cursed her limited options. Trying to escape him now would be almost impossible, so she might as well pretend to capitulate. When he dropped his guard, she could go on her way.

She stuck out her hand for him to shake. "But fine. I accept your offer."

He studied her face for an endless moment, as if he didn't trust her sudden reasonableness, but then his long fingers wrapped around hers and squeezed.

Daisy's breath hitched as she felt the power of his grip, and she sent up a silent prayer of thanks that he was wearing gloves. The thought of touching his bare skin made her a little lightheaded.

She turned and climbed back into his coach.

Chapter Four

Daisy leaned her head back against the luxurious velvet seat and tried to quash the jittery impatience plaguing her. Allowing Vaughan to escort her to Hatfield was the sensible thing to do. She *would* be safer with him than alone on horseback, and it would be foolish to refuse his help simply because he made her uncomfortable. She would accost the two runaways, take them back to London, and rejoice in the satisfaction of another job well done.

Vaughan had stalked into the inn to check on his coachman—and hopefully to keep his word about sending someone back for the highwayman she'd shot. She felt awful for hurting another human being, but she would have felt even worse if she'd done nothing to prevent the coachman's cold-blooded execution.

She closed her eyes, striving for calm, but every inhalation brought with it the ghost of Vaughan's scent, and with a groan she allowed herself to remember that fateful night five years ago.

She doubted Vaughan even recalled it. The women he'd kissed probably all blurred into one another, but it had been one of the most significant events of her life. The details were etched into her brain with cut-glass clarity.

The blame was doubtless hers. She'd been fascinated by him from the first moment she'd seen him at one of the wild parties her brothers had hosted at Hollyfield. At sixteen, she'd been told to stay in her room, but she'd always chafed at obeying orders. Besides, she was only looking. No harm in that.

She'd lingered in the shadows of the upper gallery to spy on the revelry in the ballroom below, and her heart had missed a beat when she'd glimpsed Vaughan's dark hair and saturnine features.

He invariably had a female companion in tow; her brothers never invited respectable females of the *ton*, so she could only assume the string of gorgeous women on his arm were either actresses or courtesans. The sight of his big hands casually stroking a waist, or squeezing a bottom, produced a terrible yearning in the pit of her stomach. A dark, gnawing jealousy that made her clench her fists against her skirts.

When she was seventeen, she'd stumbled upon him kissing a voluptuous blonde in one of the quieter corridors. The girl's head had been thrown back, her neck arched as he pressed his lips to her throat.

Daisy had skidded to a shocked halt on the marble floor. The girl had been so drugged by his kisses that she didn't even register the intrusion, but Vaughan's eyes had met hers and Daisy's breath had caught in her throat at the combination of amusement and burning desire in their depths.

He'd raised his brows, as if to chide her for the interruption, and she cursed the heat that scalded her cheeks as she swirled around and raced back up the stairs.

His dark laughter had followed her down the hall.

She thoroughly resented the fascination she had for him. He was debauched and wicked, clearly not the sort of man to whom she ought to be attracted, but his dangerous allure was irresistible.

After her come-out she saw him quite regularly, although he was part of a different, glittering social set. Sometimes she felt him watching her, and her pulse would thunder alarmingly in her throat, and whenever their eyes met, she'd experience a jolt in her body like a static shock. He'd raise his brows in silent challenge, and for some reason she knew it would be a sign of weakness to look away, so she forced herself to hold his gaze.

Eventually, when her skin was on fire and a wicked, heavy throb of desire pulsed between her thighs, his lips would twitch as if he was trying not to laugh, and he'd release her from her torment. His dark gaze would drop to her mouth, her throat, her breasts, and she'd feel it like a brand, a physical touch, even across a crowded ballroom.

It was a ridiculous, unspoken game between them, the rules of which she never fully understood, only that she looked forward to those wordless interactions more than anything else.

When Devlin had mentioned that he and Vaughan were joining Wellington's army to fight against Bonaparte, her heart had been seized with dread. The thought of Vaughan dying on some dusty battlefield in Portugal, of never returning to drive her quietly insane, was unbearable.

As soon as she'd heard that he was hosting a farewell party at his father's mansion in Mayfair, she'd known what she had to do. Her lack of an invitation had been no deterrent, and since Devlin had mentioned it was to be a costumed affair, it was the perfect opportunity to be bold.

Her courage had flagged a little when she saw quite

how debauched the gathering had become. She'd deliberately waited until almost midnight to arrive, certain that she had a better chance of sneaking in unchallenged if most of the guests were already drunk, but by the time she casually strolled through the side gate and into the lantern-lit gardens, it was clear that the revelry was well underway.

A giggling woman tugged an unresisting gentleman behind a yew hedge, while the unmistakable sounds of energetic lovemaking could be heard from somewhere behind the trees.

Daisy bit her lip and checked the ribbon on her mask was firmly tied. She'd borrowed the outfit from a friend who worked at Drury Lane Theatre, and the neckline of the burgundy velvet gown was far more revealing than anything she'd previously worn. She felt daring and gloriously naughty.

She spied Devlin and Dominic drinking with a group of women on the patio and gave them a wide berth as she slipped up the steps, through the open French windows, and into a crowded ballroom.

Needing some courage, she plucked a glass of champagne from the tray of a passing waiter and took a deep sip, deftly avoiding the groping hands of an inebriated gentleman dressed as a shepherd.

She weaved through the buoyant crowd, her stomach fizzing with excitement as she absorbed the hedonistic pleasure of the guests. The music was loud, the laughter louder, but there was a brittle edge of recklessness in the air, an unspoken acknowledgment that this could be the last time some of these men might truly enjoy themselves. The haunting possibility of death hovered just beyond the walls, and everyone inside was determined to seize this moment of happiness.

Vaughan wasn't in either of the rooms set aside for gaming, nor was he on the dance floor, and Daisy quashed a wave of disappointment. What if he'd already abandoned his guests and withdrawn somewhere more private with some lucky lady? She hadn't heard that he had a mistress, but it wouldn't be a surprise. He could have any woman he wanted.

She was just wondering whether to accept the offer of a dance from a handsome man dressed as a sailor when her wrist was seized in an inescapable grip, but her outraged protest died on her lips when she saw Vaughan's dark features towering over her.

He hadn't bothered with a mask. His brows were pulled down in a frown and her stomach dropped at the furious look in his eyes.

"Sod off, Gadsby. This one's mine."

The sailor sent him an amused look and shrugged. "Don't blame you, old man." His lecherous gaze slid over her exposed chest. "She's a prime bit o' muslin."

He drifted away, but when Daisy tried to extricate her wrist, Vaughan's fingers tightened almost painfully.

Her heart began to pound with excitement. Surely, he hadn't recognized her, which meant he'd singled her out because he wanted her!

She followed him, unresisting, as he tugged her through the crowd and out into a slightly less crowded corridor. Elation bubbled up inside her. Yes! This was where he'd take her in his arms and kiss her, exactly as he'd kissed that blonde at Hollyfield. She'd finally get the forbidden kiss she'd been dreaming about for so long, and since she was masked, he'd never know the identity of his conquest.

He didn't stop in the corridor. Daisy tried to angle him up against the wall, but he was so much bigger than her it was like trying to divert the path of an avalanche. She bit back a slightly panicked laugh. Perhaps he was taking her somewhere even *more* private? Oh, God! She really hadn't given this sufficient thought.

He still hadn't said a thing—he probably didn't expect conversation from his paramours—but she looked round in surprise as he finally opened a door and tugged her into a cozy-looking room that appeared to be a study.

A fire burning low in the grate provided the only illumination, but she glimpsed a heavy wooden desk and a pair of comfortable armchairs before she was swung around to face him.

The manacle-like grip on her wrist suddenly eased, and she glanced up with what she hoped was a welcoming, seductive smile.

"Dorothea Hamilton, what the *fuck* are you doing in my house?"

Daisy gasped in horror. Before she could even come up with a retort his hand shot out, ripped the mask from her head, and flung it across the room.

Oh shit.

Chapter Five

Daisy took a step back. Then another.

Vaughan was dressed in his usual impeccable black, and she had a brief, slightly hysterical thought that he must have come dressed as the devil himself. His expression was certainly one Lucifer might employ; she'd never seen anyone so angry. His eyes were almost black with rage, a muscle ticked in his jaw, and his entire body seemed to vibrate with suppressed energy.

He crossed his arms, as if not trusting himself not to strangle her with his bare hands, and positioned himself with his back to the door to prevent her escape.

Daisy's throat was suddenly dry as she cast around for a plausible explanation for her presence. She opened her mouth, but he shook his head.

"I don't recall sending *you* an invitation."

His tone was so scathing it felt like a whip across her skin, but she tried to look uncowed.

"It's Daisy," she said coolly. "Not Dorothea. And no, you didn't. But I never get invited to parties like this, and I wanted to see what all the fuss is about."

"You're trespassing. God, if you were my sister, I'd spank you!"

"You wouldn't dare!"

His eyes glittered malevolently. "You little fool. Most of the men here are drunk, and the women are here to be pleasured, and then paid. They're whores," he hissed, as if she were too simple to grasp the concept. "Courtesans. Any man who sees you will assume you're a whore too."

His lip curled as his gaze flicked over her from her head to her feet, then back up. He lingered for a thunderous moment on her cleavage, then glared at her as if she'd done something unforgiveable.

Daisy could scarcely draw a breath. If she were sensible, she'd run. Out of this room. Out of this house. But he was standing in the way. Blocking her escape even as he told her to go.

His nostrils flared. "What if someone else had caught you and dragged you in here? Or out into the garden? Would you have protested?"

She started to speak again, but he waved her words away.

"Or is that why you're here?" His expression darkened even more. "Were you hoping someone would relieve you of your virginity?"

"What? No!" Daisy couldn't decide if she was more mortified or outraged.

"If you were only looking for a kiss, then you're an idiot," he continued brutally. "No man would stop at a kiss. They'd assume any protest you made was just an act, a titillation."

He pushed off the door and paced toward her, effortlessly menacing. Daisy backed up even more, until her bottom bumped the hard edge of the wooden desk and she glanced around wildly for an escape. There was none.

He loomed over her, deliberately invading her space.

"You wouldn't be able to escape. They'd have you flat on your back with your skirts over your head before you could even cry for help."

She swallowed hard, her eyes stinging even as her body thrummed with his dangerous proximity. She hated the fact that he saw her as some helpless little fool, the pathetic, desperate little sister of his friends.

She tossed her head, feigning a bravado she didn't feel. "I have a knife in my boot."

"You'd be ruined before you even touched it."

She winced. She *had* been foolish to come here. Not for the first time, her recklessness had landed her in a dangerous situation.

He stepped even closer, and her heart pounded so hard she was sure he could hear it, but she held his gaze, defiant to the last.

His hand snaked out like lightning. He caught the back of her neck before she could duck away, his fingers threading through her hair, and her lips parted on a shocked gasp.

His mouth twisted in a mocking smile. "*Now* are you realizing how stupid you've been? Aside from your brothers, I'm probably the only man in this house who won't fuck you."

She flinched at his deliberately crude language, even as she battled a paradoxical disappointment. Of course he didn't want her. She was nothing like the women he usually chose. She gripped the edge of the desk, trying to anchor herself, determined not to show how rattled she was, how out of her depth.

"Fine. I shouldn't have come. Let me go."

She'd never been this close to him. His lips were hovering over hers, barely a sliver of air separating them. She could feel the warm exhale of his breath, smell the intoxicating midnight-forest scent of him. She was practically shaking, her blood pounding in her throat.

He shook his head. "I don't think you truly understand the danger. What you're inviting. *This*."

His lips crashed into hers, hard, an obvious punishment designed to prove his dominance and her foolishness. He leaned in, pressing her back with his weight, the hand at her neck holding her in place.

Daisy stiffened in shock, then tried to wrench herself free. She opened her mouth to tell him that he'd made his point, but the moment she did so he took ruthless advantage; his tongue slid between her lips, and the taste of him washed over her, so dark and forbidden she thought she might faint.

She made a noise, something between a gasp and a moan, and they both stilled.

Daisy thought he'd release her in disgust, but instead he made a rough sound in his throat, and kissed her *again*. His lips slanted over hers, his tongue tangling with her own, and she closed her eyes, hardly daring to believe what was happening.

Dear God, she was kissing Lucien Vaughan!

It was a revelation.

He set a deliberate, taunting rhythm, coaxing her to participate with little nips of his teeth and flicks of his tongue that caused butterflies in her stomach and a molten throb between her legs. His right hand was still in her hair, but his left came up to cradle her jaw before his fingers traced the sensitive skin behind her ear, then slid along her throat.

Fire raced through her blood.

His kisses became harder, more demanding. A wet, teasing slide toward insanity. Daisy kissed him back as though her life depended on it. A terrible urgency was unfurling inside her, a need to keep on kissing him forever. She pressed herself against him, wordlessly urging him on, and he stepped closer, between her legs, crushing her skirts between them. Even through the layers of fabric, she could feel the heat of him. The hardness.

He dragged his mouth from hers and pressed a row of searing kisses down her throat.

"Another man wouldn't stop." The words were breathed against the top curve of her breast. He sounded dreamy, almost as if he was talking to himself. He kissed his way back up the other side of her neck.

"They wouldn't resist such temptation." He kissed her jaw, the corner of her mouth.

And then his fingers tightened on her skull and his lips stilled, just resting against hers. She was panting with arousal, his chest against hers.

"They would *ruin you*," he growled, a vibration so deep she felt it right through her body. "And it would feel so *fucking* good."

Her heart skipped a beat at the raw intensity in his voice, but a splinter of alarm skittered through her. He seemed equally aroused and enraged. He was holding her precariously, bent backward over the desk at an awkward angle that gave him all the advantage of weight and balance.

"You don't even have the wits to be afraid," he whispered. "To understand how fragile you are. How easily they could break you."

Her elation vanished as reality struck her with the force of a blow. He hadn't been enjoying himself. He'd been teaching her a lesson!

His hand slid to her throat again, and her pulse pounded against his fingertips as he increased the pressure just enough to impress upon her his utter control. And her helplessness.

"You're at my mercy." He pressed the lightest, most teasing kiss to her lips, the gentleness at odds with his vicious words, and she fought back a traitorous shudder of desire. Her body still wanted him even though her mind was shrieking in outrage at his cruelty.

"And you should be thanking God that I don't want you," he growled.

Daisy wrenched her head to the side and he finally released her, stepping back and crossing his arms again. She shivered in the sudden rush of cold air.

His breathing seemed insultingly even, as if what they'd just done hadn't affected him in the slightest, but her chest felt tight and her hands were shaking against the desk.

How had the evening turned from heaven to hell in less than five minutes? She was almost reeling with the abrupt change.

"You've made your point, Vaughan." Her voice was a breathy croak, but she was proud of her composure. "Let me go."

He shook his head, his eyes still glittering dangerously. "You're not going anywhere. You're going to stay right here until I come back."

"Are you going to get my brothers?" That would certainly add to her misery.

"No. I'm going to call for a carriage."

She didn't know whether to be grateful or offended.

Thank God she hadn't compounded her humiliation by touching him back. By threading her fingers through his hair, or stroking his jaw, or sliding her hands over the hard plains of his chest. She'd saved herself that indignity, small as it was.

He pointed to her mask, lying on the floor. "Put that back on. I'll be back in a minute. Do *not* leave this room."

Daisy glared at him as he gave her one last, simmering look, then turned to the door. She rolled her eyes when he took the key from the lock and used it to shut her in, clearly having no confidence in her ability to be sensible.

Or perhaps he thought he was protecting her from encountering a less-discerning gentleman, she thought acidly. God, she hated him. High-handed, arrogant *bastard*. He'd toyed with her like a cat with a mouse, and she, like a fool, had let him.

She ignored him when he returned, gliding past him into the corridor with a regal sniff. With her mask back on, he swept her through the crowded rooms, using his big body to shove drunken revelers out of the way and shielding her from the catcalls and lewd innuendos that followed them.

A servant opened the front door to a frigid blast of air, and Daisy practically ran down the steps and clambered into the waiting carriage.

She glanced up in surprise as Vaughan followed her and caught the carriage door before it closed. His face was harsh and still annoyingly attractive in the lamplight, and she bit her lip at the horrible churn of conflicting emotions in her stomach. How could she want him and despise him simultaneously?

His gaze met hers and her heart somersaulted.

"Go home. And don't ever do something so reckless again. You won't like the consequences."

Daisy's cheeks heated, but she gave a disdainful sniff. "Consider me duly chastened."

He gazed at her for a long moment, then opened his

mouth as if he was about to say something more, but the horses rattled their harness and he seemed to change his mind. He closed the door with a resigned shake of his head and shouted up to the driver.

She almost told *him* not to do anything stupid, either, like get himself killed while he was off fighting, but pride and fury kept her quiet. The last thing she saw as she pulled away was his dark silhouette standing at the foot of the steps, the lights of the mansion blazing behind him, like Lucifer at the gates of hell.

I hate you, Lucien Vaughan.

But you'd better not bloody well die.

Chapter Six

They would ruin you.

And it would feel so fucking good.

Daisy opened her eyes and willed the heat in her cheeks to fade as Vaughan—the real one, not the memory—climbed back into the carriage and settled on the seat opposite her.

The sting of his rejection had faded a little over the years, but those particular words had continued to haunt her. She'd lost count of the number of times she'd awoken from a dark dream with them echoing in her head, her body restless and on the verge of release.

She *hated* that her unhelpful brain sometimes remembered the feel of his hand on her throat not with outrage, but with a hot, shameful pleasure that left her angry and confused.

She understood why he'd done what he had. He'd been trying to scare her into behaving. Protecting her, in his own warped, slightly perverse way. Perhaps the thought that neither he nor her brothers would be there to keep an eye on her while they were all away at war had motivated him.

And he'd been right. She'd been naive to think she could hold her own against a determined male, even one less physically impressive than himself, or with reflexes slowed with excess drink. Back then, she'd had no way of defending herself.

Not like now.

She couldn't give Vaughan all the credit for her decision to learn how to use her knives, but that night had undoubtedly contributed to her determination to develop her fighting skills.

The carriage jolted forward, and Daisy glanced over at him. "Did you tell someone about the man we left in the woods?"

"I did."

"Thank you."

He gave a disgusted sniff, apparently unimpressed by her charity.

"How bad is your coachman's wound?"

"He's had worse. Geordie and I were together at Waterloo. He took a bullet to the leg and lost half his teeth when a horse fell on him. This is nothing."

"Does he need to see a surgeon? He said the shot was still in his arm."

"Yes. He'll make his way back to London and find a sawbones as soon as it's light."

"Don't you need him to drive the carriage?"

He shrugged. "Finch can do it. Although I'm sure he'll moan like the devil while he's at it." His lips twitched, as if the thought of aggravating his friend amused him, and Daisy almost rolled her eyes. Her brothers were exactly the same, always laughing whenever some minor misfortune befell their companions. She supposed it was how men showed their love for one another.

"Violet and Peregrine will need to change horses in

another ten miles or so, at Hatfield," she said. "I wouldn't have thought they'd stop for the night so close to London, but who knows? We might be lucky and discover them there."

"Perhaps." Vaughan's expression indicated his skepticism. "But if it were me, I'd travel all night and try to put as much distance between myself and any possible pursuers." He sent her a pointed look.

Daisy sniffed. "I've been told that neither of them has been overly blessed with brains, so perhaps they won't think of that. Besides, traveling at night is stupidly dangerous. Disregarding the possibility of being waylaid by highwaymen, the chances of having an accident are much higher. Let's hope their coachman counsels staying at an inn."

They lapsed into silence, and Daisy tried not to fidget. The last thing she wanted was to converse with Vaughan, but she needed a distraction from listening to his breathing, so close, and the annoyingly delicious scent of his clothes. Besides, she might never get to talk to him in private again. She might as well seize the chance.

"Devlin was at Waterloo too. He said it was awful."

Vaughan remained looking out of the window at the darkness. "It was. It's a miracle any of us got out of there alive." His lips compressed in a dark line. "And I didn't emerge completely unscathed." He raised his gloved left hand. "My hand and forearm were burned when a grenade exploded near me."

Daisy nodded. She'd heard of his injury, and subsequent slow recovery, from her brothers. She'd even swallowed her pride and sent a sympathy card when he'd first returned to London, but she had no idea if he'd read it. He'd probably thrown it in the fire.

Still, her heart clenched at the thought of the pain he must have suffered. He might be a heartless scoundrel, but she wouldn't wish such a punishment on anyone.

"Does it still hurt?"

"Not anymore."

"Are you embarrassed by your scars? Is that why you always wear gloves?"

He gave a soft snort of amusement. "I'm not embarrassed. I don't care what people think. But they're unsightly. Wearing gloves spares me the looks of revulsion or pity from ladies with delicate constitutions."

Daisy almost dared him to show her; to say that she wasn't one to faint at the sight of a scar, or blood, but she held her tongue. She didn't need to impress him.

She cast around for another subject, but to her surprise, Vaughan turned to look at her and spoke again.

"Devlin. David. Dominic. Dorothea. What was your parents' fascination with names beginning with *D*?"

Her lips tugged upward. "I've no idea. But I wish they'd chosen something better for me. Damaris. Delilah, even. I hate Dorothea. I prefer Daisy."

He shook his head. "Ah, but the daisy is a common flower, and there's nothing common about you. You're the daughter of a duke."

She gave a bitter snort. "I'm no more a duke's daughter than you are, and the whole of society knows it. My brothers might have Dalkeith's blood, but my real father was Lorenzo Mancini, the Italian fencing master. My mother ran off with him a year after I was born. They live in Italy. Near Florence."

He tilted his head. "The duke's always acknowledged you as his, so you're legitimate in the eyes of the *ton*. You have all the wealth and privilege of the position."

"True. I can't complain. Better the secretly illegitimate daughter of a duke than the legitimate daughter of a pauper."

"Do you resent your mother for abandoning you?"

She frowned, surprised by the intimacy of the question. She'd barely discussed such things with Tess and Ellie, her best friends in the world. But Vaughan's bluntness was oddly refreshing. It was preferable to the whispers and sly innuendoes she'd endured from other members of the *ton*.

"I don't blame her at all. I understand why she made the decision."

"Was your father cruel to her? Is he cruel to you?" A dangerous edge had entered his tone.

She turned and stared sightlessly at the dark hedgerows flashing by. "He wasn't violent or manipulative, if that's what you mean. But he didn't see my mother as anything more than a means for breeding heirs. His cruelty was in his neglect. He ignored her most of the time, and treated her as a brainless fool for the rest."

"You've just described half the marriages in the *ton*." His tone was deeply cynical.

"Yes, well, after providing him with three boys and putting up with him flaunting a succession of ever-younger mistresses under her nose, I can appreciate why she decided she wanted a little pleasure too. All the luxury in the world can't make up for being unhappy. She found someone who cared for her deeply. She deserved a chance at love."

"All the more surprising, then, that you're pursuing these two runaways with such fervor. Don't they 'deserve a chance at love' too?"

Daisy glanced back at him. "My mother was thirty when she left my father. Violet's barely eighteen, and Peregrine's only a year older." She narrowed her eyes.

"People make foolish, rash decisions at eighteen that they'd *never* make at twenty-three."

His gaze met hers and she wondered if he'd catch the barbed allusion to her own embarrassing mistake. If he did, he didn't mention it.

She shrugged. "I'm proud of my mother for refusing to accept the path society laid out for her. It can't have been an easy decision."

His expression was impossible to define. "But you were an innocent casualty. She left you with the duke, to be brought up by nannies and governesses."

To be brought up without love. His inference was clear. Daisy shook her head, silently refuting the accusation. Dalkeith might have been incapable of showing affection, but she'd had a surprisingly happy childhood. Especially once she met Tess and Ellie.

"She left me in the best position she could to ensure my future prospects. I would have had far fewer opportunities in Italy. Here in England, I'm part of the *ton*. Plus, I have my brothers, whom I love—despite the glaring flaws in their personalities." She smiled, then sobered again.

"My father spends most of his time at Hollyfield, and I'm thankful for his disinterest. It's given me the freedom to work at King and Company where I can do something rewarding, instead of just flitting about, trying to snare a husband."

Vaughan's lips twitched, as if she'd amused him. "You don't want a husband?"

"Not if it means giving up what I love. I've yet to find a man who would approve of what I do."

"If tonight's an example of 'what you do,' then I'm not surprised. No man worth his salt would accept their woman putting herself in harm's way, no matter how worthy the cause."

Daisy stiffened. "Precisely my point. I refuse to become a chattel, forbidden to do anything but look pretty and arrange flowers, so I'll remain unwed."

"I'd be surprised if your father hasn't received a dozen offers for your hand, no matter how little interest you've shown. There are scores of men out there who'd want the daughter of a duke—despite the glaring flaws in her personality."

His lips twitched again, but she valiantly ignored the taunt. "Thankfully, he doesn't need to marry me off to improve the family finances, nor is he interested in making any political alliances. And unlike my brothers, I *earn* my own money. As long as I keep a low profile, he's content to leave me to my own devices."

Thank God, Daisy added silently. Ever since her come-out she'd lived in dread of her father accepting an offer on her behalf and simply ordering her to marry, without consulting her at all, as Tess's father had once done to her.

Her worry had increased every year she'd remained unwed, only tempered by the belief that the older she got, the more firmly she'd be seen as "on the shelf."

To further deter any potential suitors, she'd tried to cultivate a reputation for being stubbornly independent without doing anything so outrageous that she became the subject of gossip—thereby reminding her father of her existence.

"I doubt the duke will consider shooting a man and haring around the countryside dressed in male clothing as 'keeping a low profile.'"

Vaughan's silky drawl jolted her back from her reverie and Daisy scowled.

"Only if he finds out. Which is *not* going to happen."

Her tone dared him to contradict her.

He did not.

She nodded. "Right."

They lapsed into silence again until she bit back a jaw-cracking yawn. "What time is it?"

He checked his pocket watch. "Almost three. Why don't you sleep?"

She sent him a scornful look. "Here? With you? Ha! Besides, we'll be at Hatfield soon."

He seemed unoffended by her disdain, and merely settled more snugly into his seat.

"Feel free to close *your* eyes, though," she added sweetly. "I promise not to stab you while you sleep."

His muffled snort was her only reply.

Chapter Seven

Daisy sat up straighter as the lights of Hatfield came into view. Only sheer stubbornness had kept her awake. That, and spite. As soon as the carriage rocked to a halt she jumped down and went to speak to the two hostlers who'd ambled out of the Bell Inn to change the horses.

"Another coach, an hour ago?" The stable boy frowned. "Aye. We changed 'em." His hair was sticking up at all angles, and Daisy felt a twinge of guilt for pulling him from his bed. "We don't often 'ave *two* come through this early." He yawned. "Are you 'avin' a race?"

"Something like that." Daisy resisted the urge to kick the cobbles.

Damn. Violet and Peregrine had decided not to stop. She stomped crossly back to the carriage and Vaughan's lips twitched as he saw her expression.

"On to Stevenage?"

"Yes."

To his credit, he didn't laugh.

Daisy squashed herself into the corner of the carriage and glared dolefully out of the window, resisting the temptation to keep sneaking glances over at Vaughan as they set off again.

The excitement of the evening had ebbed, leaving her drained and desperate to sleep. She should have been back in London with the two runaways by now, not forced into sharing a carriage with the last man in England she'd have chosen as a companion.

Unfortunately, she couldn't see her luck improving any time soon. Peregrine and Violet might only be an hour or so ahead, but it was going to be almost impossible to catch them.

It was unlikely that they planned to sleep in the carriage and push through to Gretna without a single stop, but even if they decided to spend a couple of nights at inns *en route*, how could she possibly guess which ones they'd choose? The larger towns all had multiple options, and it wouldn't be feasible to visit each one in turn and ask if they were there.

And Peregrine surely wouldn't be so foolish as to book a room under his own name either, which meant Daisy would have to rely on describing them. She'd only seen Violet a handful of times at social events; apart from a riot of golden ringlets and large blue eyes, she couldn't recall much about her at all. The one time she'd met Peregrine, he'd reminded her of an enthusiastic spaniel.

Daisy sighed into the collar of her coat. The chances of her finding them before they reached Gretna were miniscule.

She *might* come upon them if they broke down and were stranded, or if she happened to glimpse a golden lion on a carriage door while passing through a town, but she didn't hold out much hope.

Still, the thought of having to admit defeat and return

to London with her tail between her legs was distinctly unappealing. Nobody could have predicted the night's unlikely turn of events, but she'd *hate* to be responsible for disappointing her friends and ruining King & Company's excellent track record.

Not to mention that Vaughan would be witness to her humiliation.

Not that she cared what he thought of her.

The landscape had been growing steadily lighter beyond the window for the past half hour, and the sun finally peeked above the horizon, spilling its rays inside the carriage. Daisy glanced at Vaughan and her heart did an odd little sputter in her chest as she got her first real look at him in daylight.

His eyes were closed, his arms folded across his chest, and she took the chance to catalogue the changes in him. Three years of war had taken its toll, not simply in his injured hand, but in the new lines that spread from the corner of his eyes. Annoyingly, the rugged maturity only served to make him even more attractive. His tanned jaw was darkened with just the hint of morning stubble, and she clenched her hand into a fist as she wondered what it would feel like beneath her palm.

He must be twenty-eight or twenty-nine now, the same age as her brother Devlin. Six years older than herself. When she'd been eighteen and stupid, that gap had seemed insurmountable, but she'd gained a world of experience since that night. Sometimes she felt decades older than her twenty-three years.

He stirred and she looked away, feigning interest in the countryside, and turned her thoughts back to her current dilemma.

She needed a new plan.

"You need a new plan." Vaughan stretched his long limbs and rolled his shoulders. "Either that, or admit defeat. The odds of you managing to overtake them are—"

Daisy ground her teeth. "I'd arrived at that conclusion on my own, thank you very much."

"There's no shame in ceding the field. Even Wellington did it on occasion."

His condescending tone made her want to pitch him out the window. He was a man crying out for defenestration. Sadly, the carriage windows were too high and too small to attempt it.

"I'm not giving up," she growled. "Violet and Peregrine are pampered aristocrats. Neither of them will be used to traveling hard. It takes three full days to get to Gretna, and even if they don't stop for food, it's highly unlikely they'll decide to spend all three nights in the carriage."

Vaughan brushed a speck of mud from his coat. "Even if they *do* stop, there's not much chance of you just happening upon them."

She nodded in reluctant agreement. "And asking after them at every inn will only waste more time. But if I head straight for Gretna, I might still arrive before them."

She looked over at him and debated the wisdom of what she was about to do. "How far north are you going, exactly?"

His dark eyes flicked to hers, and she thought she saw a glimmer of interest in their depths. "My country estate, Carisbrooke Hall, is in Yorkshire, up past Harrogate and Leeds."

"That's almost Scotland."

"It is indeed. I hope you're not suggesting that I let you accompany me—alone and unchaperoned—all the way there." Her spirits dropped, until she saw the teasing glint in his gaze. "Because that would be *scandalous*, Miss Hamilton. What if someone were to see us together?"

She indicated her outfit. Her knees and elbows were stained with mud and grass. "Anyone who sees me will assume I'm your stable lad, or a postillion. And when we stop at an inn, I'll stay out of sight. You can get a room, and I'll sleep here, in the carriage."

He was already shaking his head. "You will not. God knows what kind of trouble you'd manage to find."

"I'd offer to split the reward money with you," she winced inwardly at the very thought, "but you've already said you're not interested in funds."

"That's true. So what else are you offering as an incentive? Because as you well know, I'm not likely to help you out of the goodness of my heart."

"I can entertain you," she said, trying to sound enthusiastic. "Traveling on your own is incredibly boring. You expected to have Finch in here with you for the journey, but now he's having to drive, so you'll be starved of decent conversation."

"I'd hardly call Finch an excellent conversationalist," he drawled. "Unless it's on the topic of the French, or boxing."

"Well, then, I'm already ahead. I'll talk about any subject you like."

His lips twitched and she had the sinking feeling she was falling into a trap of her own making.

"Really? Any subject?"

She had to catch the runaways, and this was her best option. If it meant making a pact with the devil himself, she'd do it.

Daisy forced a smile. "Of course. I can't guarantee that I'll know about every topic, but I'll certainly try to engage."

Vaughan looked at her for a long moment and her heart began to pound.

"Very well."

She bit back a little smile of relief. "Excellent."

Oh, God, what had she done?

Chapter Eight

They stopped for breakfast at Stevenage. Daisy got out to stretch her legs and to check on Hero, who was still tied behind the carriage.

"I need to arrange for her to be ridden back to London," she said when Vaughan joined her. "We can't travel fast with her trotting behind, and there's no point in tiring her out for no reason."

She'd debated whether it was wise to remove a possible avenue of escape if Vaughan proved to be an impossible companion, but she could always hire another horse to ride if necessary, and she couldn't risk injuring Hero by pushing her too hard.

She removed the saddlebags, which held her coin purse, spare powder, and shot for her pistol, and stowed them in the carriage.

Vaughan nodded. "I'll do it."

"Thank you. I'll pay, of course."

He waved away her offer with a frown, as if the mere suggestion was insulting, and stalked into the inn with Finch close behind him.

Daisy tried not to brood as she waited, leaning casually against the carriage. Her stomach had been grumbling for the last thirty minutes, and she was sure the two of them were tucking into a delicious cooked breakfast and a hot mug of coffee. She let out a gasp of delight when he returned and tossed a paper-wrapped package at her.

"Breakfast."

She opened it with trembling hands, and almost groaned in happiness as the delicious aroma of freshly baked bread met her nose. There was an apple and a wedge of cheese too.

Perhaps he wasn't *completely* dreadful.

She put the apple in her pocket for later, then bit into the roll with gusto, and he shook his head, amused by her lack of delicacy. She finished the rest in short order, trying not to feel self-conscious about the way his gaze rested on her mouth. She wiped her lips roughly with her sleeve, like a stable boy, in case anyone was watching, and he turned away.

"I've thought of a way we can avoid being seen together tonight," she said as they climbed back into the coach. "We can stay at Wansford Hall, instead of at a public inn. Tess and Justin keep it staffed year-round because they're always traveling back and forth from London."

"Will they be there?"

"I don't think so, but Tess would insist that we make use of it. She'd be insulted if we didn't."

"Hollyfield's only a few miles past Wansford."

Daisy wrinkled her nose. "True. But my father might be there, getting ready for one of his parties. And if he's not, then there's still a chance one of my brothers might have decided to rusticate. Can you imagine what they'd do if we turned up together?" Her lips quirked with dark humor at the thought. "They'd probably demand to avenge my 'honor' in a duel, you'd shoot them, and there'd be a hideous scandal."

"You don't think there's a chance that they might shoot *me*?"

"Sadly not. That's not flattery, it's just that you've already killed one man in a duel, so you have the advantage. *And* I've seen them shoot. They're all terrible."

"Ah, but they'd have righteous fury on their side," he said. "That goes a long way to helping a man pull the trigger."

"Was that what motivated *you*?" she asked pertly. "Righteous fury?"

His expression darkened. "Something like that."

He clearly wasn't going to elaborate, so she let the subject drop. "So, Wansford Hall?"

He let out a resigned sigh. "Yes. I'd planned to stay at the Haycock at Wansford or the George at Stamford tonight anyway. I'll tell Finch at the next change."

The rest of the day passed surprisingly quickly. Now that Daisy didn't need to ask after the runaways at every stop, they could travel much faster. She kept an eye out for Violet's coach, but didn't truly expect to see it.

It was good to have a definite plan, despite the fact that it included someone as objectionable as Vaughan. She refused to feel guilty for roping him in—he clearly preferred to travel fast himself, and he was heading in the same direction. It made sense that they should cooperate.

His ducal crest on the carriage door assured impeccably fast service whenever the horses were changed, and the hostlers all grinned and doffed their caps when Finch tossed them some extra coins for their work.

Vaughan clearly had a reputation for tipping well, which also meant he was given the best available horses at every stop. Superior horses should give them an advantage over the runaways.

Daisy had traveled this particular route up the Old North Road countless times, both to her childhood home of Hollyfield and to the neighboring Wansford Hall after Tess had become the duchess.

Vaughan seemed disinclined to talk, so she looked out the window as they sped through Biggleswade and Alconbury. At noon they stopped at Stilton, and he emerged from the taproom of The Bell with a delicious chicken pie and a mug of hot chocolate for her, which put her very much in charity with him.

She was still surprised that he'd agreed to her scheme, but she wasn't going to question it. It was nice that he wasn't being completely obnoxious.

"Not far now," she said happily as they crossed the River Nene.

He rolled his eyes. "I know that. I attended enough of your brothers' parties to know the way."

She tensed, biting her lip as she waited for him to mention the time she'd seen him kissing that blonde, but his eyes merely glittered with suppressed amusement.

"They were always *such fun*, those parties."

"Have you ever been to Wansford before?"

"No. I know Thornton, of course, but I've only ever been to his London house."

The sun was sinking low in the sky as they traveled the few extra miles to Wansford Hall and Daisy's spirits lifted as the mellow stone building came into view down the long drive. The place was like a second home to her, and she was looking forward to seeing the friendly, familiar servants after her unsettling day with Vaughan.

Mrs. Jennings, the housekeeper, came to the door when they rocked to a stop outside, and her face creased in a delighted smile when Daisy jumped down. It was a testament to their long history that she didn't bat an eyelid at Daisy's breeches, shirt, and overcoat.

"Miss Hamilton! What a lovely surprise! I'm so sorry, but Her Grace didn't mention that you would be visiting."

"It's my fault entirely, Mrs. Jennings, a last-minute decision. I encountered a little bother on the road just outside London, but as luck would have it, I ran into the duke, who stopped to help. He was kind enough to escort me here."

Daisy had decided it was best to embroider the truth a little.

Mrs. Jennings frowned. "The duke? You mean His Grace?"

"Oh, no, not Justin!" Daisy amended quickly, realizing the confusion. "The Duke of Cranford."

Vaughan's tall, dark figure descended from the coach, and Mrs. Jennings's eyes widened before she bobbed a hasty curtsey.

"Your Grace! We are honored. Please, come inside and get warm. John will help your man with the horses."

She raised her brows and shot an intrigued look at Daisy behind Vaughan's back as they all entered the hall.

"Well, Your Grace, I'm sure you'll be wanting a good dinner if you've been on the road all day. Simmons will show you to the blue bedroom. I'll have hot water sent up for you right away."

Vaughan nodded. "Thank you."

"And Miss Hamilton, your room is always ready for you. I'll send Hannah up in a minute to light the fire." Her lips curved in a beatific smile. "I'm sure you'll want to change for dinner."

Daisy rolled her eyes at the subtle admonishment, but sent the elderly servant a fond glance. She'd have to don her stable boy disguise to continue the journey tomorrow, but there was no denying it would be nice to change into some fresh clothes tonight. She had a feeling she reeked of spent gunpowder.

Since she and Ellie visited Tess so often, they'd each been assigned their own bedroom, and Daisy kept a full wardrobe of dresses and accessories here.

Not that she cared to look remotely feminine or attractive for Vaughan's benefit.

Mrs. Jennings nodded happily, always delighted to have people to care for. "Now, if you'll excuse me, I'll go and speak with Mrs. Ward and see what we can rustle up for dinner. If I'd known you were coming, she could have prepared your favorite puddings—I know how fond you are of her desserts, Miss Hamilton—"

"Whatever you decide will be delicious," Daisy assured her. Her love of cakes and puddings was well known at Wansford.

The housekeeper nodded. "I'll make sure she makes something you like. Shall we say nine o'clock for dinner?"

"That will be perfect, thank you."

Daisy followed Vaughan and one of the male servants as they ascended the wide staircase. "Will Finch be all right? He can be assigned a room in the house if he'd prefer not to sleep above the stables with the grooms."

Vaughan shrugged. "He'll be fine. In the army we learned to sleep anywhere. I'll see you at dinner."

Chapter Nine

Lucien decided against wearing gloves down to dinner. As tempting as it was to frustrate Daisy's unashamed curiosity about the extent of his injuries, it simply wasn't practical.

Besides, she wasn't the kind of woman who'd faint at the sight of a scar. She'd shot a man to save Geordie's life, even though it had pained her, and Lucien could think of only a handful of other women of his acquaintance who would have had the guts to do the same.

He'd told her that he didn't care what other people thought, but as he descended the wide staircase and made his way toward the dining room, he found himself oddly nervous about her reaction.

He hoped to God she'd changed out of her masculine clothes. She'd removed her overcoat halfway through the afternoon to reveal a loose jacket, a white shirt tucked into a pair of soft buckskin breeches, and a pair of scuffed leather boots.

Lucien had stifled a groan. The shirt was of poor quality, thin and darned in several places, and he kept getting glimpses of the chemise she wore underneath whenever she moved. Even worse, the sleek length of her thighs was outlined with indecent clarity by the breeches.

The tails of the jacket concealed her backside when she was standing up, but when she climbed back into the coach, the curves of her buttocks were tantalizingly close and his hands had flexed with the desire to shape and stroke.

The only relief was the fact that she had no idea how much her proximity affected him. She never had, thank God.

He stepped into the dining room and almost swallowed his tongue. She was already there, waiting for him, and perhaps he should have suggested that she stay in her bloody boy's clothes after all.

"Is that one of the duchess's gowns?" he asked stiffly.

She stroked her palm down the front of it. "Oh, no. This is mine. I have a room full of things here, for when I stay with Tess and Justin."

He should have guessed that, from the way the damned thing fitted her with such delicious precision. The cobalt-blue silk dipped low at the front, hugging her breasts and hips so faithfully it was clear it wasn't borrowed. A swathe of utterly impractical fabric flowers decorated one shoulder and tumbled with apparent innocence down the neckline, irresistibly drawing the eye to the creamy swell of her left breast. It was a diabolically seductive dress.

"It's by Madame Lefèvre of Bond Street," she added absently.

Of course it was. He'd paid for a few dresses from the stylish modiste himself, for various paramours. None of them had ever looked as good in the creations as Daisy did.

Bloody woman. She didn't even *aspire* to looking good. She'd probably spent less than five minutes worrying about her hair, and he'd be amazed if she'd done more than wash the mud from her hands, but that refreshing carelessness only made her even more attractive. The fact that she clearly didn't give a fig for enticing him was both highly amusing and, ironically for her, entirely ineffective. He wanted to eat *her* for dinner.

Bloody Hell.

The servants had seated them together at one end of the vast mahogany dining table. A hovering footman pulled out the chair for her and she sank into it with a smile, while Lucien lowered himself opposite her.

Her gaze flicked to his uncovered hands as he casually rested his left on the table and used his right to take a sip of wine, but instead of glancing away, as most people did, she tilted her head and regarded him openly.

He kept his face carefully expressionless.

"Is it still healing?" she asked.

"Not really. It's been over a year. This is probably as good as it's going to get, in terms of appearance." He let her look her fill at the raised lattice of pale scars that crisscrossed the back of his left hand and disappeared beneath the snowy cuff of his shirt. "It used to be redder, but while the color has faded, the texture will always be like this."

He'd always been glad of the small mercy that it had been his left, nondominant hand that had been injured. And that fact that he hadn't lost any of his fingers.

She took a sip of her own wine. "I'm sorry you were hurt. Joining the army was a brave thing to do. Especially since it wasn't expected of you."

He frowned, thinking she was implying that he was considered a coward, but she quickly clarified.

"As the heir to a dukedom, I mean. First-born sons were expected to stay here and keep the country running."

His lips twisted. "That was certainly my father's opinion. But I couldn't stay twiddling my thumbs while other men defended my home. I was lucky to survive with such a minor injury. Thousands of men never got the chance to return."

A shadow flitted across her face. "Yes. I know. I lost a good friend at Waterloo."

Lucien experienced an unexpected flash of jealousy. Who was she talking about? Had this mystery man been just a friend, or something more?

God, he'd tried not to listen whenever her brothers discussed her various suitors, but he was sure they'd never mentioned anyone who'd been killed in action. Had she had a secret lover?

Damn it, her love life was none of his affair. It wasn't as if he'd been a saint, although in truth the rumors of his conquests had been greatly exaggerated. Since he'd been back in England, he'd been too busy recuperating for the first six months to give much thought to seduction, and after that he'd amused himself with professionals who understood that physical pleasure didn't need to be accompanied by any emotional attachment.

The arrival of the first course interrupted his brooding, and he let his eyes wander over her as she started to eat.

"That dress is an excellent disguise."

She glanced up, her brows arched in surprise. "What do you mean?"

"It makes you look sweet and docile. Not at all the kind of reckless hellion who would interrupt a robbery."

Her lips quirked in delight at the backhanded compliment, and his gut tightened in response.

"Are you still armed?" he drawled.

Her eyes flashed. "A knife in my pocket. It was hidden

in my boot. Your man failed to find it when he searched me."

He bit back a smile at her cockiness. "I'll be sure to give him a dressing-down. I doubt he's ever encountered a young lady with *three* knives on her person."

She shook her head, still smiling. "Are *you* armed?"

"Only with my wits," he quipped.

"You don't consider me any kind of threat at all, do you?"

"Physically? No. In truth, I don't."

"Not even with the element of surprise?"

She sounded offended, and he knew she still harbored a ridiculous sliver of hope that she could outmaneuver him. He should have found it ridiculous, instead of endearing.

"I doubt I'd ever let my guard down around you enough to let you get the better of me. But feel free to try, if you find it entertaining."

She narrowed her eyes at him, and he almost willed her to leap over the table and try to attack him.

She was tempted; he could see it in her face. But he also knew that it would be a fatal mistake. They'd had anger and violence between them before, five years ago, and it had only taken a heartbeat for it to turn into something equally passionate and far more dangerous. The chance of it happening again was high, even if she professed to hate him.

There was no denying the attraction that shimmered between them. It had plagued him for years, an insistent tug he'd done his best to ignore. But if she put her hands on him there was no telling how he'd react.

He saw the moment she arrived at the same conclusion. She swallowed hard and her eyes dropped from his, and she busied herself with her soup.

He ignored a twinge of disappointment.

They made it through the main course with a steady flow of harmless conversation, but when the cook brought in an impressive array of desserts, Daisy's expression became almost euphoric.

"Mrs. Ward! You shouldn't have!" She sent the cook a mock-scolding glance. "But I'm so glad you did. I've been dreaming of your crème brûlée for months."

The plump woman flushed with pride. "You know how much I like seeing people enjoy my food, Miss Hamilton. It's the highest compliment a chef can receive."

She turned to Lucien and bobbed a respectful curtsey. "Your Grace, I've made a couple of extra puddings, in case you have a sweet tooth too. That's a pear cake with custard, and this is a strawberry blancmange."

Daisy's eyes twinkled. "I hope you haven't made us the *special* desserts you made for their Graces on their wedding night?"

The cook's cheeks creased in a naughty smile that made her look more like a ten-year-old girl than an elderly matron. "Of course not. Bon appetit!" She bobbed another curtsey and sallied out.

Lucien raised his brows. "Special desserts?"

Daisy snorted. "The staff were so keen to promote a love-match between the new duke and duchess that Mrs. Ward cooked everything with foods thought to be aphrodisiacs. Tess told me all about it."

"Considering how Thornton talks about his duchess, I'd say it was entirely unnecessary," he drawled. "I've never met a man so nauseatingly in love with his own wife."

"Perhaps Mrs. Ward's desserts helped?" She used the back of her spoon to crack the caramelized sugar crust on the top of her crème brûlée, then scooped a spoonful into her mouth. Lucien watched helplessly as she closed her eyes and groaned as the first taste of the creamy dessert touched her tongue.

His cock hardened instantly.

She withdrew the spoon, pulling it slowly between her lips, and he tightened his grip on his wineglass. Bloody woman. The worst thing was, she wasn't even doing it deliberately. She had no inkling of the way she made his blood heat. Or if she did, she didn't care. He couldn't decide which would be worse.

"You like desserts?" God, his voice sounded like he'd been eating gravel. He cleared his throat again.

Her eyes popped open and she shook her head. "I *love* desserts."

"Love's a very strong word."

"I think you're underestimating the desperate lengths I'd go to—possibly just short of murder—for one of Mrs. Ward's apple puffs." She took another spoonful and ate it with salacious delight. "Isn't there a food you love?"

Lucien considered the question, mainly to stop himself from thinking of what she'd taste like if he kissed her. How much he wanted to lick that bloody cream from her skin.

"I don't think I love anything," he said truthfully. "I am fond of things. I desire things. So I have them. But I wouldn't say I *love* them."

She tilted her head. "What about people? There must be people you love."

"A select few. But loving someone opens you up to being hurt."

"It is a bit of a double-edged sword," she conceded thoughtfully. "Love makes you stronger and weaker at the same time. More vulnerable, but also invincible. That's how I feel about Ellie and Tess, anyway. I'd be lost without them."

He nodded, refusing to ask if she was also thinking about the man she'd loved and lost. "You're fortunate to have such close friends."

"I am. Which is why I can't let them down by failing to catch Violet and Peregrine."

Lucien suppressed a groan. Daisy's tenacity would be an admirable trait under different circumstances, but in this case, it was most unwelcome.

She was right to be suspicious of his motives, and he wondered what she'd do if he told her the *real* reason he was going along with her plans. Her quarry, Peregrine Hughes, was his nephew, the only son of his elder sister, Marion.

And while Daisy was determined to put a stop to Perry's elopement, Lucien was equally keen to ensure it went ahead. He was heartily sick of chaperoning the lovestruck fool around London, and selfishly keen to have his unwanted house guest out from under his feet for good.

The fact that Perry had managed to fall in love with an heiress, and not some gaudy opera singer or Covent Garden flower-seller was a miracle in itself—no less incredible than the fact that Violet seemed to return his affections.

Violet's father didn't approve of the match, but that was neither here nor there. Lucien had advised the two lovebirds to present the curmudgeonly Mr. Brand with a *fait accompli,* and since he'd had little faith that two such simpleminded individuals could get themselves to Gretna Green unscathed, he'd been following them at a discreet distance ever since they left London.

The highwaymen's attack had proved his decision to

keep a close eye on his charge was justified, but Daisy's unexpected appearance had added a new and exciting twist. Lucien's onerous task had suddenly become *far* more interesting.

His lips quirked in dark amusement. Daisy was probably going to stab him with one of her knives when she discovered the truth, but he was enjoying her company too much to tell her. She was going to be a delightful diversion.

"I hope you'll be ready for an early start tomorrow?" she said, breaking into his thoughts.

Lucien frowned into his wine. "How early, exactly?"

"Shall we say eight o'clock?"

"That's an ungodly hour."

She sent him a look full of mock-sympathy. "You poor thing. Have you ever exerted yourself to get out of bed before noon?"

He pinned her with a hot, direct look that immediately banished the teasing amusement from her face. "Only with the strongest of incentives," he drawled. "Staying in my bed is usually a far more inviting prospect."

He let that thought, that image, dance between them for a moment, and enjoyed the way her lips parted and the blood rushed to her cheeks. He stood and sent her a formal, mocking bow. "I'll bid you good night. Sweet dreams."

Chapter Ten

Daisy was up bright and early, impatient to be on the road. She'd slept fitfully, her dreams interrupted by an obnoxious number of lurid fantasies that all seemed to feature a dark, sardonic rake. She hadn't needed to see his face to know his identity. Damn him.

The servants had washed and dried her breeches and shirt, and she'd packed a small bag with some extra clothes for the days ahead. The idea of spending two nights in the far more intimate confines of a public inn with Vaughan was unsettling, to say the least, and she was determined that her identity as a woman would remain undetected.

Mrs. Jennings had miraculously produced two spare white shirts, stockings, and an extra pair of breeches for her. The shirts were so fine they must have been ordered for Justin, but the breeches had doubtless come from one of the smaller stable lads.

Daisy had debated whether to pack a dress, then decided against it, and instead included the small stoppered flask of laudanum that Ellie had once given her.

Tess had used the same concoction to subdue a man in

order to search his house for clues as to who was black-mailing Princess Charlotte, and Daisy felt better knowing she had it as a secondary kind of insurance. If she found herself needing to escape Vaughan, for whatever reason, she would have no compunction about drugging him.

To her surprise, he was already in the breakfast room when she went downstairs, and she tried not to notice how good he looked with his face freshly shaved, and his dark hair curling against the perfect folds of his snowy cravat. He'd probably slept like a log, the brute.

He toasted her with his coffee cup. "Good morning, Dorothea."

"*Daisy*," she growled. "Although you should avoid even calling me that when we're on the road."

"You're right, I should think of another name for you," he said. "Several come to mind, but none I'd want to repeat in polite company."

She gulped down a scalding sip of coffee while he regarded her with a gaze that made her wish she could read his mind. Or maybe not.

"Perhaps I'll call you brat," he murmured. "Or whelp."

"Perhaps I'll stab you in your sleep," she countered sweetly.

He smirked. "As I said, you're welcome to try."

She bit into one of Mrs. Ward's delicious apple puffs to avoid answering him, but the damned thing was so flaky that several pieces dropped to her plate and several more clung to her lips. She wiped them away self-consciously with her fingers, and glanced up to find him watching her with an intense expression that sent a shivery little thrill through her. She licked her lower lip, testing with her tongue to be sure she hadn't missed any bits, and a muscle ticked in his jaw.

He put down his coffee cup with slightly too much force. "I'll see you outside."

Daisy finished her breakfast, then went to say good-bye to the staff. Mrs. Ward and Mrs. Jennings, who were sisters, both came into the hall to wave her off.

"You take care now, Miss Hamilton," Mrs. Ward said with a stern look in her eye. "I've had Betsy pack you a hamper of food. And Lawrence has already put your bag in the coach."

"Thank you," Daisy smiled. "And would you please send this to Her Grace as soon as possible?" She pulled the letter she'd penned to Tess from her jacket pocket. She and Ellie were probably worrying themselves sick about where she might be. They would have been expecting her back at Lincoln's Inn Fields with Violet and Peregrine in tow yesterday.

As was usual when they corresponded, Daisy had given only the briefest details of the situation:

First attempt unsuccessful. Have engaged the services of a mutual acquaintance and expect to arrive at the Blacksmith's before the undesired event takes place.

Tess and Ellie would understand the reference to the fact that most Gretna Green marriages took place over an anvil, presided over by the local blacksmith, rather than officiated by any member of the clergy. Daisy had debated whether to mention Vaughan by name, or at least by allusion, as the scandal sheets did, *the D—of C—,* but decided against it.

She wasn't entirely sure why she kept the information to herself. Perhaps it was for the same reason she'd never actually told Tess and Ellie about the night Vaughan had kissed her. Which was odd, now she came to think about it. The three of them had discussed almost everything else, including details of far more graphic and scandalous experiences, but she'd always kept the dark, shameful secret of that evening locked deep inside.

Finch sent her a look that was neither friendly nor unfriendly as she stalked out to the carriage, and she supposed he was trying to decide whether she'd turn out to be trouble for his master. She rather imagined it would be the other way around.

A clatter of hooves revealed Vaughan mounted on a handsome black horse she recognized as Apollo, a slightly skittish gelding from Justin's stables.

"I would have liked to ride," she said crossly.

He glanced down at her, his brows drawn in a line. "You can't ride sidesaddle dressed like that. You'd reveal yourself as a girl."

"I can ride astride," she countered. "It's much easier than with a stupid sidesaddle."

She sent him a challenging stare, just daring him to say something obnoxious about women riding like men, but he merely calmed the circling horse with an effortless move.

"I didn't think of that. I apologize. If you still want to ride at the next stop, I'll arrange it for you."

He urged Apollo forward, leaving her open-mouthed. She watched him for a moment longer, begrudgingly appreciating the natural grace of him in the saddle—she supposed he'd ridden for days at a time during the war—before she climbed up into the coach.

She refused to long for his company. As they rejoined the road, she took the chance to make a thorough search of the interior and discovered not only that the two wall-mounted pistols had been reloaded, but also a stack of books stashed in a compartment under the seat next to the wicker basket of food Mrs. Ward had provided.

It was an intriguing glimpse into Vaughan's interests,

several of which coincided with her own. Some were predictable: a well-thumbed copy of Homer's *Iliad*—no surprise that the subject of warfare should feature in his reading matter. She snorted in amusement at the translation of *The Prince* by Machiavelli, ignored a two-week-old copy of *The Times*, and raised her brows at the copy of Byron's *Corsair*. More intriguing was the cloth-bound copy of *Sense and Sensibility* by A Lady; Daisy would bet fifty pounds Vaughan had never looked inside. Perhaps it had been left by a previous female inhabitant. A mistress? A tiny pang of envy pierced her.

She finally settled on a book on fencing by the great master Domenico Angelo and sat back to read. Vaughan's broad-shouldered figure would occasionally come level with the window, but she did her best to ignore him. She most certainly was *not* looking at the way his strong thighs flexed as he controlled the powerful horse, or how his black-leather-gloved hands rested so easily on the reins.

No indeed.

At the next stop he dismounted and came to the window. "Do you wish to ride?"

She shook her head. The sky was looking rather gray, promising rain. "Maybe tomorrow."

He shrugged, and after instructing that Apollo be returned to Wansford Hall, he joined her in the carriage.

The space immediately felt suffocatingly crowded. He gestured to the book she'd abandoned on the seat. "Dreaming of new ways to skewer me?"

"Just giving myself a little refresher. I've read it before. In fact, I've taken lessons from his son, Henry Charles, at Soho House."

To his credit, Vaughan didn't sneer at the idea of a woman learning to fence, but Daisy had the lowering thought that the graceful, precise movements she'd learned in the practice room would be of little use in a real battle, like those in which he'd been involved.

They trundled through several more villages, until the silence became unendurable. She tilted her chin at the swinging sign of an inn.

"Tess, Ellie, and I always play games whenever we're on a long journey together."

His brows rose in partial interest. "Like what?"

"Well, we try to see how many different animals we can collect from all the different pub signs we pass. I swear, sometimes you can make a whole menagerie. We've already passed The Old Bull, The Red Lion, The Eagle, The Bay Horse, and The Fox and Hounds."

She realized she was babbling, and flushed. He'd doubtless think such games incredibly childish. He probably spent *his* journeys debauching his female companions and calculating the extent of his ducal holdings to the nearest hundred thousand pounds.

"I can't say I've ever played that game," he said mildly.

Infuriating man. Still, she'd promised to provide him with interesting conversation during the journey, and she would do just that. Even if it killed her.

She cast around for another subject. "Did you know that this stretch of the Old North Road is particularly famous for its highwaymen?"

His lips twitched. "Here? Not the woods just north of Hampstead Heath?"

She ignored the taunt. "Dick Turpin is said to have galloped along here on Black Bess on his way to York."

"And every inn between here and Harrogate claims he stopped for a pint." His tone was gently sardonic. "If that were true, he'd have taken considerably longer than his famed fifteen hours."

Daisy bit back a smile. She'd always thought the same thing. "Some people say it wasn't Turpin who made the ride at all, but a man called Swift Nick, fifty years before, to establish an alibi. But everyone loves a good tale. Especially if it involves a bit of romance."

Vaughan's brows rose in astonishment. "*Romance?* There's nothing remotely *romantic* about almost being shot dead in the road, Hamilton."

"Of course there isn't. But people never focus on the unpleasant realities. Just look at the legend of Claude Duval."

"A Frenchman," Vaughan snorted.

"People romanticize him because he rarely used violence and because of the tale that he once changed his mind about robbing someone when the lady agreed to dance a *courante* with him."

"They still hanged him, though, didn't they? And that knave they called Sixteen String Jack."

Daisy sighed. "They did."

She worried her lip with her teeth. The man she'd shot might not swing on the gallows, but he might still end up dead, like his two companions, if his wound became infected.

"Stop thinking about it," Vaughan said harshly.

"What?"

"That bastard you shot. He *chose* that profession. And he would have killed Geordie. In fact, you probably saved his miserable life, because Finch or I wouldn't have spared him."

She nodded, knowing he was right—but slightly disturbed by the fact he always seemed to know what she was thinking.

The rain that had been threatening finally arrived, tapping against the windows and making the inside of the carriage seem even cozier and more private than before. Vaughan leaned back negligently in his seat.

"You promised to keep me entertained with conversation, and as fascinating as I find the subject of highway robbery, there's another topic I'd prefer to discuss."

Daisy eyed him warily. The silky, drawling tone of his voice immediately put her on guard. "And what's that?"

"I'd like to dispute a comment you made yesterday. You said you'd never use the word *noble* to describe me. And while that may be true for the most part, I believe there was one occasion, five years ago, when I acted with almost breathtaking nobility and restraint."

Her stomach somersaulted as she caught his meaning. Oh, God, were they really going to discuss this? Now? When she couldn't escape?

The man truly was a fiend.

Chapter Eleven

"You're referring to your leaving party?" Her voice didn't waver, thank God.

Vaughan crossed his legs, balancing one booted ankle on the opposite knee, the picture of relaxed elegance, but Daisy wasn't fooled. He was poised to attack.

"I am," he said smoothly.

"You call threatening me and insulting me 'noble'?"

"Threatening you, insulting you, and *kissing* you," he amended coolly. "And yes, I do. You were still a virgin when you left the house, weren't you?" His gaze caught hers and she couldn't seem to look away. "In fact, now I think of it, that might have been the first and only time I've ever denied myself something I wanted for a noble cause."

She managed a disbelieving snort. "Pfft! You didn't want me, Vaughan. It was hardly a gallant sacrifice."

Something flared in his eyes. "You think not?"

"Of course not. Why would you? You've always had women throwing themselves at you."

"Maybe that's why I didn't want *them*." His lips curved

in self-mocking derision. "It's human nature to want what you can't have."

"You said you were the only man in the house, apart from my brothers, who wouldn't fuck me." The crude word felt strange in her mouth.

"That doesn't mean I didn't want to."

It was suddenly hard to breathe, as if all the air in the carriage had been sucked out. The rain drummed against the windowpanes.

"I wanted you," he said darkly. "More than my next breath."

Daisy inhaled. Her heart was pounding against her ribs, but she forced herself to focus on his use of the past tense. He'd *wanted* her. That didn't mean he felt the same way now. Back then, she'd been forbidden, a novelty.

She feigned a nonchalance she certainly didn't feel. "Yes, well, we're both a few years older and wiser now. I'm not such an innocent fool."

"No?" His amused skepticism made her want to punch him. "I expect you've had a hundred men since then."

She clenched her fists in her lap and the reckless desire to shock him heated her blood. "Not a hundred. But I'm no longer a virgin, if that's what you're inferring."

His brows rose. She'd expected him to be disapproving, or at the very least surprised, but it was interest that flared in his eyes. He seemed intrigued.

"How very rebellious. Who was the lucky gentleman? Or gentlemen. Anyone I know?"

"It was just the one," she said, matching his cool, mocking tone. "And he wasn't a gentleman at all."

Something dark flashed into his expression. "He mistreated you? Hurt you?"

"No. Nothing like that. He was a stable hand at Hollyfield; not a gentleman."

His tension seemed to ebb a little, and she found a dry humor in the fact that he reserved his outrage for the idea of her being abused, instead of for the fact that she'd willingly surrendered her innocence to someone of a lower class. She couldn't imagine getting that reaction from any other male of her acquaintance.

"We have hours to go," he said easily. "You might as well tell me all the sordid details."

Daisy bit her lip, torn. She'd only ever told Tess and Ellie of her short-lived affair. If any other member of the *ton* were to hear of it, she'd be ruined socially, cast out as a 'soiled dove,' and her chances of marrying well would be decimated.

Not that she particularly cared about that, but she *would* care if the scandal meant that her friends were tainted by association.

And yet she didn't imagine Vaughan would spill her secrets. He had too much money to need to resort to blackmail, although he might find it amusing to threaten to expose her, just to watch her squirm.

"Your secrets will be safe with me," he said drily, reading her thoughts with uncanny accuracy yet again. "I like your brothers too much to want to plunge your family into scandal, and I don't fancy shooting one of them for having sullied your reputation."

Daisy shrugged. In fairness, Vaughan was probably unshockable. Her fumbling exploits could hardly compare to his vast worldly experience. And besides, there was still a foolish part of her that wanted to prove to him that she wasn't the naive little eighteen-year-old he'd encountered five years ago.

"His name was Tom Harding. He died at Waterloo."

"Childhood sweetheart?" His tone wasn't as cynical as it had been.

"No. But we'd known each other for a long time. He was fun. Good company." Daisy smiled as fond memories flooded her, tinged with a bittersweet sadness.

"Did you love him?"

The soft question jolted her back to attention. She searched Vaughan's face for any hint of mockery, but he seemed sincere. She turned her head and studied the raindrops snaking their way down the windowpane, and decided to be ruthlessly honest.

"You know, people always talk about love as if it's a single, fixed thing, but I don't think that's the case at all. I think there are as many kinds of love as there are people. Millions." Her breath fogged up the inside of the glass and she traced a pattern in it with the tip of her finger.

"That's not a yes."

She sighed. "I loved Tom as someone I'd grown up with, as a dear, cheeky friend. He was handsome, and strong, and when I heard that he'd be leaving to fight Bonaparte, I liked him enough to lie with him."

She'd desired Tom. Not the way she'd desired Vaughan, with that dark, heart-wrenching, pulse-pounding intensity, but in a sweeter, gentler way. And mixed in with the physical attraction had been a kind of pathos, an earnest desire to make him happy before he left for war.

It sounded strange, to call giving Tom her body a *friendly* gesture, but in a way it had been. It was as if they'd both had a premonition that their time together would be short, that they should grasp those brief moments of pleasure while they could.

"Did he make my heart beat faster when I thought about him?" she asked quietly. "Not really. I certainly never felt all giddy and foolish, like the poets describe people 'in love.' I never dreamed of being his wife. But he didn't know if he'd ever return. So I said yes."

She swallowed and braved a glance over at Vaughan—the *reason* she'd said yes. That evening with him had ignited a terrible curiosity inside her, a need to see if he was the only man who could make her feel that way, or whether she could replicate those sensations with another. A part of her still felt guilty for using Tom as an experiment, a comparison, but it had been a mutually beneficial arrangement. He hadn't wanted to leave for Portugal still a virgin.

Vaughan was watching her, his expression indecipherable, so she decided to continue.

"We discovered what pleasure was together." She sent him a challenging look. "And it *was* pleasurable. Despite the fact that neither of us really knew what we were doing."

Vaughan still said nothing, and her throat grew tight with emotion as she looked back out at the rain. The drops ran like tears down the outside of the glass. Oddly enough, the weather outside made it feel even more intimate inside, a safe, enclosed space, like a confessional.

"I cried when I heard he'd been killed. He was only nineteen. I cried for the fact that he'd never grow old, never sleep with another woman, never marry and have children. I cried at how stupid and unfair war is. *Life* is."

Daisy blinked, suddenly realizing how much she was sharing. She'd barely articulated these feelings to her friends, and now here she was, exposing herself to this man who was practically a stranger. And yet it felt easy. Right.

She clenched her jaw and sent him another defiant look. "And I was glad I'd given myself to him. I don't regret it one bit."

Vaughan nodded, but she still couldn't tell what he was thinking. She made a mental note never to play him at cards.

"Is the fact that you're not a virgin another reason you don't want to marry?" he asked. "Are you worried your secret will be discovered on your wedding night?"

Daisy suppressed a smile. Tess's wedding-night dilemma had been the complete opposite of that: she'd had to hide the fact that she was still a virgin to Justin, her second husband, after the first duke had failed to consummate the marriage.

"Not really," she said. "I doubt most men would even notice, especially if they were in their cups."

His lips quirked. "You think a man who'd just married you would need liquid courage to bed you?"

She scowled at his teasing. "No. I just think men are far less observant than women. *Especially* when they're thinking about their own pleasure."

"You wound us," he chuckled, clutching his chest as if she'd pierced him with a blade.

She refused to be charmed by his levity. "That's enough about me. I've answered your questions. Now it's your turn to tell me something personal. It's only fair." She raised her brows in challenge, just waiting for him to refuse, but he tilted his head.

"Very well. What would you like to discuss?"

She was so surprised that she said the first thing that came into her head. "Tell me about *your* first love."

"You mean the first girl I ever took to my bed?" His tone was softly mocking. "I'm sorry to say that love had very little to do with it. Not the way the poets claim it, at least. My father paid for a whore to 'make a man of me' on my seventeenth birthday."

Daisy blinked back her shock. "Oh. That's . . ."

He grinned at her expression. "I was delighted, believe me. But I certainly can't claim to have loved her. I don't even remember her name."

"Very well, but you've had other lovers. Didn't you love any of them?"

"I desired them. And enjoyed their company, for the most part. But I'd hardly say I *loved* them."

She let out a huff of frustration at his continued evasiveness. "So you've never loved a woman, ever. Is that what you're saying?" He opened his mouth to answer, but she cut him off. "If that's the case, then I feel sorry for you, Vaughan."

A muscle ticked in his jaw and she hid a smile at the fact that she'd managed to needle him.

"I loved a girl once," he said curtly. "Her name was Elaine, and she was a neighbor of ours, in Yorkshire."

Daisy crossed her arms, certain he was making it up. "Oh really?"

"Yes, really. She was my friend, like you and your Tom." His face looked suddenly stark, and she realized he wasn't making it up at all. "She was kind, and sweet, and I probably would have married her if she hadn't died."

Daisy stilled, shocked by his unexpected confession. She couldn't interpret the look on his face. Was it sadness? Bitterness? Regret?

"I'm sorry," she said, meaning it. "What happened to her? How did she die?"

His eyes flashed. "Giving birth to a child that everyone thought was mine."

Oh.

"And was it?" she managed.

His lips pressed into a thin line. "No. But . . ." He shrugged, an elegant, dismissive lift of his broad shoulders. "It doesn't matter now. The babe died too."

"How long ago was this?"

"A long time. Before the war."

Daisy bit her lip, struggling to find the right words.

She'd never expected him to reveal something so personal, and the thought of him being in love with someone, even years ago, sent an odd swoop of jealousy through her.

Now she understood the comment he'd made at dinner, back at Wansford Hall.

She sent him a tight, commiserating smile. "You were right. Loving someone opens you up to losing them. It hurts when they leave."

He nodded once and glanced away in a clear indication that he was finished with the conversation. Daisy studied him for a long moment, then looked back out at the rainy fields and hedgerows.

She'd been too young to feel abandoned when her mother had left; she couldn't recall ever having a mother, so she hadn't really appreciated the lack of one. But when Tom had died, she'd grieved him sincerely. Whenever she'd gone back to Hollyfield, his absence had seemed like an inexplicable void, something her brain couldn't quite grasp. She'd kept walking into the stables, expecting to see him, and her heart would ache anew each time she realized he'd never be there again.

She'd never been more grateful for Tess and Ellie than at that time. They were her true family, more than just friends, bonded closer than sisters, and they'd known her better than she'd known herself. They'd let her mope about for a few days, hugged her while she'd cried, and then forced her to come back to King & Co. to investigate a case involving the blackmail of a Royal Navy officer.

It had been exactly what she'd needed, given her something to focus on, and now she could look back on her time with Tom with a bittersweet smile.

He'd been her first and only lover. The only times she'd felt desire since then was when Vaughan inserted himself into her dreams, or when she happened to glimpse him in the *ton*. She hadn't been tempted to see if another man could assuage the restless ache inside her.

And yet for some time she'd been plagued by a nagging sense that she was missing something, *seeking* something she couldn't define.

She still saw Ellie and Tess on an almost daily basis, but things had changed over the past few months. First Tess had fallen head over heels in love with Justin, the man who'd succeeded her first husband as the new duke of Wansford, and then Ellie had fallen for Henry Brooke, the charming conman who'd claimed to be their fictional boss, "Charles King."

Daisy had been absolutely delighted to see her friends find happiness, but she'd also been struck by a strange melancholy. It was perfectly natural to expect that they'd spend more time with their new husbands, but that didn't stop her from feeling a pang of loss at the natural distancing that had occurred.

Her own single state had simply been thrown in sharp relief, and she'd be lying if she said she didn't envy the fact that they'd both found their perfect match.

She was lonely.

She sneaked another glance over at Vaughan. His confession had made her feel an odd sort of kinship with him. She'd always imagined him invincible, ruthlessly controlled, but he'd allowed her to see a chink in his armor, and she was struck with an incredible thought.

Despite his many friends and lovers, could *he* be lonely too?

Chapter Twelve

The rain eased a little as they arrived at Newark for lunch. Vaughan and Finch went into The Blue Bell, and Daisy grumbled to herself at the fact that she had to remain outside.

Then she remembered the basket of food Mrs. Ward had packed, and her mood improved considerably. She felt absolutely no guilt about eating the delicious array of pastries without saving a single one for Vaughan. He was probably warming himself by a nice crackling fire, while she was trying to ward off the creeping chill of the damp air.

His lips quirked as he climbed back into the carriage and saw the debris of wax paper, cake crumbs, fruit cores, and cheese rinds scattered across her seat.

"It's a miracle you still have all your teeth, considering the number of cakes you eat," he said drily.

"Life's too short to deny yourself something delicious." She shrugged, then blushed at the heat that kindled in his eyes as she realized the potential for double entendre. He didn't disappoint.

"Do you know, I'm beginning to think you're right," he purred.

She gave an inelegant snort. He wasn't flirting with her, however much she might wish he was. It was simply second nature for him to tease. He'd had no problem "denying himself" five years ago, and she doubted he'd be any different now.

She busied herself with packing the picnic away.

"It might interest you to know that our fugitives stopped here a short while ago to change horses," he said.

She glanced up quickly. "Really? How long ago? Can you tell Finch to spring the horses?"

He shook his head at her sudden enthusiasm. "No. There's more rain expected as we head north, and the roads are already bad. I won't risk an animal getting injured, or a broken wheel."

Daisy begrudgingly admitted that he was right. "I don't suppose Violet will be going any faster. At least they won't be increasing their lead."

"Glad to hear you're looking at this sensibly," he said, with a tone of teasing condescension that made her want to punch him.

But that would mean putting her hands on him, and she definitely didn't want to do *that*.

Daisy opened the copy of *Sense and Sensibility* and did her best to ignore him for the next few miles. She'd read the book before, of course—Ellie had given her a copy for her last birthday—and as ever she found herself wanting to give Marianne a good shake for being so foolish over Willoughby and for taking so long to appreciate Colonel Brandon.

The rain returned in earnest about an hour later, drumming deafeningly on the panels and tapping at the glass, and Daisy felt sorry for Finch, getting wet up on the box.

The roads became muddier, slowing their progress to

almost a crawl, and she bit her lip, wondering if Vaughan would decree that they stop at the next change.

She was about to ask, when Finch let out a shout, and the coach lurched dramatically, flinging her forward before she had time to grab the leather strap by the window. She threw out her arms to break her fall, and gave a strangled cry of horror as she tumbled onto the floor right between Vaughan's parted thighs.

Her right hand landed just above his left knee, while her left clutched his other thigh, mere inches from his groin. Her cheeks flamed as his muscles shifted beneath her hand. She tried to rear back, but he'd reached out to catch her, too; his long fingers were gripping her upper arms, holding her in place.

Her breath hitched as she realized their faces were only inches apart, and that his lips were curving into a smile of unholy delight.

"Flinging yourself at me, Hamilton?" he chuckled. "How delightful."

She pushed herself back and onto her own seat, curling her fingers into fists to banish the feel of rock-hard muscle and soft buckskin beneath her palms.

"Not in this lifetime, Vaughan."

The coach was still tilted at an unnatural angle, and Finch was swearing like a sailor above them. With a sigh, Vaughan pulled on his greatcoat and stepped out into the road. A few moments later he opened the door again and held up his gloved hand to her.

"You're going to have to get out. We're in a deep rut, at the bottom of a particularly steep section of road. The horses need to pull the carriage out, then carry on up the hill without stopping. We need to make it as light as possible."

Daisy groaned. She shrugged into her own greatcoat and stuffed her hair up under her hat, then took Vaughan's hand and stepped down into the downpour. Her boots immediately sank into the cold, sludgy quagmire of mud and water, and rain poured down the back of her neck.

Oh, wonderful.

She squelched unhappily to the side, tugging the sides of her coat around her for warmth, and found a small patch of grass on which to stand.

They were in a deep, tree-lined lane, with steep banks of earth and tall hedges on either side, and an unusually steep incline before them. Small rivers of rainwater were flowing down the hill, filling the ruts made by previous carts and carriages and adding to the muddy nightmare.

Finch remained up on the box, trying to calm the horses, but to her amazement Vaughan went round to the rear of the carriage and placed both hands on the back panel.

"Dukes aren't supposed to push carriages," she called out, just to needle him. "You're expected to get back inside and wait for someone to come and help."

"There's hardly anyone else out in this weather. We could be waiting for hours. And besides, I was a soldier before I was a duke. I've pushed plenty of carts out of ditches. At least this one's not full of ammunition. Or bodies. Ready?" he shouted up to Finch.

"Aye. Now push!"

Vaughan let out a grunt as he leaned his whole weight into the carriage. It moved forward a few inches, then slipped back into the muddy groove. He tried again. The seams of his coat strained, and mud sprayed everywhere as the wheels slid sideways, spinning uselessly.

With a sigh, Daisy trudged over to join him, enjoying

his look of surprise when she added her own weight to the effort. It wasn't much, but it was better than nothing.

They both shoved hard, rocking the carriage back and forth to gain momentum, and the wheels suddenly found purchase. The carriage bounced forward, out of the rut, and Daisy almost fell flat on her face. She threw up her hands to shield against the splatter from the wheels, but it was no good. Cold dollops of mud flecked across her face and hands as Finch sent the horses plunging on with a snap of the reins, and the carriage clattered up the hill, veering wildly.

She glanced over at Vaughan and bit back a laugh. The front of his greatcoat, from hem to collar, was covered in mud, and his face was equally dirty.

"You've got mud freckles." She snorted. "I hope you've got a change of clothes in those trunks of yours, *Your Grace,* because nobody's going to believe you're a duke looking like that."

He swiped his forearm over his face, but it only served to smear the muddy spots into long streaks. His previously pristine black boots were ruined, and she tried to ignore the way the rain plastered his dark hair to his forehead.

"Come on, let's go." He gestured up the hill, and with a resigned sigh she set off, slipping and sliding in the mud.

The track was even steeper than it looked, and when she almost turned her ankle for the second time, arms flailing as she tried to keep her balance, he gave a deep growl of impatience, grabbed her wrist, and hauled her along behind him.

Daisy was grateful for the assistance, even if the feel of his fingers made her stomach flutter. When they finally reached the crest of the hill and found the carriage waiting, she was glad to dive back inside, out of the deluge.

Her overcoat was drenched, so she slipped out of it and threw off her hat, then rubbed her hands over her arms to try to warm up.

"There are blankets under your seat," Vaughan said as he climbed in after her, also divesting himself of his coat. "There's no need to shiver like a drowned rat."

Bending over to open the storage compartment put her breeches-clad rear in scandalous proximity to his face, but the embarrassment was worth it when she pulled out two soft woolen blankets.

She tossed one at him and wrapped the other firmly around her shoulders, acutely aware that the front of her wet shirt had become almost transparent where her coat had been open at the front.

Vaughan raked his fingers roughly through his hair, and she had to turn away from how attractive he looked in such ruffled disorder. The rain seemed to have enhanced his scent, too, and her stomach curled as the delicious smell of damp earth and wet pine trees filled the carriage.

A few raindrops still clung to his temple and jaw, and she bit back a ridiculous urge to lean forward and lick them from his skin with her tongue.

Dear God, was wrong with her? She'd barely thought about such carnal things since Tom, but Vaughan's presence was making her body come alive again, all the half-forgotten feelings reemerging like a butterfly from a chrysalis.

"Thank God we're almost at Doncaster," he growled, using his blanket to wipe his face. His cheekbones were stained pink, either from exertion or the stinging rain, and she pressed her thighs together against an unwelcome throb of awareness. Why did he have to be so bloody attractive? It wasn't fair.

"Will we stop there for the night?" Her voice barely more than a croak.

"Yes. I'm not dying of pneumonia just to thwart a stupid elopement. I want a hot bath, a good dinner, and a soft bed."

She suppressed another shiver. Vaughan had seemed adamant that he wouldn't let her sleep the night in the coach, and in truth the desire to be warm and dry was a strong inducement to comply. Perhaps if the Fates were kind, she'd be able to get her own room.

Chapter Thirteen

The Fates were vindictive little bitches, Daisy thought furiously as Vaughan reemerged from the White Horse at Doncaster. This was the fourth establishment they'd tried, and there wasn't a bed to be had in the whole town.

According to a previous innkeeper, they'd arrived during the annual horse fair, which also coincided with a much-anticipated local boxing match, and every hostelry for miles around was packed to the rafters.

"No room at the inn?" Daisy had growled when Vaughan told her the news. "That's a bit biblical, isn't it?"

His lips curved. "Should I have asked if there was room in the stables? I'm sure you have fond memories of rolling around in the hay with your farm boy, but I for one refuse to sleep on a bed of straw."

Daisy clenched her teeth at his needling, wishing she hadn't told him quite so much about Tom. He'd probably tease her mercilessly forevermore.

Although, now she thought about it, she realized she and Tom had never actually made love in a bed. Their brief, stolen trysts had all taken place in either the hay barn, the woods, or out under the stars.

In truth, her amorous experience was nowhere near as wide as she'd suggested to Vaughan. She and Tom had only had full congress a handful of times. She'd refused to court pregnancy, and expecting him to withdraw from her body before he finished was a risky business. She'd trusted that he would *try,* of course, but since he seemed to forget everything, even his own name, when approaching his crisis, it had seemed like an unrealistic expectation. They'd tried using a sheath, but Tom had hated the feel of it, so most of the time they'd simply found satisfaction with hands and mouths.

"We've got a room."

Vaughan's gruff tones made her jump. He stood at the open carriage door, and Daisy hid her dismay.

"Not two?"

"I only got this one because I offered the man who'd booked it three times the original cost to give it up." He rapped the side panel of the carriage impatiently, then held out both of his arms. "Put your coat and hat back on. I'm going to carry you inside."

"What? No! Why?"

"I've told them you're my nephew. You sprained your ankle when we pushed the carriage out of the mud."

"Why would you say that?" she said, aghast at the thought of being in his arms. "Why couldn't I have just walked in there and kept my head down? Or I could put my arm over your shoulder and hobble in."

Not that the thought of putting her arm around his neck, with his arm slung around her waist, was much better.

He rolled his eyes as if she were a simpleton. "You'll be in the public areas even longer if you hop along, and everyone would see how ridiculously small you are. They might get suspicious. If I carry you, it'll be much quicker."

Daisy slapped her hat on her head and turned up the collar of her coat. "Fine."

She stood on the top step and put her arms out to catch his shoulders, but he simply swept her off her feet and started marching toward the front door of the inn before she could do more than utter a faint gasp.

Her cheeks burned in mortification. One of his arms was tucked under her knees, the other tight across her back, and her entire left side was pressed against his chest. Her cheek bounced against his lapel and her left arm was squashed uncomfortably against his stomach. She could feel the rock-hard muscles of his abdomen flexing beneath his clothes as he strode effortlessly into the brightly lit hallway.

"This way, milord," the harried innkeeper said. "Up the stairs and first right. I'll send Jenny up with a poultice for the poor lad's ankle."

Vaughan gave a curt ducal nod, and Daisy refused to be impressed by the effortless way he ascended the stairs as if she weighed no more than a feather. The fingers of his right hand were beneath her armpit, outrageously close to the swell of her breast.

She pressed her nose to the soft wool of his jacket and allowed herself one small, illicit sniff. God, his scent made her toes curl. Perhaps she could steal something of his before they parted ways? As a memento.

He deposited her on her feet with unflattering haste as soon as the door closed behind them, and she looked around the room with a critical eye. It was small, but a fire burned cheerfully in the grate and she rushed forward and spread her hands to the flames, glad of the heat.

Vaughan removed his overcoat and jacket and hung them on the hook on the back of the door, then held his hand out for hers.

"Give me your coat and hat. I've arranged for a meal to be sent up, as well as a bath. With so many guests I doubt it will be more than a hip bath, but better than nothing. We're both caked in mud."

Daisy's heart stuttered. "Bath?"

His eyes glittered with devilry. "Yes. You know. Hot water. Soap. General cleanliness. I'm sure you're familiar with the concept."

"I'm not bathing with you in the room."

He loosened his cravat, and her pulse pounded with alarm. He seemed annoyingly relaxed. "Suit yourself."

She pressed her lips together, but a knock on the door stalled her protest. She went to look out the window, turning her back to the door while Vaughan accepted the promised poultice for her ankle.

"Dinner will be coming right up, Your Grace," the maid said, sounding breathless and a little flustered at the sight of Vaughan, a real, live duke. Daisy rolled her eyes.

When the girl had gone, she turned and studied the rest of the room. A small table and two chairs had been placed by the fire, and there was a washstand with a porcelain jug and bowl on one wall, next to a tall dressing mirror.

But it was the bed that captured her attention. An ancient four-poster, its carved oak columns hung with a heavy floral brocade. At least it looked big enough for two people to share with relative ease, although her heart still gave a dangerous little thump. She would avoid that particular ordeal if she could.

"I don't suppose you're going to do the decent thing and offer to sleep on the floor?" she asked dolefully.

"You're right." Vaughan sounded entirely too cheerful. "I'm not. I slept on the ground plenty of times during the war, and I swore I'd never do it again. You can try it, if you like. Or take the chair, although neither will be particularly comfortable."

She ground her teeth. Fine. He'd left her with no other option.

She was just going to have to drug him.

Chapter Fourteen

The arrival of their meal provided the perfect opportunity. Daisy busied herself washing her hands, pouring water into the bowl while Vaughan directed the servant to put the dinner plates and glasses on the table.

When it was his turn to wash, she pulled the tiny flask of laudanum from her jacket pocket and tipped a few drops into his glass.

The liquid was clear, but she quickly topped it up with wine from the bottle of burgundy the girl had left. She slid into her seat, her heart pounding guiltily, and slipped the little vial back into her pocket.

Vaughan crossed the room and took his place opposite her, and the table was so small that his knee brushed against hers. She shifted her leg and tried to concentrate on the delicious scent of shepherd's pie, instead of the prickly heat that tingled up her thigh.

"This looks delicious," she said, taking a large sip of her own wine.

The intimacy of the scene struck her full-force. There was barely enough space for the plates and glasses, and there were no servants hovering about to act as silent chaperones. The sound of the taproom filtered up from below, a general hum of laughter and conversation, and the fire and single oil lamp provided a cozy, flattering glow.

Vaughan started on his food and she forced herself not to stare at his lips or the way the muscles in his jaw moved as he chewed. She took a bite herself, willing him to take a sip from his glass, but he seemed more intent on eating than drinking.

She'd already finished half of her own wine by the time he finally reached for his glass. His long fingers toyed with the stem, rolling it back and forth so the liquid swirled in a deep red wave, and she held her breath. She wasn't sure exactly how much he'd have to drink; Ellie had said a few drops would be sufficient to make a big man sleep.

He raised the glass to his mouth. Daisy followed the movement, but when he paused with the rim just pressed against his lower lip, she lifted her eyes and found him watching her with a devilishly amused expression.

"Daisy, my treacherous little darling, why don't you tell me exactly what's in my wine?"

She inhaled sharply. "What?"

He gave the contents of the glass a cursory sniff. "Arsenic? Hemlock?" His lips curved as she shook her head in automatic denial. "Don't bother to deny it. I saw you in the mirror."

Her horrified gaze flicked to the long cheval mirror positioned in the corner of the room. The damn thing was perfectly angled so that he would have been able to see the table—and her—while he washed his hands.

And he'd obviously been watching.

Bloody Hell.

Heat scalded her cheeks but she managed a careless shrug. She'd been caught. No point in denying it. "A sleeping potion. Ellie makes it. It contains laudanum, amongst other things."

His brows rose, but he looked more amused than annoyed. "Were you hoping to leave me here and go after the runaways on your own?"

"No. We've already agreed that would be a stupid idea."

"Ah, so you were trying to render me insensible to have your wicked way with me." There was laughter in his tone. "That's rather unsporting. I do like to be conscious when women make scandalous advances."

"I wasn't going to make scandalous advances," she said crossly. "I was trying to make sure you don't bother me in the night."

"Bother you? How do you think I might *bother* you?"

The teasing glimmer in his eyes showed just how much he was enjoying making her squirm. The beast.

"You might snore," she said. "Or steal all the covers."

"I might do those even if you drug me. And that's not what you're afraid of. You're afraid *I'll* be the one making scandalous advances."

"I'm not," she said with perfect honesty. "There must be half a dozen pretty, willing barmaids in the vicinity. You'll have no problem propositioning one of them, if you're inclined. You've no need to resort to someone like me."

He tossed the doctored wine into the fire, where it hissed and spat on the hot logs, then slid her glass toward him, topped it up, and took a healthy swig.

His eyes met hers. "I won't touch you, Hamilton."

She started to exhale, just as he added, "Not until you ask nicely."

His lazy grin was thoroughly obnoxious.

Daisy bit back a snort. She reclaimed her glass and downed the rest of the wine, but a knock on the door saved her from having to say more.

She kept her head down, hiding her face and attending to her dinner as two burly footmen carried in a copper hip bath and placed it in front of the fire. More servants followed, filling it with several buckets of steaming water, and Vaughan accepted a bar of soap and linen washcloths from the blushing chambermaid with a murmur of thanks.

The little procession filed out, and Daisy eyed the tub with a wistful pang. She was cold from the rain and achy in every muscle from bouncing around in the carriage. The water looked ridiculously inviting. But she'd stab herself with one of her own knives before she'd strip in front of Vaughan.

"Being the gentleman I am, I'll let you have the water first."

She glared at him. "I told you. I'm not bathing with you here."

"It's sweet of you to consider my modesty, Hamilton, but I'll let you in on a secret: I've encountered more than one naked female in my time. Unless you're a mermaid, I doubt you've got anything I haven't seen before."

She crossed her arms across her chest.

He gave a theatrical sigh. "Fine. I'll go and have a beer in the taproom with Finch. You've got fifteen minutes, no longer. I refuse to bathe in cold water."

Daisy held her breath as he turned and went out, scarcely able to believe that he'd conceded so easily. Was it a trick? She waited until his heavy tread disappeared down the stairs, then sprang into action.

With a glance at the clock on the mantel to gauge the time, she propped one of the dining chairs up against the door to slow him down in case he decided to come back early and surprise her. Then she stripped off her clothes.

The bath wasn't huge, not like the glorious copper one Tess had installed at Wansford Hall, but it was big enough. She could submerge her shoulders if she bent her knees, and she gave a sigh of happiness as she folded into the water.

It was almost too hot—just how she liked it—and her skin turned pink as she hastily scrubbed herself with the washcloth and soap. She was too worried about Vaughan returning to wash her hair, but she managed to step out and dry herself with five minutes to go.

Out of habit, she slipped the knife from her boot and placed it under the left-hand pillow on the bed, then dressed in a clean shift, shirt, breeches, and stockings. If Vaughan thought she was going to share a room with him wearing only her shift, he was grossly mistaken.

She'd just removed the chair when he knocked at the door, and he seemed amused to find her fully dressed again. Daisy backed up and sat on the end of the bed to give him more room, but it was only after he'd removed his boots, shrugged out of his jacket, and unwound his cravat that the true awkwardness of their situation dawned on her.

"I can't go down to the public rooms to give you some privacy."

He glanced up from untying the neck of his shirt. A deep *V* of tanned skin was already visible at his throat, and Daisy felt her cheeks heat.

"True enough. It's risky to lurk about in the corridor too. There's no end of people coming and going. You'll just have to stay here while I bath."

She tried to inject a mocking note into her voice. "Do you like having an audience?"

His lips quirked. "Not usually. I *like* having a partner, but since these are unusual circumstances, and a very small tub, I'll forgo the pleasure. I'm sure you'll spare my maidenly blushes and promise not to peek."

He tugged the shirt from his breeches and pulled it over his head without any further warning.

Chapter Fifteen

Bloody Hell, he was beautiful.

Tall and lean and ridiculously well proportioned. The curve of his shoulders flowed in a smooth line down to his biceps, and the muscled plains of his chest were ridged with intriguing hollows that made her fingers itch to explore. There wasn't an ounce of fat on him; she could see his ribs, and the slight dusting of hair that ran from his navel down, into the top of his breeches.

Daisy swallowed, her mouth inexplicably dry.

He tossed the shirt carelessly onto one of the dining chairs, then put his hand to the first button of his falls, and she sucked in a gasp.

His brows rose in subtle mockery. "Why are you looking so scandalized? You're no virgin. You've seen a naked man before. Unless you and your stable boy never took your clothes off."

He popped the button, and Daisy couldn't seem to look away.

"Was that it?" he teased. "Did you always do it fully dressed?" He shook his head in disbelief. Or pity.

His taunting snapped her out of her trance. "I've seen a naked man. More than one, in fact."

That was technically true. She'd seen Tom without his clothes. And she'd seen the ancient eighty-year-old Duke of Wansford naked, when he'd died on Tess's wedding night and they'd had to carry him into his own bed. Unfortunately, neither of those experiences bore any resemblance to the magnificent sight that was Lucien Vaughan, shirtless.

Tom had been handsome enough, but he'd still been a youth, muscled yet gangly, all elbows and knees. The old duke had been a pasty, withered sack of bones and skin.

Vaughan was . . . heart-stopping. A creature in his prime, a man in full possession of strength and vitality. The only thing marring all that tawny, sleek perfection was the scarring that ran from his left hand up his forearm to his elbow. That, at least, made him seem more like a human and less like an immortal.

With an effort, Daisy wrenched her eyes away and swung round on the bed so she was sitting cross-legged, facing the wall. She concentrated on the scrolling green tendrils of vine decorating the washbowl.

Vaughan let out a soft laugh beneath his breath. Arrogant swine. He probably thought he'd left her breathless with desire.

Unfortunately, he was right. Her skin felt all hot and itchy, and her stomach seemed to have butterflies trapped inside. She wanted to bang her forehead against the solid oak pillar of the bed. Maybe that would knock some sense into her.

She couldn't see with her face averted, but she could still hear, and her ears strained to decipher every soft, tantalizing scratch of fabric as he undressed. She bit her lip as he clearly unbuttoned his falls and pushed the soft buckskin of his breeches down his thighs. Water splashed as he stepped into the tub, and she squeezed her eyes closed tightly against the urge to peek. Maybe *she* should have taken that bloody sleeping draught and spared herself this exquisite torture.

No, being defenseless with Vaughan in the room would be a terrible idea.

His low hum of contentment made her blood thrum in her veins. She reopened her eyes and turned even further away, but a flash of movement in her peripheral vision made her pause.

Oh.

Oh no.

She could see him reflected in the mirror.

A wicked, guilty thrill made her shiver. This was completely unacceptable. She ought to look away, not spy on him like some perverted voyeur. And yet . . .

He'd spied on her, hadn't he? At dinner.

His back was to her, his arms resting along the top rim of the tub. Light from the fire licked lovingly over his wet shoulders as he rested his head against the back of the bath.

He'd drawn his knees up in front of him, as she'd done, and her eyes roamed over the intriguing swirls of dark hair on his legs. Her cheeks burned as he sat forward, took the soap, and ran it lazily over his chest and upper arms, following the movement with the washcloth. The play of muscles in his back was mesmerizing.

She was just about to look away—she *was*—when he grasped the edge of the tub and stood. Water streamed in rivulets down his back, over the curves of his rear and the thick columns of his thighs, and every good intention fled.

Bloody Hell.

She felt almost winded, as if she'd been elbowed in the stomach. Only *statues* looked like that. Idealized, marble versions of heroes, battle-honed and cold to the touch. Not glistening flesh and blood.

He reached for one of the bath linens on the chair, drying himself with brisk, efficient movements, then stepped out of the tub and wrapped the fabric around his waist.

"Seen enough, Hamilton?"

Daisy almost swallowed her tongue. She whipped her head around and found him standing, hands on hips, laughing at her.

"Wh-what?"

He pointed toward the corner. "In the mirror. Did you enjoy the show?"

Guilty heat scorched her skin. The monster! Had he known she was watching him, this whole time? *Oh God.*

She willed her flush away and produced a careless shrug. "No harm in looking."

A few droplets of water still glistened on his skin and she made a concerted effort not to look any lower than his chest.

"Ah, but are you tempted to touch?"

Yes. Absolutely.

"I think I can contain myself," she managed, with just the right amount of sarcasm.

"You don't have to."

"Don't have to what?"

"Contain yourself."

Her heart stuttered. "What?"

He sent her a dry, knowing expression. "Oh, come now. We're both adults. Aren't you curious to see what it would be like between us?"

"No!"

His brows rose in patent disbelief. "You've honestly never, ever thought about it? Not once?"

She opened her mouth to deny it, but he spoke before she could perjure herself.

"Liar!"

Daisy sought to keep her voice calm. "You don't like me, Vaughan. And I certainly don't like you."

"That doesn't matter. We don't need to be friends to fuck. It's one of Mother Nature's cruelest tricks: it's possible to lust after the most unsuitable people. You can hate me, despise my every breath, and still have the best night of your life."

She would *not* look down at his waist to see if he desired her physically.

She summoned a scornful snort. "Your confidence is ridiculous. It could be the *worst* night of my life."

"Highly unlikely. This antagonism between us only makes it more delicious." His eyes never left hers, and the intensity in them made her body tingle. "When we make love, it's going to be incredible."

"'When'?" Daisy spluttered. "What makes you think I'll ever sleep with you?"

He took a step closer. "Because you're insatiably curious. You love knowledge, and you hate a mystery. You're brave—bordering on reckless—and deep down, you know I'm right. You *want* to give in, and that's extremely vexing for you."

Daisy sucked in a breath. Damn him. He could read her like an open book.

One of his shoulders lifted in a careless shrug. "You're also not someone who lies to herself. You'll stare at the truth unflinching, even if it's an unpleasant truth. You'll acknowledge that you desire me."

He raised his hand to ward off another protest. "You're

also rebellious. You hate being told what to do, and you love the idea of thumbing your nose at convention."

God, even Tess and Ellie didn't understand her as profoundly as this man.

"And you know the final reason?" he murmured.

Daisy tried to sound bored, and not merely breathless. "What?"

"I'm safe."

A shocked laugh escaped her. "Safe? You? Ha!"

"Safe in the sense that you can sleep with me with no repercussions. I already know you're not a virgin, and I don't care. You can sleep with me and be absolutely certain I won't tell a soul. I've no need to crow about my conquests in the *ton*, so your reputation won't suffer, and I have no desire for a wife, so there's no question that I'll try to blackmail you into marrying me."

Daisy's heart was pounding against her ribs. Those were all extremely compelling arguments, and the tug of his allure was so strong.

She wanted to give in.

And yet something held her back. Pride, perhaps. Or maybe she'd finally developed the sense of caution that had evaded her for so long. Either way, she refused to be such an easy conquest.

"I don't need a man to find satisfaction. I can find pleasure on my own."

"With your hand?" He let out a good-natured sigh. "That's so lonely. And also, never as good. Someone else's hand is always better."

She couldn't help it. Her gaze dropped to his hand. The heat of the bath had turned the scars on the back of it a deeper pink, but all she could think about was how good it would feel to have his fingers between her legs. Her body clenched in response, and her gaze slid helplessly sideways, to the unmistakable bulge at the front of the bath linen.

Oh God.

He was aroused, impressively so, and heat swept over her in a fiery wave even as she told herself it wasn't for *her* specifically. Any woman ogling his semi-naked form would provoke the same reaction.

She forced a mocking smile to her lips. "Are you offering me your hand, Vaughan? Or asking for mine?"

He took another step, and she forced herself to stay still as he reached out and traced a light, teasing pattern on her knee. The heat of it seared through her breeches and sent tingles up her thigh.

"Either. Both. Whatever you want."

She ignored the desire pooling in her stomach and caught his hand to still it, and the sudden shock of skin on skin almost stopped her heart. Her thumb slid over the raised, knotted texture of his scars, and for a brief, delirious instant she fought the urge to lift it to her lips and kiss it.

Or to press it between her legs.

And then blissful sanity reasserted itself.

"Tempting, but no." She pushed his hand away, releasing him, and he turned away with a low laugh, as if he'd fully expected her refusal. Beast.

"Pity. I'm sure we'd both sleep much better if we were relaxed."

Daisy scrambled up the bed and dove under the covers. "I'm going to sleep perfectly well, thank you. And *you're* going to sleep on top of these sheets."

"Or what? You'll stab me in the night?"

She slid her hand beneath her pillow and felt the reassuring solidity of her knife. "Don't tempt me."

He shook his head with a chuckle and she turned her

head away as he pulled on a clean shirt and breeches. She did her best to ignore him as he pottered around the room, but when he sank into one of the armchairs by the fire, she watched him through half-closed lids, her nerves jittery.

This was ridiculous. She was exhausted, but how could she possibly sleep with him in the same room, let alone in the same bed?

"I'm going to sit here until my hair dries," he said. "Go to sleep, Hamilton. I promise to stay on my side of the bed."

Daisy yawned. The bed was outrageously comfortable, the weight of the covers pressing her down, and she fought the pull of exhaustion. Vaughan's perfect profile was outlined in the fireglow, and her last surprising thought was that *technically* he was going to be the first man she'd ever slept with. As in, slept beside, all night.

He was never going to let her hear the end of it.

Chapter Sixteen

Lucien stared deep into the fire and concentrated on regulating his breathing. His blood was thrumming in his temples, his cock still aching with arousal, and the infuriating cause of it all was fast asleep in the bed behind him.

He'd never seen anyone fall asleep so quickly. Daisy might claim to mistrust him, but a stupid, gloating part of him felt insanely pleased that she'd let her guard down with such astonishing speed.

Or perhaps she really was just too exhausted to fight him.

Her breathing was soft and even, and he let out a long exhale of his own as he turned his head to watch her. She lay on her side, her hands tucked neatly beneath her chin, her small body barely making a lump beneath the covers.

Awake she seemed larger, somehow, her fiery presence filling the space, filling his brain, but asleep he was reminded of how just slight she was. How fragile.

A wave of fierce protectiveness made him clench the arms of the chair. God, she was a hoyden. How in God's name had they ended up here, in this ridiculous situation?

He shouldn't have anything to do with her, she wasn't his responsibility, and yet he couldn't have left her alone in that lane if his life had depended on it.

Bloody woman.

He'd known physical agony, when the charred skin of his arm had peeled off along with the bandages, but this was torture of a different kind. To have Daisy Hamilton so close that he could smell the faint floral scent of her skin, count the individual freckles on her nose, and yet be unable to touch her. The universe had a wicked sense of humor.

When the pain of his wounds had made him want to scratch his own eyes out, he'd pictured her face. Imagined her in his bed, over him, under him, in every conceivable position, just as a distraction. And now here she was, in a room they shared, a single bed, and she'd rejected his teasing suggestion of a tryst with insulting ease.

She wanted him, though. Even if she didn't want to. It would be amusing if it wasn't so bloody frustrating. If his entire body didn't ache with the need to touch her. Possess her.

He'd reimagined that night five years ago a million times. Wished he'd kept on kissing her, ignoring everything except the ravenous urge to take what he'd been craving for so long. He could have had her right there, on the desk in his study, binding them together in an explosion of passion and heat.

He would have been her first. It would have been hot and fast and fucking incredible, but it wouldn't have been the gentle introduction to lovemaking she deserved. It would have been a mistake.

A glorious, terrible mistake.

He'd been about to leave for war. He'd had no interest in settling down, no desire for any emotional entanglements, but he would have felt honor-bound to offer for her in case she fell pregnant. She'd probably have refused him, stubborn hellion that she was, but still. The whole situation had been untenable.

Lucien raked his hand through his hair and rolled his shoulders to release the tension. She'd refused him tonight, but he'd planted the idea in her brain. Provided they were discreet, there was no reason why they couldn't explore the ridiculous attraction between them now, and he could only pray that she'd see the logic of his argument before they both went mad from frustrated desire.

Unfortunately, logic and Daisy Hamilton were only distant acquaintances.

She didn't stir as he banked the fire and carefully stretched out beside her on the mattress—on top of the covers, as she'd demanded. A faint smile touched his lips. After tonight he could say with perfect honesty that he'd spent the night with her, and there wasn't a soul in London who'd believe he'd kept his hands off her.

He wouldn't tell anyone, of course. But teasing her about it would give him an unreasonable amount of pleasure.

The bed was an ancient four-poster, and he stared up at the gathered fabric above his head, willing his body to calm. Daisy moved, her spine pressing up against his side, and it took all his willpower not to roll over and tug her into the curve of his body. She would fit perfectly in his arms.

Damn it.

With a huff, he turned away from her so they were back-to-back. Considering the amount of blood still in his cock, it was a miracle his brain was still functioning at all, but he closed his eyes and willed himself to lose consciousness.

Chapter Seventeen

Daisy groaned as a clatter from the innyard interrupted a most delicious dream. Her body was warm, tingling with suppressed energy, and it took her several seconds to realize where she was.

In Vaughan's embrace.

She stilled, hardly daring to breathe, as she catalogued the unfortunate situation. He was still above the covers, thank God, but his heavy arm was slung over her waist and her bottom was snuggled intimately in his lap. The hard ridge of his morning erection was nestled against her bottom as if it belonged there, and she resisted the wicked urge to rub herself against him.

His breathing was deep and even; every inhalation pressed his chest against her spine. She was sure he was still asleep.

Her head was tucked under his chin, and the scent of him filled her brain and made her think terrible, wicked thoughts. If she pretended to still be asleep, she could roll over and press her nose to the bare skin of his throat where his shirt lay open. She could raise her chin so her mouth brushed his.

He'd kiss her back. Even half asleep, he'd kiss her. And then he'd wake fully and roll her over and press her down and his hands would be in her hair and—

No. That would be underhanded. She was no coward. If she wanted him, she would be honest about it, not pretend she was dazed and half conscious.

And now was not the time. She had a job to do. A runaway heiress to catch.

But God, it was tempting to stay.

It was clear they'd ended up in this position unconsciously; his body was merely reacting to a female form, not her specifically, but he'd broken his promise not to stay on his side of the bed.

A wicked smile curved her lips. She'd show him.

She slid her right hand slowly beneath her pillow until her fingers closed around the familiar hilt of her knife, then stretched languidly as if trying to get more comfortable. It was hard to move with Vaughan's arm pinning her down, and his lax hand brushed dangerously close to her breast as she turned over to face him.

She held her breath as he stirred slightly, but his eyes remained closed and his breathing even as she angled her blade so the edge of it touched the skin of his throat.

A surge of unholy elation filled her as his eyes snapped open.

"Good morning," she purred.

His pupils flared as he stared down at her, and she bit her lip against the urge to laugh.

"Good morning yourself." His deep timbre rumbled against her chest and made her blood sing. "You had a knife under your pillow."

His composure was impressive, considering.

"I did." Her lips curved in triumph. "I warned you not to underestimate me."

"You did indeed."

He didn't seem appropriately concerned, so she added a little more pressure, and his eyes darkened even more. Her heart began to pound.

"I love how sneaky you are, Dorothea." The heat of him was irresistible.

"Daisy," she growled.

"It makes me want to kiss you." He leaned forward, *into* the blade, accepting the sting so their lips were almost touching.

"I'll cut you," she warned, even as her body tingled with anticipation.

His warm breath skated over her lips. "Worth it."

He closed the distance before she could disagree. His lips pressed hers, hard and warm, and for a split second she let herself melt into the kiss.

And then he moved like lightning. One moment he was kissing her, the next, she was flat on her back, his fingers pinning both her wrists to the bed, his hard body on top of hers.

Daisy gave a howl of frustration at how quickly he'd gained the advantage.

"Bastard! Let me up." Violence and desire had her almost burning up.

His laughter made her buck furiously against him, but that only served to inflame her even more. Her thighs cradled his hardness and his chest pressed down on hers, and she could only be glad that the coverlet provided a barrier between them.

She stilled, recognizing the futility of trying to make him move before he was ready and angry with herself for falling for such an obvious distraction. She'd been stupidly complacent.

"That's better," he murmured, his eyes sparkling with laughter. He gave her wrists a little warning squeeze, but she didn't release her blade, stubborn to the last.

"Nice knife. Where did you get it?"

"From an admirer," she growled. "An Italian thief."

"Whatever happened to giving a girl a nice bouquet of flowers?"

She glared up at him. "I prefer the blade."

"Such a violent little thing." He made it sound like an endearment.

His gaze flicked down to her lips, and she tensed, half hoping he meant to kiss her again, but he rolled to the side instead, easing his weight off her slowly, releasing her. She sat up, rubbing her wrists even though he hadn't hurt her at all.

He slid off the bed and stood, looking down at her, and lifted his fingers to the side of his throat, just beneath his jaw. "First blood to you."

A smear of red coated his fingertips. He angled his chin and glanced in the mirror to inspect the damage, and her heart gave an odd lurch at the sight of the thin cut she'd inflicted on his skin.

His lips curved, as if he found the injury amusing. "Pax?"

She made a point of placing her knife on the bedside table within easy reach. "Are you going to give my other knives back?"

"Eventually. When I'm satisfied you're not going to use them on me. Truce?"

She nodded, still grouchy. "Fine. Yes. Truce."

For now.

~~

Lucien tried not to laugh at the furious color that bloomed in Daisy's cheeks. She looked delicious, her eyes sparking at him, her chest rising and falling in aggravation beneath her shirt.

He turned away to hide the throbbing evidence of his arousal, although she must have felt it when he'd lain on top of her. His stupid body didn't seem to know the difference between fighting and foreplay.

With Daisy, there was hardly any difference. He wanted her with a desperation that was shocking.

He'd been awake for far longer than she had, and he'd reveled in the unfamiliar sensation of waking with a woman in his arms. He'd never invited any of his previous lovers to sleep in his bed or to linger once their mutual pleasure had been achieved.

But holding Daisy felt scarily right. Her curly mop of hair had tickled his chin, her body had nestled into his as perfectly as an acorn fitting into its cup.

Being wicked, he hadn't bothered to deny himself the temptation of touching her while she slept. He'd skimmed his palm over her thigh and into the dip of her waist, stealing the knowledge of her curves with guiltless pleasure. His finger had traced the side of her neck, and she'd shifted restlessly as he'd stroked the petal-soft skin of her cheek and touched the corner of her mouth.

When her pink lips had parted on a restless sigh, he'd snatched his hand away, fearful of being caught even as he weighed the possibility of stealing a kiss.

He'd known the instant she woke. She'd tensed, and he'd feigned sleep, his heart pounding in anticipation as he waited to see what she would do. He'd felt her slide her hand beneath her pillow, but the sweet press of her breasts against his chest and the slide of her leg against his when she'd turned over to face him had been incredibly distracting.

He bit back a smile at the way she'd outsmarted him. He hadn't expected the knife. God, he loved her spirit.

He crossed the room and kicked the fire back to life, giving her space. Distance was probably a good idea.

"I'll go and see about breakfast."

The thump of the water jug against the drawers was the only indication that she'd heard him.

Chapter Eighteen

Daisy pulled the travel blanket around her shoulders and stared sightlessly out the window as the carriage rattled and bounced along the road. She'd had numerous stupid ideas in her time, but this one, asking for Vaughan's help, was definitely the stupidest.

Why had she thought she'd be immune to him after all these years? If anything, she wanted him more than she had at eighteen, now that she knew precisely what men and women could do together.

What she could do with *him*, if she just accepted his offer.

His words had been swirling around her head for most of the day, and try as she might, she could only find one counterargument: What if she allowed herself to make love with him and it was so good that he ruined her for any other man, ever?

That was a ridiculous hypothesis, of course, but there was just something about his innate confidence that made her think it could be a possibility.

There was no danger of her falling in love with him. He was an arrogant, high-handed beast. Even if he *had* procured a hot stoneware water bottle for her feet and this lovely warm blanket to ward off the chill as they traveled increasingly farther north.

He was riding again this afternoon, almost as if he was avoiding her, but every time she spied him, her body reacted with irritating predictability. She wanted him. Just thinking about his hard frame against hers this morning made her hot and shivery at the same time, as if she had a fever. Desire pulsed low in her belly, a wicked chant that sang in her blood.

When he returned to the carriage at Harrogate she opted to ride, but the bracing fresh air didn't cool her ardor. If anything, she felt invigorated, ready for a fight. She returned to the carriage at the next stop, and her awareness of him seemed unnaturally heightened. She tensed every time he changed position, or coughed, or turned a page of his book. She kept sneaking glances at his long legs as they stretched out between them, kept thinking about those fingers of his, touching her skin.

This had to stop. She needed to get away from temptation.

"How far are we from your estate?" she demanded. "You said it was in Yorkshire. Past Harrogate. Aren't we almost there?"

He glanced up from his perusal of the *Racing Post* and blinked, as if he'd forgotten she was even there.

Beast.

"Oh, we passed the turnoff a few miles back. Just after Scotch Corner."

"But . . . why didn't you say anything?"

He shrugged. "You've been extremely vocal on how you need to arrive at Gretna before poor love-crossed Verity and Percival."

"Violet and Peregrine," she corrected.

"Whatever. I assumed that speed was of the essence. Hiring a horse or finding a carriage would just waste even more time."

Daisy narrowed her eyes at him, deeply suspicious. "To what do I owe this sudden helpfulness?"

His lips quirked. "Would you believe I'm doing it for the pleasure of your charming company?"

"Honestly? No."

He snorted in amusement. "Perhaps your comment about me lacking nobility wounded me deeply. Perhaps I've developed a desperate need to prove myself a hero."

It was her turn to raise her brows. "No one would ever confuse you for a knight in shining armor, Vaughan. Not even in the pitch dark."

"Oh no, how will I live?"

She ignored his sarcasm.

"The Scottish border's still too far away to reach tonight," he said calmly. "Your brothers would string me up if I left you to fend for yourself."

"You don't think I'm capable of getting there on my own?"

"I think you're capable of anything you put your devious little mind to, but the thought of you spending the night in a stable, or—even worse—beneath a hedgerow somewhere, makes me break out in a cold sweat."

"Worried for my safety?" she mocked.

"Worried for any poor unfortunate soul who crosses your path. I can't let you stab some innocent bystander in a fit of frustration."

"I'm not frustrated."

He sent her a knowing look that made her pulse pound. "No?"

His gaze slid to her lips, then down over her front, and her nipples tightened beneath the cotton of her shirt. He swept lower, staring at the juncture of her thighs, and she pressed her knees together, trying to ignore the flash of stomach-twisting longing that pierced her.

God, he was awful. He knew exactly how much she wanted him, and it clearly amused him to keep her teetering on the edge of sanity.

"Penrith!"

Finch's shout jolted her from her silent fuming. She turned her hot cheek to look out the window and saw they were pulling into the bustling cobbled yard of an inn whose swinging sign read THE GREYHOUND.

Two private carriages and a mail coach were all getting ready to depart, and there was an air of general chaos as passengers clambered up to sit on the roof, horses shook their harnesses, luggage was stowed, and dogs, chickens, and children darted underfoot.

Daisy almost turned away when a flash of color caught her eye. The young woman being helped up into the farthest carriage was wearing a charming lavender bonnet covered with silk flowers, but it was the riot of yellow-blond curls beneath the rim that snagged her attention. The girl settled herself on the seat in a flurry of lilac skirts as the gentleman who'd helped her in climbed up after her and pulled the door closed.

A golden lion was painted on the side panel.

Daisy gasped. The girl glanced over at her, and even from across the yard Daisy could make out wide blue eyes and a pretty rosebud mouth dropping open in a comical expression of shock.

"That's Violet!"

She shoved open the carriage door and jumped out before they came to a complete stop, stumbling as she landed. Vaughan shouted her name, but she rushed forward, dodging luggage boxes and weary travelers.

"Stop!"

The driver of Violet's coach snapped his whip, and Daisy gave a howl of fury as the conveyance clattered forward and out through the gates before she could make a grab for the horses' reins or attract the driver's attention. She whirled around and raced back to Vaughan's carriage. He'd already stepped down.

"That was them! Quick, we have to go!"

She grasped his lapels and tried to turn him bodily back toward the coach, but he simply looked down at her in amusement.

"Get in, Vaughan!" She growled. "They're getting away."

He didn't budge an inch.

She glanced up imploringly at Finch, who was still up on the box. "Mr. Finch. Please. Go after them."

Finch glanced at her, then looked over her head at Vaughan, and some silent communication clearly passed between them because he scratched his bristly cheek and shook his head.

"Can't do that, I'm afraid, Miss. The cattle are too tired. Wouldn't be right to risk 'em by carryin' on."

Daisy flapped her arms at her sides. "Well then, let's get them changed and be off." She turned and caught the sleeve of one of the hostlers who was tightening the girth of a large gray mare. "Sir, we need fresh horses immediately."

The hostler gave her an odd glance, and she ducked her head, suddenly realizing that she wasn't wearing her hat and that in her urgency her voice had risen far higher than that of the average male youth. She coughed into her hand and glanced back at Vaughan.

"Tell him!"

Vaughan stepped in front of her, neatly shielding her

from view, and the groomsman forgot about her as he took in Vaughan's height and noticed the ducal crest painted on the carriage door.

"I'm sorry, my lord, but those were the last fresh carriage 'orses." He gestured vaguely after the departed carriage.

"We'll ride, then," Daisy said, in a deeper tone. "Quick, saddle us some mounts!"

The man opened his mouth, but Vaughan shook his head. "That won't be necessary, thank you. My impetuous young nephew has clearly failed to notice how close we are to sunset, and I for one refuse to endanger either myself or an animal by riding in the dark."

Daisy elbowed him in the side, hard.

He choked off a laugh, reached back, and caught her wrist in an inescapable grip. "Come, now, boy. What kind of guardian would I be if I let you to go riding about the countryside at night? I'll not have you breaking your foolish neck while you're under my care. Your mother would never forgive me."

Daisy stepped on his foot and scowled up at him when he turned to her.

He bent so his lips were close to her ear. "Be sensible. Even if they make it to Gretna tonight, they won't find anyone to marry them until the morning. We can stay here tonight, rest the horses, and still arrive in time to stop them if we leave early enough."

She gave a soft, frustrated groan. They were *so close*. But Vaughan was right; they could get a few hours' sleep and leave at dawn. All was not lost. She could still stop the wedding and complete her mission.

"Fine."

He nodded, and she clambered back into the coach to

retrieve her hat and coat. Finch collected their luggage and she kept her head down as they entered the inn.

Her spirits rose as the innkeeper informed them that there were several rooms available, but then Vaughan spoke.

"Oh, no, I don't require a second room for my nephew. He's quite the little tearaway. Rather unhappy about being returned to boarding school, I'm afraid, and I need to keep an eye on him. We'll share a chamber. The best you have, please."

The innkeeper nodded in sympathetic understanding. "These young'uns don't appreciate how good they've got it, milord. That's for sure."

Daisy fumed silently under her hat, and trailed the three of them up the stairs and into an impressively large suite decked out in shades of warm ochre. Finch deposited their bags by the door and promptly left with the innkeeper.

As soon as they were alone, she threw off her hat and coat and turned to face Vaughan, ready to berate him about not getting her a room of her own, but his raised hand stopped her.

"Consider me duly chastened," he said, a smile ghosting his lips.

She froze in her tracks at the sudden memory of herself saying those precise words, the night he'd kissed her. Was it a deliberate taunt? Or coincidence? Surely he didn't remember it as clearly as she did.

Either way, she felt just she had back then: angry, humiliated, fizzing with nervous energy.

His brows arched at her silence. "What? No furious tirade about making you share a room? No threat to murder me in my sleep? Are you ill, Hamilton?"

He reached forward as if to put his hand on her forehead to test for a fever, but she deflected his arm and grabbed his wrist. Her fingers barely closed around it, and he could have shaken her off with the smallest effort, but he simply stilled.

Daisy could barely breathe. The room was huge, but he was so close the tips of his boots brushed hers and she glared up into his handsome, mocking face. Angry ferment mixed with frustrated desire in her belly.

Infuriating man.

She wanted him. Hated him.

God, *he* was the fever. He made her body hot and her brain stupid.

A surge of recklessness seized her. She'd thought about him all day, his closeness, his scent, his words. He was right; they didn't need to be friends. Better to regret the things she'd done than the things she hadn't.

She thought of all her childhood heroines: strong, fearless women like the warrior queen Boudica and the Amazons of myth. Women who took what they wanted, and followed their desires.

It was time to do the same.

Chapter Nineteen

"I lied." She stared up into Vaughan's face.

"About what?"

"I've imagined it. What we'd be like together."

His eyes darkened. His lips parted as if he would speak, but she didn't give him the chance. "I've thought about what would have happened if you hadn't stopped, that night in your study."

He leaned in, closing the distance between them. "And what was your conclusion?" His voice was low, almost a growl, and the sound made her knees weak.

"I think it would have been good."

"'Good'?" He spat the word as if it was an insult, but his lips curved up. "As in, average? Vaguely pleasant? A way to pass the time?"

He caught the front of her shirt in his fist, as if he were about to shake her, and Daisy's heart pounded in dark delight as he pulled her up onto her toes. Yes! She wanted him frustrated and irritated too.

"I think I can do better than 'good.'" His breath brushed her lips and her stomach somersaulted.

"Prove it."

His eyes narrowed into threatening slits. "Don't say things you don't mean. I'm in no mood to play games."

"I mean it. We're both adults. I'll be returning to London tomorrow, when I catch the runaways, but there's no reason we can't enjoy each other tonight."

Daisy bit her lip, amazed at her own daring. She'd never propositioned anyone before, but her body was on fire, tingling with anticipation. Please, God, he hadn't been teasing her yesterday when he'd given her all the reasons she should give in. If he refused her now, she'd never forgive him.

But there was no hint of gloating in his expression, only mild suspicion.

His fingers tightened on her shirt. "You're sure?"

"I'm sure."

"Because if we start this, there's no stopping."

His warning tone only made her want him more. Was this some last-ditch attempt at being noble? She didn't want noble. She wanted hot and fast and *now*.

"You promised me 'incredible,'" she taunted. "Afraid you won't be able to deliver?"

His lips quirked in an arrogant smirk. "Afraid you won't be able to get enough?"

That was exactly *what she was worried about.*

She shrugged, feigning insouciance, trying to pretend this wasn't the most exciting moment of her life. "It's just bodies. It doesn't have to mean anything."

She wasn't sure which of them she was trying to convince, but she needed to get him out of her system. Reality—however good—could never match up with her fevered imagination. They'd do this, and she'd be free of him.

The grip on her shirt loosened as he slowly flattened

his palm against her chest. His fingers splayed across her collarbones, then slid up to cradle her jaw.

"Hamilton." It was both a threat and an endearment, and her stomach clenched in dark delight. "You'll be the death of me."

"There are worse ways to go."

"So true."

He kissed her, hard, and she almost laughed in relief against his mouth. *Yes!* This was what she'd been craving. This connection, this passion. This man. His tongue tangled with hers, his taste filling her head, and it was *exactly* as she remembered it. Dark. Delicious. *Intoxicating.*

She released his wrist and slid her arms around his neck, pulling herself against him. He tilted her jaw, slanting his head for better access, and she melted, feeling her nipples tighten beneath her shirt where they rubbed against his chest.

Finally!

His left hand caught her hip, then slid around her lower back to anchor her in place, and his low growl of pleasure made her skin pebble. Liquid heat pooled between her legs.

When he dragged his lips from hers, she relished the way his dark eyes roved over her face. A faint flush of pink colored his high cheekbones.

"We're doing this more than once, Hamilton. Agreed?"

He sounded as out of breath as she was.

She pressed a kiss to the underside of his jaw. "Agreed."

Once wouldn't be enough. She wanted this man in every possible way. If they only had one night, she wanted it to be one she'd remember for the rest of her life.

He nodded. "Right. Do you see that desk over there?"

She turned her head just slightly. A handsome mahogany writing desk stood on one side of the room. She hadn't even noticed it before.

"I'm going to show you *exactly* what I wanted to do to you that night you came barging into my house uninvited."

Her pulse was pounding, but she managed a dazed nod. "Now?"

"Not yet. First, I'm going to strip off those bloody breeches of yours and pleasure you until you can't think straight. Do you have any objections?"

She almost laughed at his bossy, no-nonsense tone. It was easy to imagine him giving such clipped orders to his men during battle. As if she'd have objections to being worshipped by this man.

She pressed her lips to the place where his jaw met his ear and relished the full-body shiver that ran through him. "None at all."

"Excellent. Where are your knives?"

"I've only got one. On my belt. You have the others."

He slid his hand around her waist and pulled the blade from the sheath at the small of her back with his free hand. He tossed it onto one of the armchairs by the fire, then unbuckled her belt one-handed, and she sucked in a breath as his knuckles brushed the sensitive skin of her stomach.

She bit his earlobe in response, and the hand on her jaw tightened with just the right amount of menace. "Wicked girl."

He sucked on her lower lip, then kissed her again. She didn't often cede control, to anyone, but she loved the way he overpowered her.

He made quick work of pulling her shirt over her head and unbuttoning the falls of her breeches, and she helped him, breaking the kiss momentarily to raise her arms, tugging off her boots and wriggling out of the breeches.

She welcomed the urgency. Now wasn't the time for a gentle seduction. She wasn't a shy virgin who needed coaxing to the next step. She wanted him now. Naked, against her, *inside* her.

The thought made her pause. Her body was urging her to throw caution to the wind, but an innate thread of self-preservation still remained.

"I can't risk falling pregnant," she panted, pulling away just slightly.

"Obviously," he growled. "Do you trust me not to put you in that position?"

Daisy bit her lip. He meant: Did she trust him not to finish inside her? With Tom, she'd been afraid to take the chance, but Vaughan had far more worldly experience. He was no callow youth to get carried away and forget himself. And he'd want to avoid an "embarrassing situation" as much as she did.

"Yes."

He nodded, once, and her heart clenched at the sight he made. He'd shrugged out of his jacket and removed his cravat. His shirt lay open at his throat and her fingers itched to explore his skin. She could barely believe she was finally getting this chance. God, she'd wanted this from the first moment she'd laid eyes on him. Desire made her hands shake.

Her hair had escaped from its ribbon, loosened by his questing hands. It hung in a messy cloud around her shoulders, and he reached forward and wrapped a curl around his finger, using it to tug her forward.

She resisted, backing up, pulling him along until her thighs bumped the edge of the bed. She hadn't bothered with a corset or stays. She was down to just her chemise and a pair of white stockings now, and her skin grew hot as his gaze roamed down her throat and lingered on the peaks of her nipples clearly visible through the cream silk.

She'd bought the thing from her favorite dressmaker, Madame Lefèvre; her sole concession to feminine attire.

"Irresistible," he murmured.

He reached out and cupped her breast, holding her gaze as it filled his hand. The pad of his thumb brushed the peak, and he gave a slow smile as it tightened even more.

Daisy felt dizzy. She'd never really given her breasts much thought, but now her entire focus was on the way he touched her so reverently.

She'd expected him to take her quickly, in a passionate blur of limbs, but the bloody man seemed determined to take his time. She sighed in relief when he lifted her to sit on the edge of the bed, but instead of ripping open his falls and thrusting into her as she longed for him to do, he bent and put his mouth over her nipple, suckling her through the silk.

She nearly shot off the mattress. His hot breath dampened the material and sent a flood of warmth to her belly, and when he repeated the gesture with the other breast, she arched and leaned back on her hands, offering herself up to the exquisite, teasing pull.

Just when she was about demand that he push aside the silk and kiss her skin, he placed his hands on her thighs, spread them open, and sank to his knees.

Chapter Twenty

Daisy grabbed his hair in surprise and tried to pull him back up, but he sent her a laughing glance and pressed a kiss to the soft skin on the inside of her knee, just above her stocking.

She gasped. "You don't need to do that, Vaughan."

"No?" He turned his head and kissed the other knee, and liquid heat almost dissolved her insides.

"Really, it's fine. I'm already—"

He made a chiding little click with his tongue. "You're ready when I say you're ready, Dorothea."

"It's *Daisy*." She groaned as he slid his hands higher, over the top of her thighs, shoving the silk higher. Her cheeks burned with embarrassment. She wasn't wearing any drawers, and from his position he must be able to see everything between her legs. Tom had touched her there with his hands, but he'd never studied her the way Vaughan was doing.

She was open. Vulnerable. Exposed in the most primitive way possible. And when he slid his fingers between her legs, she let out an involuntary groan. She was already wet.

"Such a pretty flower," he murmured dreamily. He swirled his fingers, circling her with such teasingly light strokes that she ground her teeth and shifted her hips, an aching mass of want.

"Vaughan," she groaned, warning in her tone. "Stop playing."

The puff of his chuckle warmed her inner thigh. "It's *Lucien*," he chided, in the same tone she'd used to berate him. "You really should call me Lucien." He slid his thumb over the bundle of nerves at the top of her sex, then skated away. "Considering the circumstances."

Obnoxious man. She wouldn't call him Lucien. This wasn't personal. It was physical. Just bodies, mutual pleasure, not something to get emotional about.

Her heart shouldn't be singing at the hot, hungry way he looked at her, as if she were the only woman in the world. The way he breathed her name shouldn't make her wish that she was more than just a willing body to him. That way lay madness.

But when he leaned forward and put his mouth on her, she almost screeched his name. Her fingers tightened in his hair to push him away, or drag him closer, she wasn't sure which, but he placed one hand on her hip, holding her in place as he tasted her.

Daisy's eyes rolled back in her head.

"Did your last lover do *this*?" he purred.

"No!" she gasped, too far gone to even try to pretend.

Dear God, Tom had never used his mouth on her, although she'd used hers on him. Her breath came in soft pants and her stomach muscles tensed as Vaughan flicked and licked, and when he slid his finger inside her she bit her lip against the need to shout out.

It would feel so fucking good.

"God, you taste . . . so good." His words were muffled

against her skin and the vibration had her tightening her thighs around his head. She rolled her hips, trying to make him touch the place inside her that would send her over the edge.

She'd only reached the peak a few times with Tom; it had been more luck than judgment, but she could find it easily enough with her own hand. Especially when she was thinking of Vaughan.

Damn it. The real man was even better than the phantom in her dreams. He was ruining her. Not in a social sense, by taking her virginity, but by etching this pleasure indelibly into her soul. Ruining her for anyone else.

As if he could read her mind, he slid a second finger inside her and found a rhythm so perfect she could barely think. Every touch wound her tighter and tighter, like a watch spring.

"Look at you," he breathed reverently. "So beautiful."

"Vaughan, wait, I'm—"

He curved his fingers and did something wicked with his tongue and she lost the ability to reason.

"It's not all about superior size and weight," he murmured, and she could hear the teasing laughter in his tone even as her scattered brain tried to make sense of his words. "You just need to apply the right amount of pressure in exactly the right place."

The cheeky bastard! He was quoting her own words back at her. But instead of fighting, this was overpowering an opponent in an entirely different way.

Her climax rushed up to meet her. She tried to fight it, to prolong the pleasure, but it was no good. She was too close.

"Now," he commanded, low, and her brain simply shut down.

She plunged off the cliff and fell—down, down, into

that glorious, throbbing lake of pleasure that made her clench around his fingers and dig her nails into his scalp.

When she resurfaced, panting and boneless, she was lying back on the bed, and watched through half-open eyes as he stood and wiped his mouth on the sleeve of his shirt. He pulled the linen over his head, baring his chest, then unbuttoned his falls and removed his breeches, and she pushed herself up on her elbows, greedy for the sight of him.

He was as gorgeous and as intimidating as he'd been last night after his bath, only this time she could see all of him. The slope of his shoulders, the flat plains of his chest, the dark curls between his legs.

Her eyes slid lower. She'd heard a score of words for the male appendage, especially in the rougher parts of London when she, Tess, and Ellie had been working undercover. The English language had a glorious richness and range. The three of them had compiled an ongoing list of terms; there were several dozen at the last count. Rod. Shaft. Prick.

Daisy liked *cock* best. It seemed fitting for something that stood so proud and made a man inclined to strut.

Vaughan's was as impressive as the rest of him, and a smile curved her lips at the fact that at least he wasn't feigning his desire for her. A woman could pretend she was desperate for a man, but men had no such ability. He *definitely* wanted her.

And God, she wanted him.

His eyes held hers in silent challenge as he put his knee on the bed, dipping the mattress. He reached down and pulled off her right stocking, then the left, dropping them to the rug.

"I want to see you naked."

His voice was low, like gravel, and Daisy shivered as

she sat up and drew the chemise over her head, intensely aware of his eyes upon her, following every inch of newly bared skin. The drag of the fabric felt like a caress, and her nerve endings tingled in anticipation.

She tossed the silk aside without an ounce of regret.

Chapter Twenty-One

Lucien's head was spinning. Daisy was naked in front of him, and a part of his brain was still struggling to accept that this was real, and not just one of the sweat-soaked fantasies he'd conjured in his delirium when he'd been wounded.

No, he was definitely here. The taste of her was in his mouth and the soft, desperate sounds she'd made when he'd pleasured her still echoed in his ears.

This was a hundred times better than his fever dreams.

He'd removed countless female corsets and petticoats in his life, but this was the first time he'd ever divested a woman of a shirt and breeches. Her silk chemise, however, had been deliciously feminine, like water, rippling and eddying around her curves, cut low to reveal the shadowy valley between her breasts. He'd almost laughed at the way his heart had pounded against his ribs, like a youth who'd never seen a woman in her underwear before.

Daisy Hamilton had the most ridiculous effect on him. Always had. Probably always would. She was his Achilles' heel, the weak spot in his armor, but he'd ceased to question it years ago. It just was.

He had no illusions that taking her tonight would get her out of his system. If anything, it would make things a hundred times worse, because every time he looked at her from now on, he'd be haunted by the taste of her, the feel of her. And he'd want more. And more. And more.

Which was impossible. But he'd rather face another grenade than stop now.

Daisy was watching him with a combination of hunger and challenge that made him harden even more. Her cheeks were flushed, her hair a god-awful tangle of curls around her shoulders, and he'd never wanted anything so much in his entire life.

He fisted his cock as he placed his other knee on the bed, straddling her, and her eyes widened as she watched him.

"Change your mind, Hamilton?" he teased, only half joking. God, her skin was so beautiful. He wanted to lick every freckle. "No shame in ceding the field if you're outgunned."

She shook her head against the sheets. "You're not throwing me out tonight. Stop talking, and ravish me."

Bloody woman. She was so small, despite her physical toughness, and as much as he wanted to fuck them both into a glorious tangle of sweaty limbs, he didn't want to hurt her. Ever.

Daisy, however, seemed determined to make him lose control. When he leaned over her, caging her with his fists on either side of her head, she skimmed her hands over his ribs, his chest, then lower, over the ridges of his abdomen, her fingers sending shivers all over him. Her arms were too short to reach his cock, thank God, and her frown of frustration when she realized it made him bite back a snort of laughter.

If she touched him there, it was all over. He'd finish in her hand.

She reached up to his shoulders and tried to tug him down, demanding all of his weight. He could have resisted, but he let her win, and the feel of her bare breasts against his chest made him stifle a groan. Her soft belly pressed his, and she parted her thighs so that he slid between them, exactly where he ached to be.

He rolled his hips, and she sucked in a breath as his cock slid against her slick folds. He dropped his head to her shoulder, striving for control, but she kissed his jaw, her fingers clutching the hair at his nape as she tilted her hips, spurring him on.

"What are you waiting for?" she groaned, and he relished of the edge of desperation in her tone. It mirrored his own. "Do it, Vaughan, or I *will* stab you."

God, he loved her demanding.

He pressed forward, entering her slowly, savoring the incredible squeeze as her body closed around him.

So good.

He pushed up on his forearms and caught her chin, forcing her to meet his gaze.

"You feel that?" he growled, his heart pounding in fierce exultation. "That's me, Daisy, inside you. Giving you what you need."

He pushed deeper, loving the way her eyes widened and her lips parted in wordless pleasure. Her chin tilted up in his hand and he didn't look away. He wanted to burn this image, this feeling, into his soul.

"Yes." she whispered. "More."

He pulled back and slid into her full length, and she arched her back and welcomed his invasion.

He was drowning in her eyes. God, he was so fucking

grateful to be alive. To be here, in this moment. It made every second of pain he'd suffered worth it.

"So good. This . . . I . . ." Words seemed to have deserted him. All he could concentrate on was her body enclosing his, the astonishing perfection of the fit.

He pumped his hips again and the scent of her skin curled around him and his mind went a little fuzzy.

"Next time we'll take our time," he breathed, a promise and rueful apology. "But now I *really* have to fuck you."

Her lips curved up in a mischievous smile.

"Finally."

The tenuous thread he'd been exerting over his control snapped. Five years he'd been waiting for this. Five. Fucking. Years. She wasn't a virgin. She was sleek and tight and . . . *Daisy.* She could take whatever he gave.

He kissed her, plunging his tongue deep into her mouth, tasting her with a wildness that matched the rocking of his hips. She rose up to meet him with equal hunger, wrapping her legs around him and taking him even deeper and he closed his eyes and lost himself.

He squeezed her hip, palmed the sweet curves of her arse, and she gasped her approval, raking her nails down his back and matching his thrusts in the most perfect rhythm. He slid his hand between them, feeling himself sliding into her, and her fingers tightened in his hair.

"Yes. There. Please." Her throaty moans sent waves of pleasure through him, gathering at the base of his cock.

"Don't stop," she panted.

Never. He'd never stop. Whatever she wanted. He was hers.

He swirled his fingers and she went rigid beneath him, bucking against his hand as she reached her peak. Lucien tried to slow his strokes, to give her time to finish, but the feel of her clenching around him almost pushed him over the edge. He thrust hard, once, twice, remembering his promise to keep her safe only at the very last second.

Fuuuuck.

He pulled out of her an instant before pleasure washed over him like the blast of a grenade; an instant of stunned, timeless perfection, then complete annihilation.

Chapter Twenty-Two

Daisy could barely breathe.

Vaughan had collapsed on top of her, pressing her down into the mattress with a deliciously heavy weight, and she suppressed an incredulous laugh. She'd never imagined she'd see him so uninhibited, and the fact that she'd made his body so thoroughly replete with pleasure felt like no small accomplishment.

He hadn't forgotten his promise not to finish inside her, either, and her heart clenched with a traitorous little squeeze that he'd kept his word.

There were ways to avoid an unwanted pregnancy, even if he *had* forgotten. Tisanes like pennyroyal tea and the like, but she'd heard so many tales of unpleasant side effects and potential dangers that she never wanted to put them to the test.

She brushed his side with her fingertips, lightly tracing his ribs, and he rolled off her with a deep, satisfied groan. She turned her head to look at him, almost too tired to move, and found his eyes dark with satisfaction.

"*That* was . . ." Her voice was a croak and she struggled

to find the right words. Incredible? Extraordinary? He was arrogant enough as it was. He'd be obnoxious now.

"Five years overdue." He let out a deep sigh and pushed one of her curls behind her ear. "God, Hamilton. It's just as well we didn't do that before I left for Portugal. I never would have gone."

He was joking, of course, but her heart fluttered just the same.

"It wouldn't have been like that five years ago," she reminded him. "I was still a virgin."

"Only in body. In spirit, you were a shameless wanton."

She gasped, and he chuckled at her outrage.

"Don't deny it. You practically undressed me with your eyes every time you saw me across a room."

"I did not!" Her cheeks were definitely burning.

"You did. And I did exactly the same to you. You can't imagine the filthy things we were doing in my mind. I swear, one time I was talking to Lord Castlereagh about some stupid law or other and you caught my eye and I got so hard I had to excuse myself."

Daisy bit her lip, trying to quash a delighted smile. "Really?"

His eyes narrowed in mock-menace. "Really. You were the most provoking chit imaginable."

"I'm sure you found another partner to deal with your . . . little problem." Her spirits dropped at the thought of him sating himself with another woman, but she was determined to appear sophisticated.

"Nothing *little* about it," he growled. "And for your information, no, I didn't. I went and locked myself in a water closet and relieved myself with my hand, cursing you with every breath."

His dark gaze pinned her as he reached out and traced the pad of his thumb over her lower lip, dragging it down

to stroke the slick inner lining. Her stomach swooped.
"And the whole time I imagined I had you there, on your
knees, looking up at me, that wicked mouth of yours on
my cock."

Daisy swallowed. God, she could imagine it too. Her
body heated again.

"I had no idea I affected you so strongly," she managed.

He rolled over and slid off the bed, and she immediately felt the loss of his warmth.

"You affect me," he said with a dark laugh. "You drive
me bloody insane."

Her heart warmed at the backhanded compliment.
She'd take any reaction that wasn't indifference.

He padded, gloriously naked, to the linen press that
stood against one wall, opened it, and pulled out a clean
bathing sheet, which he brought back to the bed. Daisy
reached out to take it, suddenly very conscious of her na-
kedness, but he ignored her outstretched hand and sat
down next to her, using the cloth to wipe the evidence of
his pleasure from her belly.

She forced herself not to wriggle under his ministrations, and when he'd finished, she sat up and pulled on
her chemise. The flimsy barrier made her feel slightly less
exposed. She wasn't used to lolling about naked.

"We never made it to the desk," she teased lightly.

He slanted her a look as he pulled on his shirt. "The
night is still young."

She glanced at the clock on the mantel and blinked in
surprise. It was barely nine o'clock! Her cheeks heated.
They hadn't even locked the door. Finch, or any of the servants, could have interrupted them.

Vaughan was a menace. He made her forget herself.

He pulled on his breeches, jacket, and boots with swift
efficiency. Two years in the army had clearly negated his

need for a valet. "I'm going down to order some dinner. Shall I ask for a bath too?"

Visions of soaping his body, of him doing the same to her, filled her brain, but Daisy shook her head. She could barely explain it, but to bathe together somehow seemed even more intimate than what they'd just done. Losing herself in a white-hot passion was one thing. Administering to one another in the bath suggested a tenderness, a playful affection, that would be dangerous to wish for. Or encourage.

They weren't friends, merely lovers.

She had to remember that.

"I'm too tired to bathe. Just ask for some hot water so I can wash, please. And food. I'm famished."

"Worked up an appetite?" he teased as he slipped out the door.

A maid carrying a bowl of hot water arrived a short while later, and Daisy washed, then pulled on her own shirt and breeches. Vaughan had probably shared countless meals with scantily clad women, but she would feel at a distinct disadvantage if he was dressed and she was only in her chemise. Equality was important.

He reappeared just as she was starting to get bored, trailed by a servant with a tray of food, and her stomach rumbled as their meal was set on the table. She slid into her seat and attacked the steak pie and mashed potatoes with genuine pleasure.

Vaughan rolled his eyes at her enthusiasm, but his lips curved as he watched her.

Was he regretting their liaison already? Wishing he'd asked for a second room so they didn't have to share this one now that he'd sated his curiosity and lust? She couldn't tell.

He settled in the seat opposite her and made a point of

lifting his empty wineglass to the light to inspect it, and Daisy snorted when she realized what he was doing.

"Don't worry, I haven't tried to poison you tonight. I need you up bright and early tomorrow so we can catch Violet and Peregrine."

He poured them each a glass of wine. "As if I could forget. Has anyone ever told you you're relentless?"

"Many people," Daisy grinned. "As well as stubborn, pigheaded, and far too independent."

"You're positively riddled with flaws."

"Which is why I remain happily unwed."

"Retaining your independence while taking a secret string of lovers to fulfil your physical needs?"

Daisy fought a flush. No need for him to know that *he* was the only man who'd pleasured her in over two years. "Exactly."

"I must say, you've been extremely discreet. Or lucky."

"What do you mean?"

"I haven't heard a whisper about any of your previous paramours, and it's almost impossible for an unmarried woman to take a lover without someone finding out. You're running the risk of being disgraced socially."

"So sweet of you to be concerned for my reputation."

He ignored the irony in her tone. "Even if you don't want a husband to provide financial security, or to improve your social standing, have you considered marrying for physical satisfaction?"

Daisy raised her brows. "Giving someone complete control over my life for the sake of a few moments of pleasure—however delightful they might be—seems like a bad bargain. What happens when my husband loses interest and finds his pleasure elsewhere? As my father did to my mother."

"I can't imagine any man losing interest in you."

She rolled her eyes. "How many women have you said that to? A dozen? A hundred?"

He held her gaze. "You're the first."

Her heart gave a twist, but she ignored it. He wasn't being serious.

"Are you offering me *your* hand in marriage?" she teased. "Or is this purely theoretical?"

His lips gave a sardonic curl. "You've seen my hand, Hamilton. What woman would want something so scarred and unsightly?"

"Oh, I can think of a hundred girls who'd jump at the chance to be called 'Your Grace,'" she said with perfect honesty. "Scarred hand or no."

"But not you." He made it a statement, not a question.

She sent him a smile over the rim of her wineglass. "The only way I'd accept your hand, Vaughan, is if you put it between my legs."

He laughed in appreciation of her wit. "With pleasure."

Chapter Twenty-Three

Daisy disappeared into the adjoining dressing room while the dinner plates were cleared away, and when she emerged it was to find Vaughan making a circuit of the room, extinguishing the candles and turning off the lamps. Soon the only illumination came from the glowing fire in the grate.

She'd removed her breeches and shirt in preparation for sleep, but as he glanced up and saw her lingering in the doorway in just her chemise, her heart started to pound. The look on his face was the same hot, hungry look he'd sent her across a hundred crowded rooms—only now it was just the two of them, alone in the dark.

"Come here."

His low command made her stomach flip. She crossed the room, but when she got close enough to touch him, he caught her hips and pushed her back against the edge of the desk. Her pulse kicked up another notch.

"You were wearing a wicked dress, that night," he murmured. "I wanted to eat you up."

He slid the chemise off her shoulder and pressed a kiss to the side of her neck, following it with a gentle bite that sent a jolt of heat curling through her bloodstream. Daisy gripped the edge of the desk, determined not to show how desperate she was for him.

"I wanted to kill every man who looked at you." He pushed the silk down, exposing her breasts to the fire-light, and she sucked in a breath as he took one into his mouth.

Oh God. This was what she'd wanted that night. His mouth on her. His hands. Every ounce of his attention.

And now she had it. Just for tonight.

He swirled his tongue, then lightly teethed her nipple while his left hand stroked her other breast and Daisy arched up into his touch like a flower craving the sun-light. The scrape of his evening beard made goose bumps break out on her arms and she felt him smile against her skin.

He knew what he was doing to her.

His hands slid down to caress the bare skin of her thighs, sliding up under the hem of the chemise. She shifted, restless, and he caught her hips and lifted her to sit on the edge of the desk, bare feet dangling. He stepped between her knees, his soft buckskin breeches sliding against her inner thighs, and she tilted her head back to look into his face.

"I can't believe I managed to resist you." His eyes were almost black as he slid his hand up her throat and cupped her jaw. "God, Daisy. *This* is what I wanted to do."

He tilted her chin and kissed her, a kiss so blatantly carnal it was a miracle she didn't go up in flames. Daisy groaned and met his tongue with hers, savoring the edge of hungry desperation.

He unbuttoned his falls and she shifted to the edge of the desk as the hot length of him slid against her, teas-ing her with the promise of more. She wrapped her legs around his hips, dragging him even closer as he positioned himself at the entrance to her body.

"Yes," she whispered, shameless. She leaned back, bracing her hands on the desk as he cupped the back of her head, threading his fingers into her hair.

He entered her in a slow, delicious thrust. There was no resistance; she was more than ready for him, and she gasped, savoring the stretch, the incredible sensation of fullness and completion.

He was inside her, around her, commanding every one of her senses. The midnight-forest scent of his skin filled her nose, his taste filled her mouth. He made her feel overwhelmed and cherished, helpless and powerful, all at the same time.

"This is what I wanted," he repeated hoarsely, tightening his grip in her hair. He rocked his hips and they both shuddered. "You. With me. Like this."

He pulled back with almost punishing slowness, then pushed in deep again, setting a tantalizing rhythm that made her blood sing in her veins. He kissed her, his tongue tangling with hers, mimicking the thrust of his body, then bit her lower lip, sucking it into his mouth, easing the sting with another kiss that made her clench around him.

"So. Fucking. Good," he rasped.

The desk was hard beneath her, not entirely comfortable, but she wrapped her arms around him, holding him close, loving the feral way he was taking her, hard and almost desperate. She tilted her hips, trying to find just the right angle, then gasped as he suddenly caught the back of her thighs and lifted her clean off the desk.

The room blurred as he carried her over to the bed as if she weighed no more than a feather. When he laid her on the mattress and followed her down, still buried deep within her, the change of position nudged the perfect place inside and she couldn't contain her groan of pleasure.

"Good?" He pushed forward again, apparently conscious of her every gasp and shudder.

"So good," she panted, scarcely able to frame the words. "Just . . . keep—"

He didn't stop. He drove into her, a relentless pace that made everything knot tighter and tighter. She was almost there. She fisted his hair, tightening her fingers in a way that must have been painful for him, but he just let out a rough sound against her throat.

"Yes. Use me. Hurt me if you need to. Take what you want, Daisy. Take me."

She held her breath, straining against him to reach the peak. And then it came, blinding, stealing her wits in a rush of pleasure so strong she felt as if she was drowning.

He held her close as she splintered apart, but as soon as her shudders faded, he withdrew from her body. When she protested, he merely shook his head, rolling to the side and fisting his cock.

"Promised," he gasped, pumping his hand. "Not inside you."

His back arched and his hips bucked as he reached his own climax, and Daisy watched in awe at the way his muscles rippled and twitched. God, he was beautiful. Seeing him come apart, eyes squeezed closed, head thrown back against the pillows, was the most incredible sight she'd ever seen.

He let out a deep sigh and relaxed into the bedclothes, his big body suddenly lax, and she couldn't prevent the foolish smile that spread across her lips.

"Well, you certainly keep your promises, I'll give you

that," she breathed, and he let out a low, exhausted rumble of amusement.

"Man of my word. Told you."

A laugh bubbled up in her chest. "You didn't even remove your clothes."

He glanced down and seemed surprised to discover that he was still wearing his breeches, boots, and shirt. He frowned down at the damp mess he'd left on his shirt, over his belly, then pulled the garment over his head and crumpled the material into a ball.

"I'm not going to have any clean clothes left at this rate," he grumbled.

Daisy sent him a weary smile. "Don't worry. Tomorrow you can go and find all the clean clothes you could wish for. As soon as I get Violet and Peregrine, you'll be free to return to your country house."

She'd thought the reminder would cheer him, but his lips compressed, and he looked vaguely irritated for a moment before his expression cleared. "I suppose we ought to get some sleep, then, if you want an early start."

He rose from the bed and she tried not to ogle him as he tossed his shirt onto one of the chairs and stripped out of his breeches. The dying embers of the fire caressed the strong lines of his body, and she bit back a wistful sigh. She could look at him naked every single day and not get bored.

He turned and caught her eye as she tugged her chemise back up over her shoulders.

"Am I permitted to sleep *under* the covers tonight?"

She slipped under the sheet, then threw back the coverlet for him. "You might as well. It will be warmer."

She waited for him to pull on a shirt, but he padded back to her naked and slid in beside her. She shivered as he stretched out, but then he reached over and pulled her against his side and her body relaxed, melting into his warmth with a sigh of surrender.

Just for tonight.

Tomorrow they'd go their separate ways, and it was unlikely that she'd see him with any regularity once they were back in London. She'd be able to look back on this extraordinary interlude with a happy smile.

If they *did* happen to meet at some social event or other, they could just pretend to be nothing more than polite acquaintances. And if her heart felt a little pang of residual longing, then it was a small price to pay. A man like Vaughan was only ever going to be a temporary madness.

Daisy closed her eyes and allowed herself to wriggle closer to him, and she could have sworn she felt the brush of his lips against her temple as she drifted off to sleep.

"Good night, Hamilton," he murmured. "Sweet dreams."

Chapter Twenty-Four

The pale gray light of early morning was filtering through the curtains when Daisy cracked open her lids, but it was the sensation of Vaughan's lips nuzzling her neck, his hand trailing lightly over her breasts, that pulled her fully into wakefulness.

Her limbs were warm and heavy, her whole body filled with a delicious lassitude. She wanted to stay in the warm cocoon of his arms forever.

But a glance at the clock on the mantelpiece confirmed what she'd already suspected: they needed to get on their way.

Vaughan let out a disappointed groan as she pulled away from him and slipped out of the bed.

"Where are you going? Come back. I need you."

His voice was like gravel, rough from sleep, and her stomach tightened with want at his words. If only they had more time.

"We can't. We have to go. I have to stop that wedding."

He rolled over onto his front and his biceps bulged as he pulled his pillow over his head. He mumbled something incomprehensible into the sheets.

"What was that?"

He removed the pillow and turned on his side to face her, and she tried not to think about how gorgeous he looked with his dark hair mussed from sleep and the shadow of stubble peppering his jaw. He looked divine, utterly debauched. She took a step back from temptation.

"I said, forget about bloody Victoria and Peter."

"Violet and Peregrine," she corrected with a smile.

"I'll pay you five hundred pounds *not* to go after them."

"I can't do that," she countered. "And it's not just about the money. The reputation of King and Company is at stake, too. We've been hired to return Violet to London unwed, and that's what I plan to do."

"A thousand pounds," he groaned, sounding desperate. "I'll pay you a thousand pounds to get back into bed with me right now."

Daisy bit back a smile, even as she put her hands on her hips and glared at him. "You're making me sound like an *extremely* expensive courtesan."

He rolled his eyes. "You know what I mean. I'm not offering you money for sex. I'm offering you money so I don't have to leave this surprisingly comfortable bed and go haring across the Scottish border at the arse-crack of dawn. Have pity, Hamilton."

She shook her head, steeling herself against his pleading, and ignoring the twisted knot of desire in her belly.

Just one more time.

No. She couldn't let Tess and Ellie down.

"Come on, get up. Or I'll go without you."

She turned from the far-too-tempting sight of his bare chest and hastened to her bag. Keeping her chemise on, she donned a clean shirt, breeches, and stockings, then tugged on her boots.

Vaughan was still sitting in bed when she glanced back at him and she bit back a growl of impatience. He had absolutely no sense of urgency. She grabbed the corner of the coverlet and shook it, and he let out a howl of annoyance as the cold air touched his naked skin.

"God, woman! All right. I'm coming."

He threw back the sheets and stood, and her eyes widened at the sight of him. He was fully, unashamedly aroused, his cock standing proudly to attention, and he sent her a dark, sardonic look from under his brows.

"We're wasting a perfectly good cock-stand, I'll have you know."

Daisy swallowed, clenching her fists against the urge to drop to her knees and take him into her mouth. Her pulse rate doubled, and she bit her lip.

Vaughan made an anguished noise. "Stop looking at me like that, or I'm going to stop being noble, bend you over that desk, and make you forget all about your bloody assignment."

It was no empty threat. He could distract her with the least effort, and both of them knew it.

Daisy dragged her eyes from him and turned her back, shoving her dirty clothes into her bag. She fastened her belt around her waist but slid her single blade into her boot instead of the leather sheath at her back. It was more comfortable for riding in the carriage.

She let out a relieved sigh as she heard Vaughan stomp into the adjoining washroom and splash some water into the bowl.

"Where are my other two knives?" she called through the door.

"Still not ready to return them," he growled back.

She sighed, regretting the change from lovers back to reluctant collaborators.

With a final glance at the rumpled bed, she hefted her bag and unlocked the door. "I'll meet you down in the yard. There's no time for breakfast. We can eat something when we get to Gretna. It's only a few miles."

Vaughan cursed fluently, and she fled.

Finch, thankfully, was already awake and in the yard, readying the horses. He declined Daisy's offer of help, so she hopped from foot to foot to keep warm in the morning chill.

The sun was peeking over the horizon when Vaughan finally emerged, clean-shaven and annoyingly well turned out. Daisy was sure her hair looked like a bird's nest under her hat, but she'd forgotten her comb so there was nothing to be done about it.

"Let's go. Come on!" She was practically bouncing with impatience, but he was immune to being rushed.

He shook his head in clear exasperation, and glanced up at Finch. "The innkeeper says to watch out for brigands between here and Wetherby."

Finch nodded, unperturbed, and clambered onto the box, and Daisy heaved a sigh of relief as they finally got underway. She had no idea what time the blacksmith-cum-parson at Gretna opened his doors, but it surely wouldn't be any earlier than eight o'clock. They ought to arrive in plenty of time.

Vaughan seemed lost in thought, so she watched the gently undulating green and brown of the heathland beyond the window. Compared to the lush fields and forests farther south, the moors seemed bleak and unwelcoming. The only trees were low and stunted, hunched against the wind, and the ground cover was mainly wild grasses, gorse, and heather.

It was definitely colder up here, too, and she suppressed a shiver and the unhelpful thought that if she were a different kind of woman—one less driven and more open to bribery—she'd still be snuggled up, warm in bed with Vaughan right now.

Just the thought of what they'd done sent a flush of heat over her skin, as if she had a sickness, a physical yearning for his touch.

They started to slow, and she peered out the window, expecting to see another vehicle up ahead, or an obstacle, but the road was clear.

"What is it, Mr. Finch?" she called up.

The carriage came to a complete stop and rocked on its springs as Finch clambered down. She let down the step and climbed out to find him examining the leather straps that secured around the nearside horse's belly.

"The girth strap's snapped. Never seen that 'appen before." He shrugged fatalistically, and Daisy almost screamed in frustration.

"Can it be fixed?"

He shook his head and glanced over his shoulder at Vaughan, who had finally deigned to lean out of the carriage.

"Don't think it can," Finch said. "And without it, the other straps won't stay put, so the traces won't sit straight. It'll hurt the horse."

Daisy raised her eyes to the sky. "I can't believe how unlucky we're being."

"Maybe the universe *wants* those two idiots to be together? Have you considered that?"

Vaughan's lazy drawl made her temper rise even more. She swung round to face him. "Don't tell me that you, of all people, believe in fate and destiny and true love?"

His smile didn't waver. He seemed to be enjoying her ire.

"Is that so incredible?"

"Frankly, yes."

"Well, in truth I *don't* believe in fate," he admitted wryly. "At least, I don't think I survived the war because it was somehow preordained. I think there were a million different choices and events that led to me dodging death. Some of which were my own—the decision to duck left instead of right to avoid a saber, for example— but countless others were entirely beyond my control. It was just blind luck."

"Right. So by that reasoning, Violet and Peregrine can still be stopped." She glanced back along the road, hoping to see another vehicle, but the road was deserted in both directions. "Fine. I'll just have to ride."

"We don't have a saddle, miss." Finch said morosely.

"I can ride bareback, with just the reins. I used to do it all the time back at Hollyfield."

Admittedly, that was years ago, and on her trusty mare Polly, but she would not be thwarted this close to the finish line, nor admit any weakness in front of Vaughan. "We can't be more than a mile or two from the border."

She started to unbuckle the rest of the horse's straps, and heard Vaughan give a deep sigh behind her. She thought he muttered, "Un-fucking-believable," but she couldn't be sure.

"Will you ride with her?" Finch asked Vaughan.

"I suppose I must. Someone has to keep an eye on her. I'll send a man back with two horses and a new strap when we reach Gretna."

When both mounts had been unhitched, Daisy accepted a boost up onto the gray and watched with reluctant admiration as Vaughan swung himself up and onto the larger chestnut. He wheeled the animal around and sent her a bored glance.

"Ready?"

Daisy wasn't ready at all. She'd forgotten how much harder it was to stay atop without stirrups or saddle. Still, she gripped the reins and pressed her heels to her mount's sides to get him to move forward, and soon they left Finch and the stranded carriage behind.

After a mile or so she forgot her nerves as the familiar sensation of riding bareback returned, and she increased the pace, laughing as the wind tore at her hair. For a brief moment she felt like a girl again, wild and free, galloping around the estate, or heading into the village to call on Tess.

She glanced over at Vaughan, trotting easily beside her, and wished they'd had more time together. She hadn't expected to enjoy his company quite so much.

And then the village of Gretna appeared in the distance, and she forgot about everything except the mission.

"There it is! That river marks the border between England and Scotland."

She didn't dare urge the horse into a canter, since she was sure she'd fall off, so she curbed her impatience as they ambled over the bridge and joined a steady stream of carts and pedestrians who all seemed to be heading toward the center of the bustling little village.

The first building they passed was the toll house—also a place where she'd heard marriages could be performed—and she checked the yard to be sure Violet's carriage wasn't there, then continued down the narrow street.

"What time is it?"

Vaughan took a gold pocket watch from inside his jacket. "A quarter past eight."

The street widened as they passed a series of small

shops and inns, mostly built of pinky-gray stone, and Daisy felt almost sick with nerves as she spied the smithy up ahead at the crossroads.

The building itself was tiny, a single-story white-painted affair with black window frames, and to her utter dismay she saw that smoke was already billowing from the chimney.

She slid from her mount just as the front door opened and a small group of people came out, including a girl in a pretty lavender dress. Her heart dropped as she recognized Violet Brand's cheery blond curls.

"Noooo!" she groaned.

Violet's hand rested possessively on the arm of the handsome, brown-haired man Daisy vaguely remembered as Peregrine Hughes, who was gazing down at his beloved with a besotted smile. Daisy glanced at Violet's left hand, and groaned again at the flash of a gold band on her fourth finger.

Married. She was too late.

The three people flanking them were clearly the "anvil priest" who'd performed the ceremony, and two random witnesses, paid to attend to make things official.

"Bloody, bloody hell," Daisy growled.

Vaughan came up behind her and took the reins from her hand, then tied the two horses to a nearby hitching post.

"Too late?" he asked mildly.

She resisted the urge to take a swing at him. He sounded as if he wanted to laugh.

And then the couple at the door glanced over at them, and Peregrine's face broke into another smile. He lifted his hand and sent them a cheerful wave.

"Uncle Lucien!" Peregrine shouted. "You're just in time to congratulate us! Violet's just made me the happiest of men."

Chapter Twenty-Five

"'Uncle'?"

Daisy froze, convinced she'd misheard. She glanced over at Vaughan, then back at the lovebirds, who were now crossing the street toward them. "Did he just call you *uncle*?"

Vaughan took a cautious step back, but the glitter in his eyes made her heart begin to pound. A strange buzzing noise filled her ears.

"My decision to escort you has not been entirely motivated by altruism," he drawled.

Daisy stared at him, incredulous.

"Peregrine Hughes is my nephew."

"Your nephew," she said levelly, somehow managing not to raise her voice to a screech.

"I'm afraid so. Marion, my elder sister, threw herself away on a mere Captain of the Guards, one Charles Hughes. Perry's their only child. They spend most of their time at Carisbrooke Hall and rarely come to London, but a few months ago Perry was sent to stay with me for a little town bronze while his parents went on an extended tour of Italy."

Daisy narrowed her eyes. "You were supposed to be looking after him, and he's eloped with an heiress right under your nose."

Vaughan's lips curved. "Oh no. He eloped with an heiress with my full knowledge and consent. I'm the one who told him to do it."

Fury was bubbling through her veins, but Daisy pushed it down, conscious of not making a scene in such a public place, even as she wanted to scream at him like a fishwife. Then fillet him like a fish.

"Why in God's name have we been chasing them the length of England, then?" she hissed.

"Because as much as I love the boy, neither he nor Violet have the wits of a peahen. I wanted to make sure they arrived unscathed and actually managed to tie the knot."

Perry and Violet were almost upon them, so Daisy pinned him with a look that promised violent and painful retribution and turned to the happy couple.

A grinning Perry shook hands with Vaughan, who clapped him on the shoulder, while Violet gave Daisy's outfit a slightly confused look before she bobbed a curtsey.

"Hello again, Your Grace." She smiled prettily at Vaughan. "We took your advice." She held out her left hand to show them both the ring.

"Congratulations," Vaughan said silkily. "I hope you'll both be very happy."

Perry glanced down at Daisy. Now that she saw the two men together, she could see a certain similarity. Perry was like a watered-down version of his uncle. Where Vaughan's hair was almost black, Perry's was a rusty brown, his eyes a warm hazel instead of a piercing dark coffee.

"And who's this?" Perry asked with a friendly smile. "You're definitely not Finch."

Vaughan grinned. "May I present Lady Dorothea Hamilton."

Unwilling to curtsey in her male attire, Daisy awkwardly held out her hand and Perry shook it. He sent her an intrigued look, then shot Vaughan a questioning glance, and her cheeks heated as she realized the conclusion he was drawing: that Vaughan had brought her along as his mistress to keep him entertained.

"Why aren't you wearing a dress?" Violet asked, her forehead wrinkling in confusion. "Did you have an accident? Were your clothes stolen, or something dreadful like that?"

"I'm undercover," Daisy said stiffly. "On behalf of the investigative agency King and Company. Your father hired me to prevent your marriage."

Violet's big blue eyes widened, and a regretful smile curved her pink lips. "Oh, poor Papa. He's going to be dreadfully cross. But he'll forgive me, I know he will. He always does."

"Aren't you worried he'll cut you off?" Daisy asked. "Isn't that what Robert Child, the banker, did to his daughter Sarah Ann when she eloped with the Earl of Westmorland? He cut her out of his will, and left all his money to her second son, or her eldest daughter, so that no one bearing the Westmorland title would ever see a penny of it."

Violet gave a trill of laughter that sounded like tinkling bells. It made Daisy want to elbow her in the throat.

"Oh, no. Papa would never be so cruel. He dotes on me, you see. And the only reason he objected to Perry was because he thought he was a fortune hunter. Which isn't true in the least, is it darling?"

"Certainly not," Perry said, looking offended. "I might not have your vast inheritance, but with Uncle Lucien's thousand pounds a year, we'll be perfectly fine."

Daisy turned and gaped at Lucien, but he merely bowed slightly to Violet.

"Don't worry about your father, Violet. I'll make it right with him when I get back to London."

Violet's ringlets bounced as she nodded earnestly. "Eloping is all the rage nowadays. The Duke of Wellington's niece, Anne, married Charles Bentinck, brother to the Duke of Portland, here, you know."

"And one should always strive to keep up with the latest fashions," Daisy muttered. Her sarcasm was lost on everyone except Vaughan, who smothered a laugh behind a cough, but she was far too furious with him to feel any sort of kinship. The bastard had been lying to her for *days*.

His meddling meant she'd have to admit her failure to Violet's father. King & Co.'s reputation could be severely damaged if Brand started telling people about this disaster and her professional incompetence. Much of their custom was from word-of-mouth recommendations, so his dissatisfaction would not be a good advertisement.

Damn Vaughan.

"We've taken rooms at the inn over there," Perry said, gesturing across the road to a slightly shabby-looking establishment called The King's Head. "I've ordered breakfast. Let's all go and have something to eat."

Daisy's stomach gave a traitorous little growl, and since there was nothing to be done but accept defeat, she traipsed across the street after Violet and Perry, trying to ignore the nauseating way they were fussing over one another.

Instead of following them through the front door, however, she tailed Vaughan as he led their two horses through the arched entrance and into a stable yard at the rear. A scruffy stable hand took charge of them, and when they stepped inside, she caught Vaughan's sleeve, preventing him from going through to the breakfast room.

Instead, she opened the first door on her left, which let into a storage cupboard, stepped in beside the mops and sweeping brushes, and pulled him in after her. She closed the door, then fixed him with a narrow-eyed glare.

"I could kill you," she growled. The room was so small they were barely two feet apart.

"I don't doubt it. In a hundred different ways."

She shook her head at his flippancy.

"Now you see why I've been reluctant to give your knives back," he said.

Her fingers twitched with the impulse to pull her remaining blade from her boot and stab him with it. Nowhere fatal. Just his shoulder, maybe. Or his thigh.

"I trusted you, you arse!" she fumed. "And you've been lying to me from the moment we met in that bloody lane."

Her initial disbelief at his deception had been replaced by a volcanic anger and a sickening knot of hurt in her belly.

"God, I've been so stupid! You've been trying to delay me for *days*." She glared up at him. "You've been laughing at me, stringing me along, making me think I had a chance of catching them, when all this time you've been sabotaging me for your own twisted amusement!" She sucked in a breath. "There was nothing wrong with the bloody girth strap this morning, was there? You told Finch to come up with something to stop us getting here on time."

"Well . . ." Vaughan had the grace to look guilty, and she let out a growl of annoyance. And then a new, even worse, thought struck her. She stabbed him in the chest with her finger.

"Oh God, you tried to keep me in bed this morning. Did you only seduce me to slow me down? To distract me?"

His brows lowered. "No! Absolutely not! I seduced you, if that's how you want to put it—even though I seem to remember you being just as much of an active participant—because I've wanted you for fucking *years*."

He reached up and wrapped his hand around hers, engulfing the finger poking him in the sternum. "I still want you. Every second of the day."

She shook free of his hand, ignoring the way her stupid heart twisted in her chest at his words. He was a lying toad. She couldn't trust a thing he said.

"Stop it. Just tell me why you told Perry to elope. Why couldn't he stay in London and earn Brand's approval?"

"Because I was sick and tired of him moping about my house like a lovesick puppy." Vaughan said crossly. "It was a purely selfish gesture. The two of them are ideally suited—they're both equally silly—and since Brand's only real objection was the fact that Perry didn't have an income of his own, I promised to give them a thousand pounds a year simply to get him off my hands."

"That's . . ." Daisy struggled to find the words.

"Practical," Vaughan supplied. "I knew Brand would come round eventually, so I told Perry to elope, then present him with a *fait accompli*. Easier to apologize for something you've done than to gain permission for something you haven't. The two of them can find a nice little house in Mayfair, and I'll get the pleasure of a solitary existence once again."

"What about your sister? Won't she be upset that her only son's married in her absence?"

Vaughan shook his head. "Of course not. The only thing she'll care about is that he's married someone he loves, who loves him back. She married for love herself. She'll understand."

"I don't suppose the fact that Violet's almost as rich as the king will hurt either," Daisy said cynically.

"Her wealth doesn't matter. I've got more than enough to help them if Brand chooses to cut them off, and don't forget that for all his money, Brand's still the son of a wool merchant, whereas Perry's uncle is a duke. Marrying into an aristocratic family has a cachet all of its own."

Daisy knew that well enough. She'd been avoiding socially climbing suitors for years. But Vaughan's perfidy still stung. "Your scheming has wasted my time and ruined my professional reputation."

"Which I genuinely regret," he said. "Look, I'll pay you the five hundred pounds you would have had from Brand. And I'll talk to him when we get back to London. Let him know it was entirely my fault that you couldn't stop the wedding. King and Company's good name won't be adversely affected."

"I don't want your charity. Or your company, for that matter." She stepped around him and pushed open the door.

"Where are you going?"

"I'm not staying here. I'll take two fresh horses back to Finch, and he can take me back to London in your carriage. It's the least you can do. You can share a coach

with Violet and Perry as far as your estate. I'm sure they'll
be wonderful company."

Daisy hastened back through the inn's central hallway
and emerged in the cobbled courtyard at the back. The
stables were off to one side, with a trio of rough-looking
stable hands loitering below the arches, but the arrival of
a carriage through the arched gateway impeded her progress. She waited for it to stop, but as soon as it did, a
woman dressed in a deep green velvet cape and matching bonnet stepped down in front of her.

Daisy moved back into the doorway to give the new
arrival room just as the woman glanced up. Mutual recognition was instant, and Daisy's blood froze as horror
filled her.

The new arrival's eyes widened, and her thin brows
rose in astonishment.

"Dorothea Hamilton? Good Lord, what on earth are
you doing here?"

The shrill tones carried across the yard as the woman's
fascinated gaze swept over Daisy's jacket and breeches
with almost comical slowness and her nose wrinkled in
well-bred disdain. "And wearing *that*?"

Daisy willed for the ground to swallow her up. It did
not oblige.

Bloody Hell.

Letty Richardson was the worst gossip in the whole
of London. She'd come out the same year as Daisy, Tess,
and Ellie, and her spiteful gossiping was legendary. She'd
always seen other women as a threat to her own marriage
prospects, and her sly smugness when she'd accepted an
elderly baron at the end of the season had been unbearable, despite the fact that her new husband was an overbearing letch no other woman would have wanted.

Now, as a married woman, Letty loved to feign pity

for "poor unfortunate spinsters" like Daisy, while simultaneously whispering about all her unfeminine flaws behind her fan with her little coterie of petty-minded friends.

This was, without doubt, a nightmare.

Chapter Twenty-Six

Daisy cursed her monumental bad luck as a litany of excuses ran through her brain. Madness. Amnesia. Kidnap. A lost twin. Sadly, none of them sounded remotely plausible, so she squared her shoulders and lifted her chin.

"Letty, what a surprise!" Her tones indicated it was anything but pleasant. "I say, you're not here to commit bigamy, are you?"

Letty let out a fake little laugh, even as her eyes narrowed. "Of course not. I'm on my way back from visiting my sister. She lives up past Dumfries."

She waved vaguely northward with her white-gloved hand, but her eyes glittered with malicious delight. It was clear she suspected a scandal.

"But this is marvelous!" Her eyes roved Daisy's features again and she gave a gleeful chuckle. "From the looks of you, I do believe I've stumbled onto an elopement! How famous. You've finally found someone to marry you."

Her tone was so condescendingly saccharine that Daisy clenched her fingers into her palms against the urge to shove Letty into the steaming pile of horse manure just to her left.

"Who's the lucky man?"

Daisy opened her mouth to tell Letty to mind her own business when she felt a presence behind her and saw Letty's eyes widen to the size of saucers.

"I am."

Vaughan's deep, amused tone made Daisy's heart stop in her chest.

"What?" Letty squeaked. She recovered from her surprise almost immediately and sank into an obsequious curtsey. "I mean, Your Grace! How wonderful to see you again."

She couldn't seem to decide where to look; her eyes kept bouncing between Daisy and Vaughan.

"But I'm not sure I understand," Letty simpered. Her entire attitude had become flirtatious and cloying. "This must be the most bizarre coincidence. You're not here with *Dorothea,* are you?"

She made it sound as though associating with Daisy was one step worse than contracting the bubonic plague.

Daisy stood stock-still as Vaughan casually slipped his hand around her waist and tugged her back into his chest in a move so naturally possessive it was as if he'd done it a thousand times before.

"You heard me. Yes, you've stumbled on an elopement. And yes, I'm the lucky man. Daisy, here, is going to be my duchess."

Daisy kept her expression completely serene as Letty gaped at her. Her brain didn't seem to be able to come up with an alternative suggestion.

"So you're not married yet?" Letty managed.

"Not yet. But we will be," Vaughan said.

Letty's forehead wrinkled. "Is this true?"

"Of course it is." Vaughan's other hand stroked Daisy's cheek in a gentle caress. "I've been in love with her for years. It's just taken me this long to convince her to accept me."

Letty looked as if she was about to expire. She gaped at Daisy as if seeing her for the first time. "Years?" she croaked. "You've been asking her for years? And she refused you?"

Daisy lifted her brows, as if she was the sort of cool, irresistible female who refused offers from gorgeous, wealthy dukes like Vaughan on a weekly basis.

"Years," she lied firmly.

"Luckily, I'm very stubborn," Vaughan drawled. "And *very* persuasive." There was no mistaking the amused innuendo in his deep voice.

Letty's mouth dropped open in a perfect little *O*, and Daisy would have relished the sight if her own reputation wasn't being comprehensively shredded by this little charade.

Vaughan's hand tightened on her waist as he gave her a little squeeze. "Now, if you'll excuse us—"

"Do you need a witness?" Letty blurted out. Her eyes shone at the prospect of playing a key role in what she obviously believed to be the scandal of the century. She was doubtless cataloguing every single detail to recount it to anyone who would listen when she got back to London. "I'd be more than happy to—"

"That won't be necessary, Lady Richardson," Vaughan said firmly, cutting her off. "My nephew and his wife have kindly agreed, and we're not having any other guests."

He pressed Daisy's waist and pulled her gently to one side so that the doorway was clear. "I'm sure you're desperate to get to your room and rest after your journey. You look a little tired. We won't detain you any longer."

Letty looked as though she'd happily stay forever, but she must have realized that she'd been neatly dismissed, as well as deftly insulted, and gave a little shrug.

"Yes. Of course. In that case, please accept my congratulations." She bobbed another curtsey and swept past them with a final disdainful glance at Daisy's outfit.

"Perhaps when you're a duchess you'll give some thought about improving your wardrobe, Dorothea," she said snidely. "Do let me know if you'd ever like some pointers."

She sailed past them before Daisy could say that she'd rather leap naked into a vat of boiling oil than go shopping with the likes of her.

Daisy waited until the sound of Letty's footsteps had disappeared behind her before she stepped out of Vaughan's hold and whirled around to face him. She'd thought she'd been angry before, when he'd revealed his role in the elopement, but *this* was beyond the pale. Blood seemed to pulse in her throat and swish in her ears.

"What the bloody hell was that?" she hissed, almost incandescent with fury. "Letty's the worst gossip in the whole of England, and you just told her we're about to be *married*!"

She turned and stormed toward the stables, certain that he would follow. "She's going to be charging back to London as fast as she possibly can to share that delicious piece of news."

Vaughan caught her shoulder and swung her back round to face him.

"I was trying to save your reputation!" he countered crossly. "What else would you have had me say? That you're my mistress? That we're having a torrid affair?"

"Yes!" Daisy fumed. "That would have been better. Everyone knows I don't give a fig about getting married, and nobody in the *ton* will be surprised to hear that I've become your mistress. They've been expecting me to do something like that for years. I've heard the whispers. They say I'm just like my flighty mother, a slave to my passionate nature, a scandal waiting to happen."

He reached for her again, but she stepped back, away from his touch, and took a deep inhale, trying to calm her hectic breathing and her pounding heart.

"Now everyone's going to think we've married in secret, even if we don't announce it to the world. Letty's more efficient at spreading news than a full-page advertisement in *The Times*!"

Vaughan shook his head, but she wasn't finished.

"I don't care if I'm ruined. I'm not marrying you. You're going to go straight back to London and tell everyone that we've broken off our engagement."

"And what good will that do? I'll be branded a wicked cad who seduced then abandoned you—and get hounded by your brothers who'll probably shoot me before asking for an explanation—or, worse, I'll be seen as an object of pity and scorn because everyone thinks you've jilted me at the altar. Neither of those options particularly appeal to me, Hamilton."

He raked his hand through his hair. "And what about you? If you return to London unwed, you'll be branded a harlot. You'll be blacklisted from society."

"I can lay low until all the fuss has died down," Daisy muttered. "Tess will let me stay at Wansford Hall. And when everyone's forgotten about me and moved on to another scandal, I'll quietly move back and start working for King and Company again. I can live above the office. Tess bought the building years ago."

"What about your father?" Vaughan demanded. "Or have you forgotten about him? Because I'm sure he'll have something to say about his daughter disgracing the family name."

Daisy's spirits plummeted. Oh God. Her father would be livid. He didn't care what she got up to in private, but he'd abhor having the whole world gossiping about her. What if this proved the final straw and he forced her to marry some doddery old letch just to salvage her ruined reputation? She could end up with someone as dreadful as Letty's husband.

And what about Tess and Ellie? Word *would* come out if she returned to London, even if she waited a whole year, and she'd rather live in seclusion forever than have the business they'd all worked so hard on sullied by her involvement, or her friends shunned because of their continued association with her.

Bloody Vaughan.

The man in question tilted his head and the thoughtful, calculating expression on his face made her pause.

"What?" she demanded.

"Is it really that bad an idea? Getting married, I mean. Socially we're equal. I'm a duke, you're a duke's daughter."

It was Daisy's turn to gape at him. "Of course it's a bad idea. The worst."

"It would save both our reputations."

Disbelief and humiliation roiled inside her. God, was there anything worse than his pity? "I'm not entering a marriage of convenience just so you can be seen to be doing the honorable thing, Vaughan."

"It's not just that. I have to marry sometime. I'm expected to make an effort to keep the ducal line going." His dark gaze burned into hers, and she ignored the little frisson of awareness his attention always produced. "I honestly don't care about producing an heir, but I'm more than willing to enjoy the attempts to make one with you."

Her stomach somersaulted at the tantalizing thought of making love with him again—multiple times, over several months, years possibly—but she ignored it. She had too much to lose.

"I'm not denying the physical chemistry between us," she said, as calmly as she could. "But passion like that doesn't last. There needs to be something more. A deeper respect and enjoyment of the other person's company. Shared humor and interests. If I'm going to marry and have children it will be because I love the other person, and know that they love me. Not because society demands it."

Vaughan let out a frustrated sigh, but he clearly realized further argument was futile. "Fine. But let me escort you back to Wansford Hall. It's not safe for you to travel alone with just Finch, even with all of your knives."

He was right, curse him, and he must have sensed her indecision, because he pressed home the advantage.

"At the very least, come with Perry, Violet, and me to Carisbrooke Hall and stay there tonight," he coaxed. "I'll ask one of the female servants to accompany you as a chaperone for the rest of the journey, and provide an extra coachman and outriders for protection."

She frowned, but was secretly glad of his offer. And since they wouldn't be alone together, she wouldn't be tempted to change her mind.

"I'll even give you back your knives," he said, before she could refuse. He reached into his jacket and withdrew the two he'd confiscated, holding them out with the handles facing her like a peace offering.

Daisy raised her brows. "Brave of you. You must be very sure I'm not going to stab you."

His lips twitched. "If you're going to do it, you should

marry me first. That way, you'll be a duchess as well as a widow, and I'll die with the satisfaction that at least you're protected by my name and fortune."

She scowled at his levity. Tess had become a widowed duchess on the night of her first wedding when the old duke had cocked up his toes, but she hadn't been the one to kill him. He'd died of natural causes.

"I don't want to kill you, Vaughan. Just stab you somewhere painful."

"My death could be your freedom."

"You're too wicked to oblige me by dying early. You'd live to be a hundred, just to annoy me."

He chuckled. "Same goes for you. You're too stubborn to die first. Maybe we should marry just to see which one of us wins?"

Daisy shook her head. Despite the fact that he didn't love her, there were undeniable advantages to marrying him, not least his sense of humor.

The problem was, she'd probably end up falling in love with him, which would only lead to misery when he inevitably lost interest in her and took his attentions elsewhere. Even the position of duchess, and the possibility of having children to love, wouldn't make up for the heartache. Her mother had discovered that. A gilded cage was still a cage.

She took the knives. Since she wasn't wearing her holsters, she tucked them into her jacket pockets, one on each side, and the finality of the gesture made her heart sink. Vaughan had no excuse to seek her out now that he'd returned them.

"Thank you," she said stiffly. "And I'll accept your hospitality at Carisbrooke Hall. But only because I want a nice hot bath and a clean bed, neither of which I imagine this place can provide. I am *not* forgiving you."

"Understood." He nodded, once, then stepped past her and approached one of the stable hands who'd been forking hay in one of the stalls. "You, there. Can you ready two carriage horses and take them about five miles back along the road to Carlisle? You'll find my driver and carriage waiting for a new pair."

"'Course I can, milord."

"Thank you." Vaughan reached into his pocket and pulled out a coin that he flipped to the groom, who caught it with a deft swoop of his hand. "For your trouble."

"Thank you, sir." The man nodded his appreciation and gave a gap-toothed grin. "I'll get right to it."

Satisfied, Vaughan turned back to her and gestured toward the door. "Shall we? Perry and Violet will be wondering where we are."

"Perry and Violet won't even have realized we're not there," Daisy said grouchily. "A grenade could go off next to them and they wouldn't notice."

As soon as the words were out of her mouth, she realized how insensitive they were, considering Vaughan's wartime experience. She clapped her hand over her mouth with a gasp. "I'm so sorry! It was just a figure of speech. I never meant to make a joke about your injury."

Luckily, he seemed amused, and not mortally offended. "It's fine. Really. You don't have to watch what you say when you're with me."

"I really am sorry," she repeated.

He laughed at her mortification. "You promised to discuss any topic with me on this journey, Hamilton. That includes this. Nothing is off-limits. Not with me."

Something squeezed in her chest at his words, and she felt the oddest pang of melancholy. She'd loved that aspect of the past three days. The unexpected liberation of being able to say whatever she wanted without watching her tongue. Without worrying that she'd be judged for being too inquisitive, too brash, too curious. Too educated. The fact that their journey together was over left a hollow ache of regret. She'd miss their candid conversations. She'd miss him.

Damn it.

She turned away to hide the ridiculous prick of tears that suddenly burned her eyes. "You go inside. I need a bit more time out here to get the stink of Letty Richardson out of my nose," she muttered.

He paused, as if to argue, but she hurried off down the row of stalls and stopped to pat the nose of a friendly black mare. She saw him leave from the corner of her eye and pressed her forehead to the rough boards of the stable door with a choked little sob.

She'd just refused to marry Lucien Vaughan.

Five years ago, she'd have said yes in a heartbeat.

Three days ago, she'd have happily stabbed him through the heart.

Now she said no, even when half of her wanted to say yes.

Bloody Hell.

Chapter Twenty-Seven

Daisy surreptitiously wiped her eyes as two more grooms entered the stables and started speaking in low tones with the man Vaughan had asked to take the horses to Finch. She'd spent long enough moping about in here. It was time to go back inside and pray she didn't encounter Letty again before they left.

She straightened her spine and turned, only to see the three men blocking the doorway.

"This the one?" the tallest of the three asked his friend.

"Aye. That other lady called 'im 'Yer Grace,' which makes 'im a duke. And I 'eard 'im say *she* were to be 'is duchess."

Daisy took a step back as the back of her neck began to prickle. It was a sensation she'd experienced several times before, in places like Limehouse and Seven Dials, where danger lurked in every alley. There was something about the attitude of these three that made her distinctly uneasy.

She slid her hand into her pocket and palmed one of her knives as the second man took another step toward her. He sent her an insulting, appraising full-body glance and his top lip curled in a sneer.

"Duchess, eh? 'Ain't no accountin' for taste. I like a woman with a bit more meat on the bone. You sure she ain't just 'is fancy piece? Look at 'er. Why's she dressed like a boy?"

The first man gave a snort. "Maybe 'e's a molly? You know what these nobs are like. Bunch o' perverts, the lot of 'em. Either way, 'e'll pay a pretty penny to get 'er back."

Daisy's heart sank. She put her left hand in front of her, palm out, in a placating gesture. "Now, gentlemen, there's clearly been a misunderstanding. I'm not his lordship's woman. I only met him this morning. He let me sit up on the box when I was walking from Carlisle."

The man Vaughan had paid spat into the straw. "She's lyin'. They was just arguin' about gettin' married."

Daisy glared at him. "If you were eavesdropping, then you presumably also heard me refuse him. I'm not his fiancée. We're not even friends. In fact, he *kidnapped* me. That's why I'm here, in this godforsaken place."

The second man scratched the stubble on his chin. "If 'e kidnapped ye, then 'e wants ye, don't 'e? Man like 'im can get any woman 'e wants for the toss of a coin, so if 'e's gone to all the bother of kidnappin' ye, 'e must want ye somethin' fierce."

Daisy almost rolled her eyes at this skewed male logic.

"He didn't mean to kidnap me. He thought I was someone else," she lied desperately. "He'll be glad to see the back of me, I swear."

None of the three men seemed to be listening.

"Even if she's just 'is piece o' muslin, he'll want 'er back." The tall one said. "Nobs like 'im 'ave a code of honor."

The near-toothless one nodded. "Aye. We'll take 'er, and send 'im a ransom. A fine fellow like that's goin' to be mighty keen to get 'er back safe and sound."

The three of them all nodded in agreement, and Daisy cursed beneath her breath as they began to approach. A row of stalls hemmed her in to the left, a stone wall with just a few small windows to her right, but the narrow aisle also prevented the men from fanning out. It was only wide enough for two of them abreast.

She pulled her first blade from her pocket and held it high, then dipped her left hand for the second, and the sight of her brandishing them made the trio pause.

"You're making a big mistake," she hissed. "I know how to use these."

It was clear they didn't believe her. They came closer, and she cursed inwardly at the need to hurt them.

"I warned you!"

She threw the first blade, and the toothless one let out a howl of pain as it plunged into the meaty part of his thigh. He stumbled to the floor, but the other two were too close for her to throw the second one. She slashed a wide arc around her as they rushed her, trying to keep them at bay. She caught the tall one's forearm, cutting through the cloth of his jacket and shirt to draw blood, and he leapt back with a curse, but the third man managed to grab her wrist and slammed it against the hard wooden panels of the stall.

Daisy let out a cry of pain. She didn't drop the knife, but the horses reacted to the commotion. They reared and whinnied in agitation, tossing their heads, and the one in the nearest stall bucked and kicked the boards with a sound like thunder.

She tried to free her hand, but the man's grip was too strong, and the two of them grappled in the restricted space. Daisy tried to twist away, sweeping her leg behind his knee to try to topple him to the floor, but he used the weight of his body to slam her into the siding and she screamed as a bolt of pain streaked through her shoulder.

She twisted away, panting in agony, just as the tall one rejoined the fray, his face twisted in a rictus of fury.

"Little bitch cut me!" he panted, and the last thing Daisy saw was the knuckles of his closed fist coming toward her face.

And then everything went black.

Chapter Twenty-Eight

Where *was* the bloody woman?

Lucien raked his hands through his hair and scowled around the deserted courtyard. A deeply disinterested cat sat atop the stone mounting block in one corner, licking its paw, but there weren't any stable hands to question about where Daisy had gone.

He shouldn't have let her out of his sight. She was Daisy Hamilton; she couldn't be trusted an inch. She was reckless, stubborn, and infuriatingly self-sufficient. He should have known her easy acceptance of his offer to stay at Carisbrooke Hall was suspicious.

Bloody woman.

She'd probably saddled a horse the minute he'd gone back inside and set off toward Carlisle on her own.

Unacceptable.

He marched back inside to find Perry and Violet feeding one another bites of teacake in the front room of the inn.

Lucien suppressed a shudder. This was precisely the reason he hadn't wanted the boy in his house for a moment longer. Perry had been mooning about, trying to engage him in discussions about which of Shakespeare's sonnets best described Violet's quivering lips or cornflower blue eyes until Lucien had been forced to lock himself in his own study with a seventeen-year-old malt just to get some peace.

Unfortunately, his study held the desk on which he regretted *not* debauching Daisy Hamilton every time he entered the room, which had done nothing to improve his temper.

"Have you seen Miss Hamilton?" he growled.

Perry brushed a crumb from his upper lip. "Sorry, no. She hasn't been in here."

"Have you lost her?" Violet asked, blue eyes wide with concern.

Lucien bit back a sarcastic retort. *Of course I've bloody well lost her. Why would I be asking you about her if I knew where the bloody hell she was?*

No. It was their wedding day. He had to be nice.

"I have," he said coolly. "I think she must have set off back toward Carlisle. You two take the carriage and head to Carisbrooke Hall. I'll find her and meet you there."

He headed back out to the yard, and since there was still no sign of the stable hands he'd seen earlier, he set about saddling a horse himself. He was just adjusting the girth on a feisty-looking chestnut when a shuffle of straw caught his attention and he turned to see a small, nervous-looking housemaid lurking just inside the doorway.

"Can I help you?" he growled.

The girl sent a hurried glance back over her shoulder, then shuffled forward. "Happen it's the other way round, sir," she said. "Are you the duke? 'Is lordship?"

"I'm *a* duke," Lucien qualified, speaking more softly so as not to frighten the girl. She couldn't have been more than fifteen, and she looked like she might flee at any moment. "And since I'm probably the only duke here, I expect I'm the man you're after."

The girl wrung her hands in a nervous gesture. "I'm sorry, sir, but your lady? The one wearing the breeches? She's been taken, sir. I seen it."

Every muscle in Lucien's body tensed. "What do you mean, taken? By whom?"

The girl shrank back at his harsh tone, and he forced himself to try to look less menacing. "Please, tell me what you saw."

She pushed a thin strand of mousy-brown hair behind her ear. "It was the Maxwell brothers, sir. The three of 'em work 'ere in the stables, when they're not drinkin' an' fightin'. Mistress Gordon is their aunt. But they're nothin' but trouble, sir. Connor just got out of jail for stealin' a goat from the magistrate. And Jem, the youngest, 'e's not right in the head. Always tryin' to take advantage o' the maids."

She shuddered, and Lucien winced inwardly at the bleak look in her eyes. Jem had doubtless managed to corner her somewhere, and he sent up a silent prayer that she'd escaped with nothing worse than an unwanted kiss. His blood ran cold at the thought of Daisy in the hands of such men.

"Why would they do anything to my . . . woman?" he demanded.

"Happen they'll want a ransom," the girl said sorrowfully. "I saw the three of 'em leave with an open-top cart, and your poor lady lyin' in the back, not movin'. Alan, the middle one, is 'andy with 'is fists."

Lucien's chest felt like it was being ripped open, but a cold fury was building behind his breastbone, the same sensation he'd always felt when he'd seen his comrades die, or witnessed the senseless carnage after a battle. "When?"

"A few minutes ago, sir."

"Which way did they go? Do you know where they'd be taking her?"

The girl glanced over her shoulder again, clearly uncomfortable with telling tales on her employer's nephews but determined to prevent another injustice. Lucien delved into his pocket and withdrew a handful of guineas.

"Here. Take this. Just tell me where she might be. Please."

"The Maxwells live over at Blackford, 'bout ten miles east," she said quickly. "Take the Carlisle road, but after 'bout six miles there's a crossroads for Todhills and Rockcliffe. Head toward Todhills, and Blackford's another few miles after that. The Maxwells farm all the land thereabouts."

Lucien nodded and shoved the coins at her. "Thank you, miss."

"Elsie," the girl mumbled.

He compressed his lips. "Elsie. If you want to leave here, use that money and make your way to Carisbrooke Hall, near Barnard Castle. I'll make sure you're found a position that doesn't include being molested by the stable hands, you hear me?"

The girl nodded again and a relieved smile brightened her face. "Oh, yes, sir. Thank you, sir!"

Lucien didn't listen to the rest of her gratitude. He led the prancing chestnut into the yard and mounted in one swift move, then clattered out onto the road, his heart pounding against his ribs.

God, Daisy would never have succumbed without a fight, which meant those thugs would have had to hurt her. He kicked the horse into a canter. He *would* find her. And he'd make the men responsible for taking her wish they'd never been born.

Thoughts of bloody retribution filled his brain as he galloped back toward Carlisle, and after a few miles a familiar figure sitting atop his ducal carriage came into view.

Finch sent him a wave, but Lucien cursed as he realized the toothless stable hand he'd ordered to bring replacement horses must have been one of the bastard brothers who'd abducted Daisy.

He reined in and Finch's brows rose as he saw his expression. Years of fighting together meant he immediately grasped the seriousness of the situation.

"Where's the trouble?" he demanded.

"Daisy's been taken. Three men and a cart. Did they come this way?"

Finch's brows rose. "Aye. At least, two men with a cart and another on horseback passed by, not twenty minutes ago. I asked if they'd come from Gretna, but they didn't stop."

"Did you see her? In the back of the cart?"

"No. It was filled with straw. They must have hidden her under it."

"Fuck." Lucien shook his head. "I should have brought another horse for you. I didn't think."

"You want the pistols from the carriage? They're primed and loaded."

"Yes."

Finch had just handed them up when a faint sound caught Lucien's attention and his spirits rose as they both turned toward the south. A lone figure on horseback was approaching, and as it got closer Lucien could see that it was some kind of cleric, dressed in the distinctive black robes, white ecclesiastic collar, and flat-crowned hat associated with the profession.

The man was proceeding at a glacial pace, and Lucien curbed his impatience as they waited for him to draw level.

He wasted no time with niceties. "Ten pounds for your horse, sir."

The vicar, or curate, or whatever he was, looked confused. "I beg your pardon?"

"I'd like to buy your horse for ten pounds. Right now." Lucien thrust his hands in his pockets, then cursed inwardly as he realized he'd given his last coins to the maid back at the inn.

"That scrawny nag's not worth ten shillings," Finch muttered. "Let alone ten pounds."

Lucien sent him a quelling glare.

"But how will I get to Gretna if I sell you my horse?" the vicar asked.

Lucien ground his teeth. "My nephew will be coming along shortly in another carriage. He'll stop when he sees *this* carriage. You can tell him his uncle orders him to convey you to Gretna, to procure two horses and a coachman, bring them back to be hitched to this carriage, and to continue to Carisbrooke Hall."

The vicar sent him a dubious look. He was clearly a man who liked to debate every matter under the sun. "But if he takes me back to Gretna, and your man leaves with you on my horse, this carriage will be left unguarded. Someone might come along and steal it."

"Without any horses?" Lucien growled. "That's extremely unlikely. And in all honesty, I don't give a fig for what happens to this bloody carriage. You can have it, for all I care."

The curate looked shocked, but Lucien couldn't tell if it was because of his language or the sentiment.

"That carriage must be worth hundreds of pounds!" he gasped. "Who are you, sir, that you would give it away so carelessly?"

Lucien sent the man his finest ducal glower, and he'd never been more glad of his title and its ability to impress. "I'm the Duke of Cranford, and the cost of this carriage is nothing compared to the cost of a woman's life."

"You need my horse to save a soul?" the vicar gasped. This, clearly, was familiar territory, even if the saving was more temporal than spiritual.

"I do. And your arguing is impeding that task. Now, are you going to give me that damned horse, or not?"

It obviously occurred to the man that Lucien didn't truly need to ask for permission; he could simply take the horse by force if he wished. He dismounted and handed the reins to Finch, who nodded.

"Thank ye, Vicar."

"You can sit in the carriage until my nephew comes," Vaughan ordered as Finch mounted up. "And make sure he pays you that ten pounds."

The vicar nodded, still looking bemused, as Lucien turned his mount and galloped away with Finch close behind.

"So, where are we off to?" Finch demanded when they'd settled into a steady rhythm.

"Some place called Blackford to find three brothers by the name of Maxwell. They've kidnapped Daisy and mean to hold her for ransom."

Finch let out a low whistle. "That woman certainly has a knack of getting herself into scrapes."

Lucien frowned. "It wasn't her fault this time. It was

mine. Those bastards overheard me say she was going to be my duchess."

Finch gave an astonished cough. "Your duchess? And why would you say a thing like that?"

"To salvage her reputation. It's my fault she chased Perry all the way to Gretna. I could have sent her back to London any time these past three days. But I didn't. Which means it's my fault some silly bitch of a gossip saw her at the inn and assumed she'd eloped."

"With *you*?" Finch chuckled, then shook his head. "Dear God!"

Lucien scowled at him. "What?"

"It's unlike you, that's all. Since when have you cared about a woman's reputation?"

"Daisy's not some bored society wife or professional courtesan. She's the daughter of a duke. My friends' sister. I'll not have her ruined and cast out of society on my account."

"But offering to *marry* the girl? Surely there's another option?"

"None that wouldn't hurt her, or ruin her life."

"From what I've seen, she'd think marrying *you* would ruin her life."

Lucien grimaced. "That's what she said."

Finch sent him a thoughtful look. "It might be the best thing for you, though."

"What do you mean?"

"You've never had an ounce of interest in marrying any o' those society chits. But I've seen the way you look at her. How you talk to her. It's different."

"How?"

"I've watched you with scores of women over the years. And you treat 'em all the same. You're cool and suave, and they fall right into your lap. You converse, but neither of you really listen, because it's all just shallow, frivolous things like *ton* gossip."

"What's your point?"

"You talk with her, really talk. *And* you listen. You discuss important things, like the war, and your scar, and losing friends. You're polite with every woman you meet, except her, because she's the only one who makes you feel things. She makes you angry. She makes you hard. She makes you jealous."

Lucien's heart was pounding at being so unexpectedly scrutinized by one of his oldest friends. Finch had never said anything so personal in all their years together.

"Been eavesdropping from up there on the box, have we?" he retorted, stung into defensiveness by the accuracy of the words.

"Just giving you my observations," Finch said serenely.

"Since when did you become her greatest admirer?"

"Since she threatened to stab you on the Hampstead road." Finch grinned. "I've had the same impulse myself, on occasion. The girl's got pluck."

"She's a bloody menace."

"She'd have made a good soldier. She's loyal. Driven. Gets the job done. Never complains."

Lucien rolled his eyes. "She does nothing *but* complain. At least to me."

Finch sent him a smug look. "Exactly. How many women have you met who agree with every word you say, *Your Grace*? Who don't have a single opinion of their own? A thousand. And they bore you to tears. That girl argues with you just for the fun of it. Out of principle. Even when she secretly agrees with you."

Lucien frowned. Finch was right. Daisy would argue the moon was made of cheese if he said it was butter, and she'd come up with some amusing almost-believable reasoning for her position too.

God, he'd do anything to hear her complain again. Or argue with him.

Anxiety tightened his chest as an awful sense of familiarity closed over him. He'd galloped across country like this a decade ago, a youthful knight filled with righteous fury, riding to the rescue of a different woman.

He'd failed. Elaine had died.

He would *not* let history repeat itself.

Chapter Twenty-Nine

Daisy awoke to pain. A throbbing in her jaw and a stabbing ache to her shoulder.

She was lying on the ground—she could feel that without opening her eyes. Cool grass pressed against her cheek, a chill wind fanned her skin, and the scent of woodsmoke stung her nose. She was outside, and from the flickering light filtering through her closed lids, it was late in the day, and someone had lit a fire. She was too far away to feel its heat.

Recollection returned in flashes. The stables at the inn. Vaughan. The three men.

Bloody Hell, she was in trouble.

She strained her ears, listening for clues as to where she was and where her captives might be. She couldn't sense anyone close by, or hear breathing, but that was no guarantee that she wasn't being watched.

Footsteps crunched behind her, then to the right, and she cracked her lids a tiny amount, still feigning unconsciousness. It was almost dark; the sun was setting. God, had she been senseless the entire day? How far had they taken her?

Don't panic. Think. Assess the situation.

She was lying on her side in some sort of clearing, but when she tried to move her arm to relieve its discomfort, she realized her hands were tied in front of her. A new bolt of alarm shot through her, but she took slow, calming breaths.

They'd left her feet unbound. That was something. Escape might still be possible.

The toothless stable hand sat across the fire from her, on a large boulder in front of a cottage-like structure the Scots called a bothy. The place had seen better days. It lacked a door and half the roof was gone, and ferns jutted out from between the stones.

The one who'd punched her stepped around her and went to squat next to his accomplice. Neither of them glanced at her, and Daisy dared to move her head a fraction. Trees ringed the clearing, sheltering them a little from the wind, taller than the stunted ones she'd seen out on the moors, and the soft sound of horses indicated there were some tethered nearby.

A glint near the fire drew her attention. The toothless one was admiring the two knives she'd had in her pockets, holding them up to the flames and testing the edges with his thumb. Daisy scowled, even as she felt a flash of grim satisfaction. At least he'd had to pull one of them from his leg. She'd made him hurt.

Had they found the blade in her boot? She didn't dare move enough to check, in case they realized she was awake, and it would be better to retain the element of surprise.

If they were anything like Finch, they wouldn't have expected her to have three knives on her person. That might be her salvation. But she had to wait for her chance.

"Why ain't she woken up?" the toothless one said, his

voice a petulant whine. "You 'it 'er too 'ard, Alan. What if you've broken 'er 'ead? We won't get no ransom if she don't wake up. They'll 'ang us for murder."

"Shut up, Jem," the bigger one replied crossly. "She'll come round. And if not, we'll just bury 'er up on the moors where nobody'll ever find 'er."

Toothless—Jem, apparently—wiped his nose on his sleeve and glanced over at Daisy. She forced herself to stay completely still.

"Think Connor's delivered the note yet?"

"Should've done. Unless the duke already left The King's Head. 'E might've 'ad to track 'im down."

"Five 'undred weren't enough to ask," Jem complained. "Even if she's just 'is whore." He sent a calculating look over toward Daisy. "Ain't no reason we can't enjoy 'er before we give 'er back, right? A duke's fancy piece must know a trick or two. You should've let me touch 'er."

Daisy's stomach curdled at the thought of either of them touching her, but at least she hadn't been molested while she was unconscious. Small mercy.

Her leg suddenly cramped and she straightened it in immediate reflex, and both men turned to look at her.

Shit.

"There, you see. She ain't dead." Alan didn't sound as if he cared one way or the other.

Since the ruse was up, Daisy rolled onto her back, then managed to shuffle to a seated position, pushing up with her bound hands against the dirt. Her vision swam at the sudden change and she sucked in a few deep breaths against the urge to faint.

"Welcome back, milady," Jem said with a mocking flourish of his hand. "I trust ye slept well?"

She scowled at him and worked her jaw back and forth,

testing it with her fingers. It was painful, and felt swollen, but it didn't feel as though it was broken. Her lip was split, though; she tasted blood, and her head was pounding in a most unpleasant way.

"You'd better hope that man o' yours is good for the money," Jem sneered.

Daisy drew her knees up in front of her and sent him a stony stare. "Oh, he's rich enough. He's also not a man to be trifled with. He'll track you down and see you hanged for this."

Jem snorted in derision. "'E'll 'ave to catch us first."

Alan rose and Daisy tensed, but he only sent his brother a look. "I need to piss. Don't touch 'er while I'm gone."

Jem rolled his eyes, but Daisy's dread increased at the thought of being left alone with him. "I need to piss too," she said, and Alan laughed at her unladylike language.

"Fine duchess you'd make, with a mouth like that."

She held up her bound wrists in front of her. "Untie me so I can undo my breeches."

"I can 'elp you with that," Jem leered. "Be my pleasure."

She kept her gaze on Alan. He seemed the lesser of two evils, despite how generous he was with his fists. She widened her eyes and tried to make herself look as pathetic and helpless as possible, no threat at all.

"Please. I swear I won't try to escape. I don't even know where we are, or which direction to go."

Alan gave a sigh and plucked one of her knives from Jem's hand, ignoring his grumble of protest. Daisy pushed herself to her feet as he crossed the clearing toward her, unwilling to be at a disadvantage by staying seated.

He grabbed her wrists and sliced through the twine bindings with ease—she always kept her knives sharp—and she flexed her fingers to regain some feeling in them.

"Go behind the barn," he said roughly. "But I warn

ye, if you try to run, I'll let Jem 'ave ye. And 'e won't be gentle."

Daisy nodded meekly. "Understood. Thank you, sir."

Her heart was pounding as she started toward the corner of the little building. She didn't know what she'd do if her knife wasn't still in her boot, but even if she had to fight these men with her bare hands, she would. She made a big show of walking slowly, as if she were almost crippled in pain, and raised her voice as she stepped out of sight.

"Still here!" she called, reaching down to check her boot, and her heart gave a leap as she found the familiar solidity of the handle. She had a blade. But when best to use it?

Since she really did need to relieve herself, she did so, squatting awkwardly to avoid the stinging nettles as she kept her ears pricked for Jem. When she was done, she took a quick glance around to see if there was anywhere to hide, but apart from a small stand of evergreens behind the cottage there was nothing but a low stretch of drystone wall trailing off toward the horizon.

She considered trying to climb one of the trees, just to inconvenience her captives, but they'd doubtless just come up after her and not be gentle in tossing her back to the ground.

If she palmed her knife now, it might be noticed. Better to retain the element of surprise. She found a small, sharp rock and concealed it in her hand instead. It would be better than nothing.

She stepped back around the corner of the ruin just in time to see the dark shape of a lone horseman galloping over the crest toward them. Alan reemerged from the trees near the fire, tugging up his breeches, and waved his arm in greeting.

The light was almost completely gone now, and Daisy slipped into the doorway of the cottage, recognizing the third man who'd abducted her, the one they'd called Connor. All three men looked quite similar, with reddish-brown hair and deep-set eyes; they were probably brothers, or kin of some kind.

"Why ain't she bound?" the new arrival glowered, pointing at Daisy as he slid from his mount.

Jem sent her a scornful look. "Alan knocked the fight out of 'er. And besides, where's she going to go?"

He indicated their bleak surroundings and Daisy's spirits dropped as she saw his point. It the fast-fading light she could see no other buildings nearby, no friendly lights that suggested help or habitation. They appeared to be in the middle of nowhere. Still, if she could manage to steal a horse . . .

"Did you deliver the message?" Alan asked.

Connor spat a glob of phlegm onto the ground. "Weren't no one to give it to. Aunt Rachel said the duke rode out barely half an hour after us, alone. I went back along the Carlisle road, thinkin' to find that carriage of 'is, the one we passed before, but it were nowhere to be seen."

Jem glared at Daisy, as if this was somehow *her* fault, and she hunched her shoulders and ducked down, trying to look as cowed and unassuming as possible.

The two horses that had pulled the cart had been let loose to graze, but their legs had been hobbled to stop them from straying too far. It would take her too long to untie them to escape.

Damn.

Perhaps she could steal Connor's horse.

"So now what?" Alan demanded as Connor strode to the fire and stretched his hands out toward the flames. "'Ow are we goin' to let 'im know we've got 'er?"

Jem leapt to his feet and pointed toward the horizon. "No need. The bastard's found us!"

The others turned in alarm, and Daisy's heart skipped a beat as she saw two horsemen galloping toward them at speed. Vaughan's unmistakable silhouette was in the lead, with Finch close by his side. They were riding as if hell itself was after them.

"You stupid bastard!" Alan swore at Connor. "You've led 'em straight to us!"

"I never saw 'em!" Connor countered, equally incensed. "Someone must've told 'im. Or he's got the luck o' the devil."

He strode over to the cart and pulled a rifle from beneath the hay, which he proceeded to prime with a measure of powder from a copper flask on his belt. Alan pulled Daisy's knife from where he'd tucked it in the back of his belt and held it ready, while Jem caught up her other knife from a stone by the fire.

Daisy cursed at the horrible irony of two of her own blades being used against her rescuers. God, if either of them hurt Vaughan or Finch, she'd go mad.

They were still advancing, and although it was getting harder to see them as the darkness increased, they still had a good half mile to cover. The barren location had given them no chance of a surprise attack, and they were easy targets for Connor's rifle.

Daisy sprang forward just as he shouldered the weapon. She sprinted the few yards from the cottage and flung herself against his back, barreling into him with her shoulder, using all her weight and momentum. His finger tightened on the trigger and the rifle fired with an ear-splitting roar, but he stumbled forward with a furious oath as his shot went wide, snapping a branch of a nearby evergreen.

Daisy staggered and went down on one knee, then rolled to the side as he swung around to wallop her.

"Little bitch!" he roared.

She rolled again, trying to get clear of him, then flung the rock at his head, forcing him to duck, but Alan had already raced across the clearing. He caught the collar of her shirt, yanked her roughly to her feet, and gave her a backhanded slap across the face that made her ears ring and her knees buckle.

Behind her, she heard Vaughan roar with fury, and she sank down, letting Alan take all of her weight as she reached blindly for the knife in her boot.

A pistol shot cracked the air behind her. Alan jolted, and she didn't think; she pulled the blade from her boot and thrust it upward. There was a sickening give as it embedded itself in his arm, then a jarring resistance as it hit bone. She tugged it free and slashed again, but he'd already released her and was staggering backward, toward the cottage, blood pouring from both her handiwork and a fresh bullet wound in his shoulder.

He'd dropped her second blade in the dirt, and she snatched it up, her lungs heaving with exertion, ready to go at him again, but he sagged against the doorframe, then collapsed.

Satisfied that he was no longer a threat, she swung back around to see Vaughan's horse clearing the low stone wall in a graceful arc. He fired a second pistol as soon as he landed, and Connor staggered back as he was hit at almost point-blank range. Vaughan flung himself from his mount, taking Connor to the ground, and they grappled for possession of the rifle.

Vaughan wrenched it from Connor's grip and smashed him in the face with the butt. The dreadful crunch of bone and cartilage breaking turned Daisy's stomach, but she felt a rush of savage satisfaction as Connor slumped down onto the grass.

Still-mounted Finch had cornered Jem against the far wall. Jem took a wild swing with Daisy's last knife, barely missing the horse's nose, but Finch kicked him in the face with his boot still in the stirrup, and Jem's chin snapped up as he crumpled to the ground.

Daisy glanced back at Vaughan. His face was harsh in the firelight, savage fury glimmering in his eyes. This wasn't the cool, cynical duke familiar to the *ton*. This was the seasoned soldier, a man who'd faced death a hundred times. His chest was heaving with exertion as he pushed himself off Connor's lax body, but the darkness in his eyes faded, replaced by a desperate urgency and concern as he rose and started toward her.

"Daisy. God, where are you hurt?"

Chapter Thirty

Daisy's knees threatened to buckle as Lucien came toward her. Her hands were shaking in reaction, and she took a deep breath to steady her pounding heart.

"Where are you hurt?" he commanded again. His gloved hand came up to cradle her jaw before she could answer, his thumb sliding over her cheek, and his eyes darkened as he catalogued her split lip and the bruising to her jaw.

"Bastards," he growled. "They hit you." His eyes narrowed even more. "Did they do worse?"

Daisy shook her head. "Only tied me up. I'm fine. Truly."

He glanced back over his shoulder, as if debating whether to go back and inflict more damage. "I should kill the bloody lot of them."

She caught his wrist and shook her head. "No. No more killing. Not for me."

A lump formed in her throat as she looked up at his profile and a thousand conflicting emotions tangled in her chest. "It's good to see you. I didn't think you'd—"

"Come for you?" he finished. A muscle ticked in his

jaw as he glared down at her, as if mortally offended. "I'll *always* come for you, Daisy."

His gaze burned into hers for an instant before he looked away, as if realizing what he'd just said. How it could be construed. He cleared his throat. "We never leave a man behind."

He removed his hand from her cheek and stepped back, and her stomach swooped in disappointment. She wanted him to wrap his arms around her for comfort. To forget the panic in the safety of his embrace.

She wanted him to kiss her.

Stupid.

Finch caught Lucien's loose horse by its reins and brought both mounts to a stop, then dismounted and gave Jem a none-too-gentle kick in the ribs to make sure he was definitely unconscious.

Daisy retrieved her last knife from near the fire where Jem had dropped it, every muscle aching now that the excitement was over. She watched impassively as Finch found a coil of rope in the back of the cart and made short work of tying Jem's ankles and wrists.

Lucien stalked over to Connor to do the same, but when he knelt down beside him, he glanced back at her with a guilty look.

"He's dead."

Alan was still conscious, slumped in the doorframe, and he made a low sound of anguish. "Connor?" He glared at Lucien. "Dead? Ye've killed my brother!"

Lucien returned his glare. "He shot at me first. And he would have hanged for kidnapping if I'd sent him to the magistrate."

Alan snapped his mouth shut, clearly realizing the same fate still awaited him. He was bleeding from the pistol shot Lucien had inflicted, and Daisy's stab wounds, and he groaned as Finch bound his shoulder roughly with his cotton neckerchief.

"Why bother to patch me up if ye're plannin' to see me swing?" he groused.

Lucien stared down at him irritably. "I'd gladly send you to the gallows, but the lady, here, prefers mercy." He gestured toward Daisy. "You'll live. But don't forget that every breath you take, from this moment until your last, is because *she* spared you."

Alan nodded, his face white, and glanced over at Daisy, who sent him an impassive stare.

The knowledge that Lucien wasn't going to execute the remaining two men made her almost giddy with relief, but it warred with an angry frustration that their stupid actions had resulted in the death of their brother. Perhaps this loss would be enough to stop them trying something so foolish again. She certainly hoped so.

Connor's mount had galloped off at the first sound of gunfire, and neither of the horses that had pulled the cart had saddles.

"Shall I drive the cart back to Gretna?" she asked, already dreading the task. She just wanted to lie down and sleep. Her head was throbbing, her knee hurt where she'd grazed it, and she was feeling distinctly lightheaded. She hadn't eaten anything all day.

Lucien shook his head. "You're in no state to drive, or ride, for that matter." He remounted his horse in a fluid move and held his hand down to her. "You'll ride with me."

His tone brooked no argument, and she didn't have the energy to object. She simply grasped his hand and placed her foot on top of his, using it as a step as he pulled her up to sit in front of him, astride.

The horse pranced in protest at the additional weight,

but he quieted it, and she quashed a shiver of awareness as his arms came around her on either side. She wasn't used to riding like this. Her bottom nestled snugly between his thighs, in his lap.

She swallowed as an unwelcome jolt of awareness skittered through her. "Are we going back to Gretna?"

"No. Perry and Violet have gone to Carisbrooke Hall to let them know to expect us. It's only a few more miles."

Daisy was feeling so bad she didn't want to go even *one* mile, but she certainly didn't want to stay here, so she simply nodded as he wheeled the horse and urged it away from the cottage.

"Hoi!" Alan shouted, aggrieved. "Ye can't just leave us 'ere."

Lucien didn't even spare him a look. "I'll tell someone you're here when we get to the next town. Bury your brother wherever you see fit, and if I ever see you or him"—he nodded toward Jem's prone body—"ever again, I'll see you both hanged. That's a promise. Do you understand me?"

"Aye," Alan muttered. "Understood."

"Good."

Lucien kicked the horse forward.

"I'm sorry you killed again because of me," Daisy said softly.

He transferred the reins to one hand and wrapped his free arm around her waist, tugging her back so her spine pressed more securely against his chest.

"I'm not going to lose sleep over it, Hamilton," he said, a hint of irony in his tone. "And neither should you. He deserved it. Which is more than I can say for most of the poor bastards I killed in the name of King and Country. None of them wanted to be in a war, any more than I did.

They were just doing what they were told. *Those* three were stupid, greedy bastards. It was justice."

Daisy nodded wearily. She could hear Finch's horse following somewhere behind them, and hoped the rising moon would provide enough light by which to see.

"The first man I killed was justice too."

Lucien's quiet comment made her stiffen in surprise. "What?"

"That duel you asked me about. The one before the war. You called it cold blood. But it was justice."

Daisy frowned at the horse's ears, amazed that he was finally answering her question. Was it because of their recent close shave? Had their moments of shared danger somehow bonded them together?

"The man I killed was Elaine's stepfather."

The girl he'd said he'd loved. "Why?"

"Elaine came to me when she discovered she was pregnant. The child wasn't mine—we were friends, like you and your Tom, but we'd never made love. She was desperate, distraught. She said the child's real father would never offer for her, and she begged me to marry her and protect her with my name."

Daisy didn't dare to move. Perhaps the darkness, and the fact that he wasn't looking at her made it easier for him to talk? Either way, she was keen to hear the truth from his lips.

He let out a huff of self-derision. "I refused. Told her I was too young to marry, too busy living my life in London. I assumed she'd got involved with a married man, or someone equally unsuitable. A servant, maybe. I pitied her, but not enough to tie myself to her for the rest of our lives."

He shook his head, his chin rubbing the top of her hair where she rested against him. "Her family bustled her away up here, to Fountain's Court—their estate shares a boundary with Carisbrooke Hall—to hide her situation. She was an embarrassment, an unwed girl in the family way. They told everyone she was ill."

He sighed. "In truth, I forgot about her. Out of sight, out of mind. When I finally came back up here to visit my sister, months later, I learned the truth from one of the servants. Elaine's stepfather was the father of her child. He'd forced himself on her, and her own mother had refused to believe it when she'd told her. She blamed Elaine for seducing her husband."

Daisy bit her lip in horror, her heart aching for the younger woman. This wasn't the first time she'd heard of such a sordid case; instances of familial abuse were tragically common if one read the newssheets or followed the criminal cases at the Courts of Justice. Worse still were the thousands more cases in which the perpetrator was never brought to justice. It made her blood boil just thinking about it.

It struck her how easily *she* could have shared a similar fate. The Duke of Dalkeith was not her real father, but he'd never once treated her with anything other than the respect due to a daughter. He'd certainly never tried to rape her or hurt her in any way. She'd been incredibly fortunate in that regard. Better his careless inattention than such a sick, unhealthy "love."

Lucien adjusted the reins, steering the horse over the springy heather and through a shallow stream.

"When I heard that, I went a little mad. I rode over to Fountain's Court like a stupid knight errant, convinced with the arrogance of youth that I could save her. I demanded to see her. Her stepfather refused. I offered to marry her, but he wouldn't give her up. I challenged him to a duel. He and four of his men beat me to within an inch of my life. They left me in a ditch, lucky to be alive." His low laugh was hollow, bleak.

"By the time I'd recovered, Elaine was dead. The baby came early, and she died in childbirth, along with the child."

Daisy closed her eyes tighter against the knot of emotion in her chest. Not just for Elaine and her child, but for Lucien, too, racked with guilt for not caring enough, for doing too little, too late. "I'm so sorry."

His chest rose and fell in a deep breath.

"What happened to him? Her stepfather? You eventually got that duel."

"I did." His tone was harsh now, bitter with recollection. "It took two years, but I finally encountered him in London, at a club. I beat him, fairly, at cards. Won a fortune off him, in fact. But ruining him financially wasn't enough. Why should he live when Elaine was cold in the ground? So I taunted him until he accused me of cheating. He was drunk, but we both knew it had nothing to do with cards.

"I demanded the satisfaction of a duel, knowing he couldn't refuse in public without looking like a coward. A gentleman would have waited until he was sober, but I didn't care about being a gentleman. We pushed back the tables and each nominated a second. Your brother Devlin was mine."

Daisy tightened her grip on his jacket. She hadn't known that particular detail. Devlin had never mentioned it.

"He must have realized I meant to kill him. He fired early, winged me in the shoulder. I shot him through the heart."

"Good," Daisy muttered fiercely.

She felt him look down at her, but didn't lift her head.

"He deserved it," she continued, "but I'm sorry you were the one who had to deliver justice."

"Killing him didn't bring back Elaine."

"No. But her spirit can rest in peace, knowing you avenged her."

She twisted round to finally look him in the eye. "I'm sorry I said you weren't noble."

He brushed a tangled curl of hair from her cheek, careful not to press on the bruised skin. "When I heard those men had taken you, it was like hearing about Elaine all over again. I wanted to kill them all."

How had she ever thought him cold? The emotion burning in his eyes was unmistakable. God, this man. He'd killed for her. Blackened his soul even more to protect her. But he'd also lied to her, deceived her, and then casually announced their engagement.

What on earth was she going to do?

Chapter Thirty-One

Daisy recognized the ominous signs about an hour later. At first, she'd dismissed the headache and the stiffness in her shoulders as a result of being slammed into the stable wall, then tied up in the cart, but the worsening pain in her head brought a horribly familiar sense of impending disaster.

She was about to be extremely unwell.

To call the episodes she occasionally suffered "just a headache" was like calling a severed limb a "little graze." The pain in her head would gradually increase, and she'd start to see dark spots in her vision, or little flashes of black and white, like spinning discs, in the periphery. Soon the pain would get so bad she'd vomit.

She was almost at that point now. She tried breathing through her mouth and ignoring the pounding in her skull, but her head felt like it was being crushed in a vise.

"Stop. Let me down!"

Lucien reined in immediately and she slid from his lap as quickly as she could.

"What's the matter?"

She couldn't answer him. She simply staggered a few

feet away from the horse, sank to her knees in the scratchy heather, and retched up what little was in her stomach.

She heard him dismount behind her as Finch said, "Maybe it was the blow to her head? Sometimes make's 'em sick like that. I've seen it before."

Daisy shook her head, feeling utterly miserable. "It's not that. It's a dreadful kind of headache that makes me ill. It happens a few times a year."

Her stomach rebelled again, and she spat into the grass, humiliation warring with the throbbing pain. "Go away, Vaughan."

She heard him snort. "Don't be ridiculous. You think I've never seen anyone cast up their accounts before? I've dealt with all three of your brothers when they couldn't handle their drink. Do you need to eat something? Drink?"

"It won't help. I just need to lie down in a dark room until it passes."

"We're only a few miles from Carisbrooke Hall. Let's get you there and put you to bed. Is there some medicine you can take? A tincture of some sort?"

"Laudanum helps." Her sluggish brain made it hard to think. "Wait! There's some in that vial I tried to give to you, at the inn." She patted her jacket pockets in sudden recollection, but they were frustratingly empty except for her knives. Anger made her head throb even more. "Those bastards must have taken it." Or perhaps it had fallen out during the fighting.

"There's laudanum at the house. Can you stand?"

She nodded and rose on shaking legs. She felt so unwell she could barely see straight. Lucien took her arm and guided her back to the horse, and she managed to support herself long enough for him to haul her back up.

Instead of placing her astride, he positioned her sideways, across his lap, her head resting against his chest as his arms came around her to hold the reins. It felt precarious, but she didn't object. He wouldn't let her fall.

The wind blew her hair against her cheek, and she pressed her face into his jacket and took deep, calming breaths.

"Close your eyes." His deep voice rumbled in her ear. "Don't worry about trying to stay upright. I've got you."

The world was spinning unpleasantly, so she did as he suggested, trying not to wince as her head pounded with every jolt of the horse's hooves.

The rest of the journey passed in an endless, pain-filled blur. She concentrated on counting each individual breath. In. Out. Exhale the pain. When that didn't work, she savored the reassuringly steady thump of Lucien's heartbeat, then catalogued the delicious scent of him instead of the pressure hammering her skull.

Perhaps she should ask Finch to choke her unconscious again?

She was barely aware of their arrival at Carisbrooke Hall. At any other time, she would have been craning her neck to note every detail of Vaughan's ancestral lair, but she barely opened her eyes. She had a brief impression of a long, tree-lined drive, tall stone walls, and a set of wide, curved steps.

A huddle of servants appeared. Lucien passed her down into a pair of waiting arms, then dismounted himself, and Daisy only managed a murmur of protest as he swept her back up into his arms. She was too exhausted to walk, too dispirited to argue. Everything hurt.

He strode through a huge doorway and into an echoing marble hall, and the agonizing flare of lanterns inside made her squeeze her eyelids tight again. There was a flurry of concerned conversation, his commanding tones a low rumble where she rested against his chest.

She would not be sick on his coat. It probably cost more than she earned in a year.

"Master Peregrine and his new bride arrived earlier," someone said. "But they've already retired."

"Not surprisin', on their weddin' night," Finch snorted with a chuckle.

"He said you'd be bringing a guest," an older, female voice said. "I've readied a suite in the east wing, Your Grace."

Daisy didn't care where they put her, as long as it was dark and had a bed. The blessed oblivion of sleep beckoned.

Lucien carried her upstairs, just as he'd done at the inn, only this time she was grateful for the assistance. When he finally stopped moving, she opened her eyes to a pretty room decorated in shades of cream and gold. A servant rushed to light the lamps, but she groaned in protest.

"No light, please. It hurts my head."

The servant paused, and she felt Lucien's arm tighten around her as he adjusted his grip.

"Dark," Daisy mumbled. "It needs to be dark."

"We have darker," he said decisively. The world spun as he turned and marched back out onto the corridor. The servant scurried after them.

"Fletcher, bring me a bowl in case she needs to be sick again. And laudanum."

"Yes, Your Grace."

Daisy cringed inwardly. God, she hated to be so weak, so helpless. Why was her body being so bloody uncooperative?

Dark paneling, gilt mirrors, and huge paintings passed by in a blur as Vaughan strode along a hallway and entered a room that was blessedly, deliciously dark. No lamps or candles pierced the Stygian gloom, and she moaned in relief as she was deposited gently onto a bed, and sank into the heavenly softness.

"Oh, thank you."

The pain in her head was so intense she wanted to cry. She curled up onto her side and pressed the heel of her hand into her right eye socket to try to relieve the pressure.

"What else helps, other than darkness?" Vaughan's voice was low, but brisk, and she appreciated his no-nonsense approach. If he showed her any pity she would crumble.

"Cold things. Like ice wrapped in a cloth on the back of my neck."

He glanced at the door as the servant returned.

"Laudanum, my lord."

"Thank you. Do we have any ice?"

"I'm afraid not, Your Grace. We haven't restocked the icehouse, since we didn't expect you or Master Peregrine to be here until the end of the season."

"Fine. Go and wet a cloth. With the coldest water we have, from the well in the orchard."

"Yes, sir."

"Daisy?" Lucien's voice was softer as he spoke to her. "Can you sit up and drink this laudanum?"

"Yes."

She might be sick again, but it was worth trying. She'd drink hemlock if it made the pain stop. There was the sound of a bottle being unstoppered and the faint glug of liquid as she pushed herself upright, keeping her eyes closed.

"Open your mouth. I have a spoonful of it here."

She obeyed, dutifully swallowing the bitter-tasting medicine with a grimace.

"It tastes vile," he murmured. "I know. I used to take it for my burns. But at least it should help you sleep."

She nodded and lay back down, stretching out against the blissfully cool pillows. The mattress sagged as he sat down next to her, but before she could protest, his big hands were on her head, massaging her skull with just the right amount of pressure. She managed a groan.

"Ohhhh, that's nice. Thank you."

He'd removed his gloves. His fingers circled the tense muscles of the neck and she arched up like a cat in silent appreciation.

"I wish Ellie and Tess were here." She sounded pitiful, but she didn't care. She was beyond mortification. Lucien had seen her at her absolute lowest ebb. There was no point in trying to be brave or sophisticated now.

"I'm sorry they're not." He sounded genuinely regretful. "But is there anything else I can get for you?"

The laudanum was beginning to work. The sweet lassitude was creeping over her, the pain starting to dull just a fraction. It was like floating on a pitch-black tide. Her body felt as if it was made of lead; it was a struggle to lift her arm, but she managed to reach up and encircle his wrist.

"Stay."

The tendons in his hand flexed. "Here? With you?"

She managed to nod, fighting the urge to slip under the beckoning wave of darkness.

"Please," she whispered.

The mattress shifted as he lifted his legs onto the bed and propped himself up against the headboard, his hip next to her head. He twisted his hand so she released her grip on his wrist, and she felt the brush of his fingers smoothing over her hair.

"I'll stay, if you want me to. Sleep now."

With a deep sigh, Daisy allowed herself to drift off, her lips curving wryly despite the lingering pain. Who'd have imagined she'd ever find Vaughan's presence *relaxing*?

Well, maybe "relaxing" wasn't the right word. He was not a relaxing person. But there was no denying that the thought of him there, watching over her while she slept, brought her a great deal of comfort. He was like a fierce and loyal watchdog, lethal to everyone but her.

Chapter Thirty-Two

Lucien stared down at Daisy and something tightened in his chest. She was alarmingly pale; all the color had left her face and her freckles stood out in stark relief against her milky skin. Her curls were a dark puddle on the navy bedding, almost invisible in the gloom, and he smoothed a wayward tendril with his finger, straightening it out against the velvet and watching as it snapped back into a lazy helix when released.

He'd seen men mortally wounded, bodies writhing in pain, but watching her suffer tonight had been a torment all of its own. He hated feeling so powerless, hated that there was so little he could do to make her feel better. There was nobody to punish, as there had been for Elaine. No way he could take the pain on her behalf. All he could do was sit in the dark with her, and wait.

This was his room. His bed. And the sight of her on his deep velvet coverlet made his stomach twist in primal satisfaction.

Logically, it was the best place for her. The midnight blue hangings were infinitely darker than the pastel guest room she'd been taken to first. With the door closed and the curtains drawn, it was like the underworld. He'd always liked it that way.

She was curled on her side, burrowing into the fabric. Her slim shoulders rose and fell with every breath, and he was fiercely glad that she'd found relief in sleep. Glad that she'd found it here, in his personal space.

He'd never had a woman here, in this bed, before.

Daisy looked as if she belonged.

She didn't move when he pulled the sheets up and around her body. In the faint light from the hallway, he could see a purplish bruise developing on her jaw, and his blood heated again at the knowledge that she'd been mistreated. He should have killed all three of those kidnapping bastards and left them to rot. He lacked her benevolent streak.

Unable to help himself, he reached out and gently traced the slope of her nose, the silky softness of her lips. She didn't stir. She was beautiful, even battered and bruised, and his heart swelled with an odd kind of pride, the kind he'd felt for his scrappy young recruits when they'd come through some testing skirmish.

She was a fighter, brave and merciful in equal measure, and he found he was properly in awe of her. Her dogged persistence was infuriating at times, but the thought of a world without her in it was utterly bleak.

He could have lost her tonight. So easily.

Lucien frowned. Claiming her as his fiancée at Gretna had been a spur-of-the-moment decision, the only way he could think of to limit the damage to her reputation. Being thought to have eloped with him would cause a minor scandal, but at least if they wed, she'd be a duchess. The position would afford her an extraordinary amount of protection.

If they didn't marry, society would treat the two of

them very differently. If they said that she'd jilted him, he'd get little more than mockery for "losing his touch," but she'd suffer a far worse fate. Since they'd been seen together, unchaperoned, everyone would assume that they'd been intimate. She'd be considered a lightskirt. Men who might previously have offered for her would move on to other, "purer" candidates, and she'd be fair game for the lecherous cads who prowled the dance floors and drawing rooms of Mayfair.

Daisy was more than capable of putting such idiots in their place, of course, but the thought of her being shunned and gossiped about by the bitchy women of the *ton* made him want to crush something. What was the point in being a duke, with all the power the position commanded, if he couldn't force people to accept her, be kind to her?

It was infuriating.

Marrying him was her best option, however much she might resent it. True, she'd be tied to him, but he was probably the one man in society who'd let her continue her work for King & Co. He'd never deny her the satisfaction of doing something she loved, and at which she clearly excelled.

Provided she didn't go anywhere too dangerous, of course.

She'd probably refuse to let him employ a bodyguard to accompany her on her missions, but perhaps *he* could go with her and watch her back. They'd make a formidable team. And he was more than happy to kill anyone who threatened her.

As his duchess she'd have his fortune at her disposal too. His father had left the duchy in a solid financial position, and his own transactions on the stock exchange had garnered him more money than he knew what to do with.

The thought of showering Daisy with clothes and jewels pleased him in ways he couldn't quite explain. She looked delectable in a muddy pair of breeches, but he wanted to see her wearing a dress that he'd chosen for her, with the Cranford diamonds sparkling at her throat.

The fact that she clearly didn't give a fig for such things was highly amusing. It would be his pleasure to indulge her. She'd huff and complain—and then steal everyone's breath.

Society was so fickle he knew he could paint their elopement as desperately romantic. If he said he'd been so in love with her that he hadn't wanted to wait the traditional three weeks for the banns to be read, the dowagers and matrons would smile indulgently at his masculine impatience and overlook the fact that he could have just purchased a special license in London.

Daisy would make a remarkable duchess. Fierce and unexpected, passionate and loyal.

She was also intelligent. Once she'd had time to consider all the ramifications, she'd come to see that marrying him was by far the lesser of several evils.

His pride rebelled a little at the fact that she hadn't jumped at the chance—a hundred other women would have done so—and then he snorted softly in self-mockery.

Of course Daisy would make things difficult. Her insistence on only marrying for love made her an anomaly in the *ton*. Marriages were usually more social and financial contracts than passionate unions, but he admired her optimism.

Even if it made his own life bloody difficult.

She moved, twisted, so her forehead pressed against the outside of his thigh. Her hand lay near his knee, half curled, and he gave in to the temptation to stroke her palm lightly with his finger. Her fingers closed around it, trapping him.

"Lucien."

He stilled as she murmured his name. And then his heart missed a beat as she pulled their joined hands toward her and pressed her lips to the scarred back of his hand, then tucked it beneath her cheek.

She was asleep. She didn't know what she was doing. It wasn't a kiss. She was just seeking comfort.

He still didn't move his hand. He simply sat there in the darkness, his heart hammering as if he'd run the full length of a battlefield under fire, pierced by a sensation that was half pleasure, half despair.

When Daisy woke again it was still dark, and she had absolutely no idea what time it was. The pain in her head had receded to a dull ache; still there, but lurking in the background so she could finally think of other things.

She rolled onto her side, and in the strip of light that glowed from beneath the door she saw the dark shape of a man sitting in a wing armchair just to the right of the fire. Her heart gave a little skip. She knew who it was.

"You're awake," Vaughan said softly. "How do you feel?"

She rubbed her hands over her face. "Better. Thank you."

He uncrossed his legs and rolled his shoulders, and she had the impression that he'd been sitting there for quite some time.

"Have you ever figured out what causes these headaches?"

She tilted her head to stretch the muscles of her neck. "I wish I could. I've tried to see if it correlates to food that I've eaten, or some activity I've done, but I've never found anything."

"Could it be related to your monthly courses?"

Her brows rose. Most men would be too ignorant or too embarrassed to bring up such a topic, but Vaughan was not most men. He seemed genuinely interested in finding the root cause.

"I don't think so. I tried tracking that, too, but there was no pattern. I've thought there might be a link to times when I've been particularly busy, working long hours and not sleeping enough, but who knows?"

"Could it be that you haven't been eating regularly?"

Daisy yawned. "Perhaps."

"Can you eat something now?"

"What time is it?"

"A little after midnight." He didn't seem annoyed that she was keeping him awake.

"The servants will have retired for the night. Don't wake them up just to make me some food."

"It's no bother. I told them to leave some soup on the stove for you, in case you woke up. I'll go and get it."

He stood, a tall shadow in the darkness, and when he opened the door, she saw him silhouetted against the faint glow from the hall. His hair was mussed, as if he'd been running his hands through it, and the collar of his shirt was standing up at an odd angle. It made him look appealingly disheveled.

Daisy propped herself up against the pillows when he'd gone. There was a candle in a brass holder by the bed, and she lit it with the tinderbox that sat next to it.

She was still almost fully dressed. Someone had removed her boots and her jacket, but left her in her shirt, breeches, and stockings. For comfort, she wriggled out of her breeches, confident that Vaughan wouldn't see what she had on beneath the covers.

He returned a short while later, carrying a tray that he placed on her lap, and she quashed her guilt at having him play nursemaid and servant for her. It was nice to be coddled for a change. The inviting aromas of warm bread and vegetable soup made her mouth water, and she dipped the spoon into the bowl with a happy little sigh.

"Thank you," she mumbled.

He resettled himself in the chair, and she tried not to feel self-conscious as he watched her eat.

"There's no need to stay," she said, swallowing a mouthful of bread. "You can go to bed if you want."

His mouth curved at the corners. "You asked me to stay. Don't you remember?"

Heat warmed her cheeks. Had she said that? She'd certainly *wanted* him to stay. But had she actually said such a thing out loud?

"You called me Lucien."

Oh God. When had she started thinking of him as Lucien instead of Vaughan?

"You probably misheard. I expect I said Lucifer."

He sent her a sardonic look, brows raised.

"If I *did* ask you to stay," she said quickly, "then it must have been the effect of the medicine. It makes a person say all sorts of bizarre things."

His eyes glittered in amusement, as if he knew she was hedging. "That's true. I thought I was a horse at Waterloo, once, when I'd been on the laudanum. And I'd be happy to go to bed. You're in it."

Daisy glanced around, taking in the sumptuous velvet hangings and subtle hints of gold. The understated masculine elegance. She should have known. Even the bedclothes smelled like him. No wonder she'd wanted to bury herself in them.

A shiver of awareness ran through her. His bed. The intimacy of it made her head spin.

She placed the tray on the bedside table and pushed back the covers. "I'm sorry. I'll—"

"You'll stay right where you are," he said firmly. "I'll go and sleep in one of the guest rooms."

Guilt at turfing him out of his bedroom warred with indignation that he'd put her there in the first place. She narrowed her eyes, determined not to be swayed by his apparent generosity.

He slanted her a sly, sideways smile. "Unless you're feeling so glad to be alive that you want to celebrate in the time-honored way?"

Daisy bit back a snort. "You think such a heroic rescue deserves a physical reward?"

His eyes sparkled, and she appreciated his teasing attempt to make her feel better.

"There's a lot to be said for a gratitude fuck. I know plenty of soldiers who swore by it, after a battle. It's an excellent way to relieve stress. Might help stave off another one of those headaches."

"Thank you, Dr. Vaughan," she said drily, "but I think I'll just try to sleep."

"I'm only thinking of your health." He shrugged. "Any time you feel the slightest twinge, I'd be more than happy to help."

"Don't think I'm going to forgive you, just because you've taken care of me," Daisy said, determined not to cave to his insidious charm. "You've made my life an absolute nightmare."

"Likewise," he countered. "I left London to rid myself of a nephew, not saddle myself with a wife."

"I'm not going to be your wife," she growled.

He rose, and she pulled the bedsheets back over her legs, slumping down in the pillows, thinking he was going to come near her, but he merely strode across to a large mahogany linen press that stood against one wall. He selected a clean shirt from within, and sent her an enigmatic smile.

"We'll talk about it in the morning."

Chapter Thirty-Three

It was full light when Daisy woke again, and a servant scratched at the door with a steaming bowl of porridge. The girl drew open the heavy curtains, and Daisy blinked in the bright sunlight that streamed through the tall windows. Her head, mercifully, didn't object.

"Morning, Miss. I'm Jenny. His Grace said you'd be wanting a bath."

Daisy smiled. "A bath would be lovely, thank you. But breakfast first. I'm famished."

"I'll come back up in twenty minutes or so to assist you." The girl bobbed a curtsey and slipped out the door before Daisy could object.

The porridge was delicious, made with extra cream and a swirl of honey, and Daisy ate the lot, glad that she was feeling almost back to normal. When Jenny returned, clutching an armful of bathing sheets, she gestured to a doorway Daisy hadn't noticed, set into the wooden paneling.

"The bathing room's through there."

Daisy almost laughed when she saw the enormous copper tub set in the center of the tiles. Tess had a similarly luxurious bath back at Wansford Hall, and it was clear that Vaughan had spared no expense when it came to his own creature comforts. No measly, cramped hip bath in front of the fire for His Grace, the Duke of Cranford.

The tantalizing image of him, steam beading his skin, rippled in her brain like a mirage before she forcibly dismissed it as *not helpful.*

An ingenious series of pipes brought both hot and cold water up from the kitchens, and when it was half full Daisy sank into the most welcome bath of her life. She slid under the surface and fanned her fingers through her hair, washing the dirt and dust away.

The maid had left a bar of delicate, rose-scented soap, and she lathered it over her whole body, reveling in the sensation of feeling fully clean once again. Her knees were grazed from the fight, and there was a faint purple bruise on her right cheekbone, but otherwise she didn't feel too bad.

When she finally emerged, cheeks glowing from the heat, it was to find Jenny laying what looked to be a dress, petticoats, and other pieces of feminine clothing on the bed.

Daisy's brows rose in surprise. "What's all that? Do they belong to His Grace's sister?"

The maid smiled. "No, Miss. Mrs. Hughes is quite a bit taller than yourself. Her things would be far too long and I've had no time to alter any of them. These are from Master Peregrine's new wife. She said you didn't have any dresses of your own, and asked me to give this to you."

Daisy bit back a small groan, even as she forced a sunny smile. "How kind of her."

The chemise and silk stockings were lovely, but her spirits plummeted as she got a closer look at the dress. Violet's sartorial preferences were diametrically opposed to her own. She cast a desperate glance around the bedroom for the clothes she'd just discarded. She'd rather put on soiled garments than don the pastel horror Violet had sent.

"I've taken your breeches and shirt downstairs, to be washed," Jenny said cheerfully.

Damn it all.

"Would you like me to help lace you up?"

"No thank you, I can manage. Do you happen to know where His Grace is?" Perhaps she could linger up here and avoid seeing him altogether.

"He's in the breakfast room, miss. He told me to tell you to get dressed and meet him there at eleven o'clock."

Daisy glanced at the clock. It was already half past ten. She was going to have to wear the blasted dress.

"Thank you, Jenny. I'll find my own way down."

Daisy descended the stairs twenty minutes later, her heart pounding oddly in her chest. Carisbrooke Hall, from the little of it she'd seen, was undeniably impressive. The hallway she'd just traversed was huge, littered with priceless paintings and antiques, and the gardens she'd glimpsed through the windows spread out as far as the eye could see. There was an entire herd of deer.

She'd given in to the temptation to snoop before she left Vaughan's room, of course. They'd be on their way back to London soon, and she might never have another chance, and she wanted to know as much about him as possible.

A peek inside the huge linen press had produced a waft of his familiar scent that made her stomach do a little somersault, but a quick search of the drawers, writing desk, and dressing chests proved unproductive. Paper, ink, a block of sealing wax. Some bills from his London tailor. He paid an exorbitant amount for his boots.

She wasn't sure what she'd expected to find. He wasn't the sort of man to keep incriminating love letters. And it wasn't as if he'd have a sheaf of erotic drawings hidden somewhere, when he'd probably done all the scandalous things depicted in them in real life. The memory of him doing several of those things to *her* brought an extra flush to her cheeks.

No. However tempting his body might be, the rest of his personality left a lot to be desired. He was sneaky, manipulative and . . . he'd given her the best climaxes of her entire life.

Not helpful.

The man in question was seated at one end of a large mahogany breakfast table, a cup of steaming coffee in his hand, and his eyes widened as she appeared in the doorway.

"Good God."

"Don't you dare laugh!" Daisy ordered fiercely. She'd never felt so self-conscious.

His gaze raked her from head toe, and he pressed his beautiful lips together into a thin line. It was clear he was holding back laughter as she stalked the length of the table toward him.

"You look . . ."

She sank into the seat next to him with a disgusted snort. "Go on, say it. Like a jellyfish. Or a strawberry blancmange. I can't decide which." She gave one of the frills that adorned her neckline a disgusted flick.

The gown Violet had provided was the most hideously unflattering thing she'd ever worn in her life. No doubt the pale pink color looked wonderful with Violet's cornflower blue eyes and golden ringlets, but it didn't suit Daisy's darker coloring one bit. To make matters worse, the fussy proliferation of lace, bows, and frills made her look like the result of a terrible accident in a haberdashery shop.

Vaughan took a sip of coffee, but his eyes laughed at her over the rim of his cup.

"I think it's safe to say that pale pink is not your color."

The amusement he was deriving at her expense was obnoxious. Daisy narrowed her eyes. "I couldn't agree more."

"And the style suggests a certain girlish innocence that strains credibility."

She poured herself a steaming cup of coffee. "I'll take that as a compliment."

"I won't object in the slightest if you want to take it off," Vaughan said. "In fact, I'd be happy to assist."

"I still have a knife," she reminded him, even though his suggestive words brought a flash of heat to her skin.

He grinned. "You can't stab me, Hamilton. I played your knight errant. I rescued you. It would be exceedingly ungrateful."

She added two lumps of sugar to her cup. She needed the energy to argue with him. "You're the reason I was kidnapped in the first place, *and* the reason we're in this ridiculous situation now."

"Perhaps," he conceded. "But I had noble intentions. I was trying to make the best of a bad situation."

"Wasn't it Samuel Johnson who said that Hell is paved with good intentions? We're clearly well on the way."

Daisy had spent much of the morning trying to decide what she should do. "The way I see it, there are several ways this 'situation' can progress. Option one would be the worst for you. We could say that you lied to Letty, that we were never engaged, and that you forcibly abducted me and took me to Gretna as your mistress."

He raised his brows. "You're right. That doesn't reflect well on me at all. Especially if everyone thinks I'm subsequently refusing to marry you. Not that I particularly care about my reputation, but even cast as the poor, unwilling victim, you'd still be ruined."

"True."

"Besides, that doesn't make any sense. Why would I bother to take you all the way to Gretna if I had no plans to marry you? I could have just stayed in London and debauched you there." He slanted her a wicked, knowing look. "In my study. Against the desk. Multiple times a day."

Beast. Why did he have to taunt her so?

"That's also true," Daisy conceded serenely. "And anyone who knows you would instantly realize you'd never put yourself to so much trouble for a woman."

He ignored the unsubtle dig. "I suppose we could say I was in Gretna because I was chaperoning Perry and Violet. And that I took you along for my entertainment. But again, why would I bother abducting someone unwilling when there are so many *willing* ladies who would gladly fill your place?"

Daisy's heart gave a jealous little clench at the truth of that, but she forced herself to match his flippant tone.

"Would it be too much to pretend that your desire for me was so insatiable that you lost all sense of reason and resorted to kidnapping?"

He sent her an amused, ironic look. "What do you think?"

"You're right. Nobody would believe it."

She quashed an irrational sense of disappointment. Of course it was too much. She'd never inspire such passion in a man like Vaughan. That fact that he'd even desired her *once* was a miracle.

"What's option two?" he asked.

"We let everyone think I *agreed* to an affair with you, and Letty caught us."

"That's a terrible idea. Not only would you be ruined socially, but every unscrupulous cad in London would start pestering you in the hopes of making you their mistress once I'd finished with you."

"I think you're overestimating my appeal," Daisy scoffed.

"And I think you're *underestimating* it. Even in a dress as hideous as that." His eyes flashed.

"Either way," she said, ignoring the way her stupid heart gave an irregular little thump, "if I'm thought to be a lightskirt, Ellie and Tess will suffer by association, and so will King and Company. I don't want that."

"So what's option three?"

She huffed out a breath. "We say we *were* engaged, like you told Letty, but that I changed my mind when we got to Gretna. That's not much better than the other two options, really, except that people might give me the benefit of the doubt and think I'm still a virgin, despite being unchaperoned with you for several days."

"You're clutching at straws. Society gives women far less leeway than men. You'll still be seen as soiled goods. But you might still find a man willing to overlook the fact that you're not a virgin and marry you."

"I'm not interested, if it still affects my friends and my business." Daisy took another sip of her coffee. Her nerves were jittery, her thoughts spinning with the ramifications of every possibility.

"Can't we just agree that marrying me is your best option?" Vaughan said irritably. "If we say we were married at Gretna, there'll be a bit of scandal, but people will forgive it as the impetuosity of two people in love."

"Again, straining the bounds of credibility. And we *aren't* married," Daisy said stubbornly. "Are you saying we should pretend that we are?"

"No. How would that work? If we say we're married, you'll have to come and live with me at Cranford House. We'll have to act as man and wife in public."

"I could do that without actually marrying you," Daisy said, just to be pedantic.

"No, you couldn't. Your father is going to demand proof of a wedding. He'll want to see a copy of the register, and he'll expect to discuss settlements and negotiate a dowry."

Daisy bit her lip. He was right, damn it. There was no way she could lie about something so monumental to her father. The truth would come out.

Vaughan placed his cup carefully back into its saucer. "We have to get married. Properly. It's the only solution that stops you from being an outcast and protects your business and friends. You'll have all the social and legal benefits of being the Duchess of Cranford."

And all the heartache of being married to a man who doesn't love me.

"A marriage of convenience," she said hollowly. "Which you're only suggesting because of what happened all those years ago, with Elaine. You feel guilty because you didn't save her by offering to marry her, and now you see a way to redeem yourself. You can save my reputation by marrying me, and while that's a very noble sentiment, I don't want to marry someone because of a sense of duty or guilt."

He opened his mouth to argue, but she shook her head. "Have you ever listened to the actual marriage vows? The groom has to promise to 'forsake all others . . . as long as ye both shall live.' Do you honestly think you could be faithful to just one woman for the rest of your life?"

"Is that your only objection?" His brows lifted, as if her answer intrigued him. "That you don't think I could be faithful?"

"That, and the fact that you don't love me," she said, with brutal honesty.

"Interesting."

She started to ask what he meant by that, but it was his turn to interrupt her.

"You know, the bit *I* remember is the groom saying, 'with my body I thee worship.'" His dark gaze bored into hers. "Just so you know, Hamilton, I am *more* than willing to worship you with my body at any time of the day or night." His eyes held hers. "As many times as you like." His lips quirked and she ignored the corresponding tug in her belly. "As hard and as fast, or as soft and as slow as you like."

Daisy rolled her eyes, banishing the wicked enticements he painted with his words.

"You've already 'worshipped' me, Vaughan. And as fun as it was, I'm sure the novelty will soon wear off. You'll lose interest, and then we'll both be trapped."

"So you're refusing me?"

His tone was impossible to decipher. She couldn't tell if he was angry, frustrated, or simply relieved.

"I am. I'd rather be ruined than tie myself to a man who doesn't love me. But I appreciate the offer."

He poured himself a second cup of coffee, and the look on his face gave her a moment of disquiet. He didn't look like a man who'd been granted a reprieve. He looked . . . calculating. Which, in her experience of Vaughan, did not bode well.

"Have you seen Violet and Perry this morning?"

He accepted the change of topic with a comical grimace. "I have. Thankfully, it was before I'd had my breakfast, so I didn't cast up my accounts at their nauseating display of postnuptial satisfaction. They've gone for a picnic somewhere in the grounds. We can only pray they don't fall in the lake or get trampled to death by cows because they're busy plaiting flowers into each other's hair and composing sonnets."

Daisy bit back a smile. "Will they be coming back to London? I'd like to leave as soon as possible."

"Yes. Violet wants to explain things to her father, and I've said I'd be there to back them up. If you'll deign to travel with us, we can all leave this afternoon."

Daisy nodded. "As long as they have their own carriage."

"Agreed."

"We can all stay at Wansford Hall again tomorrow night, but we'll still have to spend tonight on the road. Will we stay at the same inn we were at before?"

The one where she'd watched him bathe.

"Yes. I'll get you your own room. Jenny can come as your maid."

"Yes, please. I'll write to Tess and ask her to meet us at Wansford. She can tell us what rumors are flying round London. If the worst comes to the worst, I suppose I'll just go and visit my mother in Italy for a few years."

Vaughan's eyes narrowed in displeasure. "Are you honestly saying you'd leave the country—leave your job and your life and your friends for *a few years*—rather than marry me?"

Daisy lifted her chin and lied through her teeth. "Absolutely."

Chapter Thirty-Four

The journey back toward London was very different from the one they'd taken north. Finch drove one carriage, containing Daisy and Jenny, while a second coachman drove Perry, Violet, and the small mountain of hat boxes, trunks, shoe boxes, and suitcases that made up Violet's luggage.

If that was Violet's idea of packing light, Daisy snorted to herself, she dreaded to think how much the girl would take when she went away for more than a week. Napoleon and his armies had probably traveled with less.

Vaughan, mercifully, elected to ride, and despite Jenny having altered a very fine riding habit for Daisy, she declined to join him outside. Being near him was both pleasure and pain, since she spent every moment vacillating between being certain she was making the right decision to refuse him, and the niggling feeling that she was being a complete and utter fool.

Vaughan might not love her, but was her insistence on such a thing truly realistic? Could a woman in her position expect the man they married to love them, heart and soul? Tess and Ellie were almost certainly the exceptions in the *ton*. Perhaps Daisy should just be grateful for the fact that Vaughan desired her, and abandon herself to the passion—however fleeting it turned out to be.

She seemed to change her mind with every rotation of the carriage wheels.

When they reached the White Horse at Doncaster, Vaughan joined Perry and Violet in the public dining room to eat, but Daisy took her evening meal alone in her room. It was not the same one she'd shared with Vaughan, thank God, but she was still plagued by memories of him.

She hoped Tess and Ellie would be able to meet her at Wansford Hall. She'd never been more in need of their support and advice.

The following morning, Vaughan sent Jenny up to ask if Daisy was going to "hide in the carriage all day," and despite knowing he'd made the taunt deliberately to goad her, she told Jenny to unpack the riding habit. Avoiding him simply betrayed the fact that he had the power to affect her, and she refused to admit to such a thing.

The knowing curl to his lips as she stormed to the mounting block was irritating, but Daisy's heart beat hard in her chest at his proximity.

Their horses fell into step some way behind the carriages to avoid the dust kicked up by the wheels.

"Not tempted to sit in with Perry and Violet?" he teased, keeping his expression impassive.

"And play gooseberry? No thank you."

"You're the one who supports marrying for love. That's what you get. Kissing and crooning and holding hands."

She rolled her eyes. "Not always. Tess and Justin aren't like that. Nor are Ellie and Harry."

"Exceptions."

"I thought of another option last night," she said. "What if you deny everything? Say Letty made the whole thing up. You're a duke. She's a known gossip. Your word will carry more weight than hers."

"Letty Richardson's obnoxious, no doubt about it, but painting her as an out-and-out liar seems a bit harsh. She *did* see us. Besides, people are bound to ask why she'd concoct something so extraordinary—especially about me. In case you weren't aware, I have a reptation as a man unwise to cross."

"I'm well aware of your reputation," she said primly.

"Well, then. Even if I deny it, they'll say there's no smoke without fire."

Daisy suppressed a frustrated groan. She'd have no qualms about ruining Letty's reputation to salvage her own. The woman didn't deserve her mercy, but he was right. There would still be endless gossip and innuendo.

Her spirits rose when the warm sandstone walls of Wansford Hall finally came into view. She spurred her mount forward, galloping down the long drive and leaving Vaughan and the carriages behind.

Tess must have been watching for her arrival, because she hurried out onto the front steps as Daisy slid from her mount. She took one look at her face and enfolded her in a hug, just as Ellie appeared behind her.

"We came as soon as I got your letter," Tess said breathlessly. "What on earth have you been up to? London's awash with all sorts of ridiculous rumors."

There goes the faint hope that Letty had decided to keep her mouth shut.

"Long story," Daisy panted, conscious of Vaughan and the others drawing closer. "I'll tell you everything as soon as we're alone. Are you here on your own?"

Ellie gave a wry laugh. "Hardly. Harry and Justin

insisted on coming with us to find out about the drama firsthand. They said they might be *useful*, if you can imagine such a thing."

Daisy managed a smile. "More likely neither of them trusted you not to get into trouble without them."

The carriages were almost upon them, so Tess turned to welcome her guests. Daisy hadn't actually told them who she was traveling with, and she heard Tess's shocked gasp as she and Ellie caught sight of Vaughan's unmistakable figure.

They both dropped into welcoming curtseys.

"Your Grace! Welcome." Tess said smoothly.

"A pleasure." Vaughan nodded and made the extra introductions. "My nephew, Peregrine Hughes, and his new wife Violet, lately Brand."

Tess sent the couple a wide smile. "Congratulations. And welcome to Wansford Hall. I wouldn't dream of having you all stay at an inn, not when we have so many spare bedrooms. Please, come in and get settled. Mrs. Jennings will take you."

Violet and Perry were ushered inside, and Daisy glanced back at Vaughan, trying to gauge his mood.

"Justin is inside, Your Grace," Tess said easily. "Playing billiards, I believe, with Ellie's husband, Harry, Earl of Cobham. Would you prefer to be shown to your room or be taken straight to them?"

"I'll go and see them first, thank you."

"Simmons will show you the way. Dinner will be at eight."

Vaughan nodded again. "Very good."

He strode into the house after the footman, and Daisy let out a soft breath. She felt tense every time he was near. Every part of her body tingled with awareness.

Ellie linked their arms, her eyes sparkling with good humor behind her glasses. "Dorothea Hamilton, I have a feeling this is going to be your best adventure yet. Come in and tell us *everything*."

Daisy allowed her two friends to sweep her up to the bedroom she used whenever she was a guest. As soon as they were inside, Tess seated herself in one of the arm-chairs beside the fireplace and Ellie threw herself onto the end of the bed, exactly as she'd done when they were girls.

Their twin expressions of anticipation made Daisy grin, and she deliberately turned and washed her hands and face, using the pitcher and bowl on the washstand, simply to make them wait some more.

"You are a dreadful tease," Ellie scolded with a laugh. "That note you sent to Tess was a masterclass in mystery. All you said was, *'Disaster. The hermit may have been right. Meet me at Wansford as soon as you can. Expect additional guests. D.'"*

Daisy suppressed a snort. She'd known the oblique message would bring the two of them quicker than a full explanation. There was nothing they enjoyed more than a mystery, except maybe a challenge.

Tess frowned. "I assume the hermit you were referring to is the one we visited in Vauxhall Gardens a few years ago? The one who said your ideal match would be with a highwayman?"

"I think the actual wording on her scroll was that she'd 'meet her true match on a dark highway,'" Ellie said. "But what has that to do with anything? Why is London abuzz with rumors about you and the Duke of Cranford—the man currently playing billiards down-stairs with our husbands?"

"The man who looked at you as if he couldn't decide whether to strangle you or drag you off into the nearest dark corner and ravish you," Tess added gleefully. "And believe me, I'm familiar with the look. It's one my husband employs on an almost daily basis."

"Mine too," Ellie chuckled. "Come on, out with it!"

Chapter Thirty-Five

Daisy sank onto the bed next to Ellie and drew up her knees. "First of all, tell me exactly what rumors you've heard concerning myself and Vaughan."

"There were a score of them flying around Cecelia Lambert's card party last night," Tess said. "You're either his mistress, his fiancée, or his wife, depending on who you ask. Everyone kept asking Ellie and me to confirm something, but of course we pleaded ignorance."

Daisy groaned. It was as bad as she'd feared. "Thank you. But I'm afraid there's no stopping this now. You've already seen the happy couple, Peregrine and Violet, downstairs, so you know I failed to catch them before they tied the knot at Gretna Green."

Tess shrugged. "Who cares about them? We care about *you*. What's going on? Are you having a torrid affair with Vaughan? Please say yes. That man is glorious."

Heat warmed Daisy's cheeks. "Not exactly. I mean, I *did* allow him to seduce me. Just once—I mean, on just the one occasion—one night—"

Ellie's mouth opened as if she were about to ask a question, or ten, but Daisy rushed on.

"—but the real disaster happened when Letty Richardson saw us together at Gretna Green. Vaughan told her we were engaged, thinking that would save my reputation."

Ellie's eyes widened behind her gold-rimmed spectacles. "Oh goodness."

"So what did you do?" Tess demanded, her voice rising in excitement. "Go to the blacksmith and say 'I do'? Are you Her Grace, the Duchess of Cranford?"

"I am not. Before I had the chance to think, I was kidnapped by three idiot brothers who'd overheard Vaughan saying I was to be his duchess. They planned to hold me for ransom."

Daisy recounted the subsequent events in as much detail as she could remember, and when she was done the two of them stared at her in bemusement.

"So now I don't know what to do," Daisy finished. "I've gone through all the possible options, and not one is satisfactory."

Ellie wrinkled her nose. "Wait a minute. Can someone explain to me why marriage to Lucien Vaughan—Duke of Cranford, handsome as sin, rich as Croesus—is *unsatisfactory*? I'll admit he's tall, dark, and terrifying, and known to shoot people at the slightest provocation, but I've never heard of him mistreating a woman. Far from it. He has the reputation for keeping women *extremely* satisfied. At least until he gets bored and leaves them. What happened? You say he seduced you. Was it a disaster?"

"A complete disaster," Daisy admitted. "But not in the way you mean. It was a disaster in the sense that I hoped it would banish the ghost of him from my foolish brain. I thought one night with him would prove that he was nothing special."

"Ah." Tess managed to imbue the single syllable with a world of meaning.

Daisy sighed. "I thought it would work in the same way as those inoculations invented by Dr. Jenner. If I deliberately infected myself with a small dose of the disease—Vaughan, in this case—I'd be able to fight off a much more serious case in the future. But I was wrong. I didn't make myself immune. All I did was give myself a full-blown case of him. He's all I can think about. All I want. I am *infected*, and the worst of it is, I don't think it's simply incurable lust. I have all sorts of other complicated feelings about him."

Tess and Ellie were both regarding her with fascinated, rapt expressions.

"What other sort of feelings?" Tess asked.

"I *like* him. Even though he's an absolute monster." Daisy shook her head, disgusted with herself. "He fought for me, risked his life for me. Cared for me when I was ill. He was kind."

Ellie frowned. "Well, that's not fair. It's bad enough him looking like he does, and being all brooding and masterful, but if he's secretly *nice* beneath all that sarcasm, how were you supposed to resist?"

"Everything conspired against me," Daisy wailed. "There was only one bed. Only one horse. He *bathed* in front of me, for heaven's sake."

"Oh, bloody hell," Tess muttered. "Baths are notoriously dangerous. There's not much he could do to make you change your opinion now either. Maybe if he went about kicking dogs, or assaulting his staff?"

"He doesn't," Daisy said dismally. "His staff all dote on him, and so does his nephew. And he's kind to animals. He refused to let the carriage horses be overworked, or travel at night, and I saw him give the crust of his pie to one of the dogs in the yard at the White Horse."

"He did lie to you all the way to Gretna," Tess rallied.

"But then he proposed to save her reputation," Ellie countered. "That was very noble."

"Exactly!" Daisy cried. "He only offered out of duty. He doesn't want me, except physically. If we marry, it will be nothing but a marriage of convenience, and after my mother's experience, I always said I'd only marry for love. And he doesn't love me."

"It sounds as if *you're* already halfway there, though," Ellie said bluntly. "You're in love with him, aren't you?"

Daisy gave a heartfelt groan. "Ugh. Yes. Not that the idiot deserves it. He's arrogant and overbearing and positively riddled with flaws. It's not fair."

"Love isn't fair," Tess said with a grin. "It's inconvenient and disruptive, but life would be very dull without it. People were moaning about it a thousand years ago, and they'll be moaning about it a thousand years from now."

She tilted her head. "You know, Justin only wanted a marriage of convenience when we first met, but he ended up falling for me. Couldn't that happen with Lucien? Why can't you make him love you?"

"A strong physical attraction is an excellent start," Ellie agreed.

"But physical attraction doesn't last. He'll tire of me eventually, and then I'll have the agony of knowing he's seeing other women."

"Perhaps. But you'd have the protection of his name and the cushion of his fortune. You'd still have your friends and your job. And you could always take a lover of your own," Tess suggested. "Besides, there's no guarantee that he'll be unfaithful. Men like Vaughan don't fall easily, but when they do, there are no half measures. It's all or nothing."

"And you're not the sort of woman to accept defeat either," Ellie said bracingly. "You like nothing better than a challenge. Why not see marrying Vaughan in the same vein? Think of him as a case you have to crack, or a puzzle you need to solve. You're inventive, clever. Fascinate him. Be like Scheherazade, in *The Arabian Nights*. Be so brilliant that he won't look at another woman for as long as he lives."

Daisy bit her lip. "You think I should just marry him, then?"

"I don't see a better alternative. Not unless you want to be banished from society."

"I could take an extended trip to go and see my mother in Italy. Maybe by the time I come back people will have forgotten?"

"Unlikely. The *ton* has an incredibly long collective memory. Besides, if you're married to Vaughan, you won't have to worry about your father trying to foist you off on someone worse."

"That's true."

Tess got to her feet. "So, we have a plan. You're going to bring Vaughan to his knees, both literally and metaphorically."

"He hasn't actually proposed, you know," Daisy said crossly. "He just keeps announcing that we should get married. I'd give one of my knives to see him on his knees, begging for my hand."

"You've seen my hand, Hamilton. What woman would want something so scarred and unsightly?"

Daisy bit her lips as his previous words rose up to haunt her. She'd laughed at him then, deflected him with a flippant joke. Now, she'd do anything to have him ask again.

Tess caught her hand, interrupting her reverie. "The first step in your campaign can be to dazzle him at dinner." She sent the hastily altered riding habit a scathing look. "Lucky for you, we squeezed in a trip to Madame Lefèvre's before we left town. She gave us that new dress you ordered last month. We'll help you get ready."

Chapter Thirty-Six

"Why on earth would she refuse to marry you?" Justin potted the green ball in the middle pocket of the billiard table, then glanced at Lucien. "You're a better catch than half the royal dukes. You're solvent, sober—most of the time—and you're not entirely hideous to look at."

Lucien shrugged and took a sip of his brandy. "She doesn't care about being a duchess. Or for my fortune. The only reason she'd consider it is to salvage her reputation—and even that doesn't seem to be a strong enough factor."

Harry sent him a sidelong glance. "Is that why you want to marry her? To prevent her from being ruined?"

"It's one factor," Lucien said slowly. "But not the main one." He twisted the chalk on the end of his cue and frowned at the table, then waited until Justin was about to pot the blue. "I want to marry her because I can't imagine marrying anyone else."

Justin missed the cue ball entirely. He straightened. "Are you serious?"

"Absolutely."

"Are you in *love* with her?"

Lucien bent over the table and casually potted a ball in the corner pocket. "I am. I've been in love with her for years, only I was too pigheaded to admit it."

"Have you told *her* that?" Harry demanded.

Lucien potted another ball. "God, no. She wouldn't believe me, even if I did. She thinks I've only asked her out of some misguided sense of guilt."

Harry and Justin both nodded, as if this made perfect sense.

"Does she love you?" Justin asked.

"I doubt it," Lucien said, a faint smile toying about his mouth. "But I fully intend to remedy that."

"Do you think you can?" Harry raised his brows. "Because from what I know about Daisy, she's not easily swayed. Once she's made her mind up about something, there's no stopping her."

"I stopped her," Lucien said mildly. "She was all set on ruining Peregrine's wedding, but I managed to get the better of her."

"How, exactly?"

Lucien grinned. "A gentleman never tells. Needless to say, our marriage will not be lacking in passion."

"I'm amazed she didn't stab you with one of those knives of hers," Harry chuckled.

Lucien's fingers touched the side of his throat, just below his jaw. "Oh, she tried."

"So, you want to marry her, even though she's said no," Harry said. "Fair enough. Have you considered kidnapping? Forcing her in front of a vicar? Better to ask for forgiveness than permission, and all that."

"You should know," Justin said wryly.

Harry gave an ironic bow.

"She's already been kidnapped once this past week," Lucien said. "Twice, if you count me spiriting her up

North. I don't want to force her into anything. If she *truly* doesn't want to marry me, then I'll accept her decision. Even if it's a stupid, wrong decision."

"Really?" Justin drawled. "You'll let her walk away? Be ruined. Marry someone else?"

Lucien growled, annoyed at how well his friend knew him. "No, damn it, of course not. She needs my protection, whether she admits it or not. She's not going to be someone's mistress, or relegated to the demimonde, or turn into some sad, neglected spinster. I'll accept her decision *temporarily*. I'm going to marry her. Even if I have to spend the next fifty years convincing her that I'm serious."

"Actions speak louder than words," Justin said. "How about a grand gesture? I bought a washed-up racehorse and tried to lose a fortune, just to prove to Tess that I loved her more than money. It was a bloody disaster, because the stupid thing ended up winning by mistake, but it all worked out in the end. It was the gesture that counted."

"I *didn't* steal the crown jewels." Harry nodded. "Despite having the perfect opportunity. Not one single piece. In fact, I didn't steal anything from anyone—unless it was on behalf of King and Company—to show Ellie I was serious about leaving my old life of crime behind."

"Daisy isn't the sort of woman who appreciates dresses and jewels," Lucien said. "She'd prefer a small arsenal of sharp weapons. But I didn't survive three years of Frenchmen trying to kill me just to get stabbed by an angry female in my own drawing room. Arming her would be a stupid idea."

Justin glanced at the mantel clock and put down his cue. "We'll have to think about this later. It's time to get ready for dinner."

Chapter Thirty-Seven

Dinner was a surprisingly amiable affair. Everyone seemed to have tacitly agreed not to mention anything about Daisy and Vaughan's predicament, for which Daisy was profoundly grateful.

Logic insisted that marrying him was her only viable option. She had to be practical. Sensible. But her heart ached for impractical, illogical things.

Stupid heart.

She'd derived a startling rush of pleasure from the simmering look he cast her when she'd first appeared in the dining room with Ellie and Tess. She'd ordered her damson silk gown from Madame Lefèvre, intending to wear it to the opera, or the next time King & Co. had a case that required her to extract information from some hapless male who could be counted on to pay more attention to the cleavage on display than to the words coming out of his mouth.

The low neckline was wonderfully distracting, so expertly cut that it seemed as though one false move would expose her completely. It wouldn't, of course. The boned corset beneath made sure of that, but Madame Lefèvre was quite deservedly one of the most expensive dress-makers in London. She didn't just sell dresses. She sold fantasies. Fever-dreams. Miracles of illusion.

It certainly seemed to have captured Vaughan's attention. Despite being seated at the opposite end of the table, Daisy could practically feel the heat from his regard. Every time she heard the low rumble of his voice, or the gruff bark of his laugh, her stomach clenched.

When dessert arrived—Mrs. Ward had excelled herself with both summer pudding and crème brûlée—she glanced over at him and found his piercing gaze fixed on her mouth. She tortured him by licking the back of her spoon with deliberate lasciviousness, and gained the delightful reward of a muscle ticking in the side of his jaw and a glare that promised retribution.

Excellent.

She dropped her gaze to the almost-healed nick on the side of his neck. A casual observer would assume he'd cut himself shaving, but a wicked, possessive thrill raced through her at the memory of how he'd received it. It was an intimate secret between them, something only the two of them knew.

Worth it, he'd said.

Well, she'd just keep reminding him of that. She was worth more than just his kisses. She was worthy of his heart. His life. His love.

The men lingered at the table when the ladies withdrew, and Daisy couldn't decide if she was relieved or disappointed when Tess suggested they retire to their respective rooms. She was tired after the long day of traveling, but still craved more interaction with Lucien.

Here, in a private setting with friends, the rules of propriety were more relaxed, but she was already dreading the return to London. The stifling social restrictions there would mean her every move would be watched and commented on.

Life would be unbearably dull if she had to avoid Lucien. What was the point in attending a ball without the possibility of catching his eye across the room and seeing if she could drive him to distraction? She wanted to make him abandon all good sense, and drag her away into a broom closet or hedge maze and show her exactly how men like him treated provoking women like her: with the delicious "punishment" of debauchery.

Tess and Ellie offered to come into her room to talk, but for possibly the first time in their acquaintance, Daisy pleaded fatigue. She adored them both—but she needed to think.

Jenny helped her undress and get ready for bed, and when she was gone, Daisy looked around the room she'd used for years with fresh eyes. Had it really been only five days ago that she'd slept here last? Before she'd given herself to Vaughan.

It seemed a lifetime ago, and she a different woman.

She couldn't regret what had happened. Wicked she might be, but in the darkest, most secret recesses of her mind, she was glad that things had come to this. If she was completely honest, she'd spent years fantasizing about belonging to him, of possessing him in return. Of having him thoroughly entwined in her life.

Even if he *had* only offered marriage because he was being noble, she'd make sure he never had cause to regret it. They were well suited. Both of them were capable of being sneaky, stubborn, and manipulative. Both of them liked to win. She was more than a match for him.

Tess had put him in the room at the far end of the corridor, just two doors down from Daisy. They were the only two guests in this particular wing of the house. Ellie and Harry had been moved to a larger set of rooms in the east wing, near Tess and Justin's own master suite, and Daisy didn't know whether to curse Tess for her unsubtle encouragement or to laugh at her silent approval.

Lucien's tread sounded on the boards outside her door an hour or so later. Daisy held her breath, but while his steps slowed, he passed by without stopping and she ignored the little tug of disappointment that snagged in her chest.

She'd rejected him. She couldn't complain if he did the noble thing now and gave her some space. Even if she wished he'd stay true to form and simply barge into her room and ravish her.

Pride demanded that she keep refusing him until he at least proposed properly, but it was clearly up to her to get him to that point.

Something had to be done.

Daisy waited another twenty minutes, then slipped out of bed. Her silk dressing gown matched her scandalously sheer nightgown, both a glorious emerald green, edged in black lace. Madame Lefèvre had insinuated that such styles were all the rage in Paris, especially among the beautiful courtesans at the Palais Royale.

Most noble ladies would have been offended to have been shown such harlot's garments. Daisy, Tess, and Ellie had ordered three sets each. Madame knew her clients' tastes to perfection.

No doubt Justin and Harry had already been brought to their knees by the seductive silk and their respective wives. Now it was Vaughan's turn.

Daisy's heart was in her throat as she turned the brass doorknob as quietly as she could and stepped out into the dimly lit hallway. A single oil lamp had been left burning at the far end, and its flame flickered as Vaughan's own door suddenly opened too.

Daisy stilled.

He glanced up, his hand still on the door handle, and his eyes darkened at the sight of her, caught motionless in exactly the same position down the hall. He was wearing a banyan robe of deep burgundy, with a sash tied around his waist. A tantalizing *V* of bronzed skin showed at the neck. Was he naked underneath? She hoped so.

"Going somewhere?" she asked innocently.

"Just looking for a glass of water."

She bit back a snort at his innocuous tone. "That's odd. There's nearly always some in every room. Tess is an excellent hostess."

"I've a decanter of brandy, not water."

"There's a bell pull. You could have called a servant."

"Didn't want to bother them so late. What are *you* doing?"

Daisy let her gaze drop to his lips, then back up. "I was hungry. I thought I'd sneak down to the kitchens and see if there was any leftover dessert."

She pressed her lips together to stop a giggle escaping.

His teeth flashed. "Liar. You were coming to my room to tell me you accept my proposal."

She lifted her chin. "I was not. *You* were coming to *my* room to actually propose. Because you haven't, you know. You just told Letty I was going to be your duchess."

His brows quirked. "What's the point in proposing? You've repeatedly said you'll only say yes to a man who loves you."

"That's true."

He took a step toward her. "Then humor me. How will you know when a man loves you?"

His question caught her off guard. In truth, she'd never actually thought about it, beyond a vague feeling that she'd somehow just *know*. Tess and Ellie presumably knew that Justin and Harry loved them, but Daisy had never asked them to explain how. That omission was something she needed to rectify if she had any hope of making Vaughan fall in love with her. She'd need to know when her efforts had been successful, after all.

"Well, I suppose he would have proved his love for me in a hundred different ways," she temporized.

"How? By filling your house with so many flowers you get hay fever? Composing sonnets to your eyebrows?" His tone was sardonic.

"Well, no," she admitted. "I can't say either of those would convince me. Quite the opposite."

"What, then? Would he build you a house? Plant you a garden? Give vast sums to a charity close to your heart?"

"Fund a home for soiled doves, wounded veterans, and stray dogs, you mean?" Daisy saw his look of confusion and laughed. "That was what Tess, Ellie, and I said we'd do when Tess first became the Duchess of Wansford. We didn't end up with quite that combination, but we do support two different boardinghouses in Covent Garden. The Traveler's Rest is for veterans, and the Golden Hart is for soiled doves. Both of them accept dogs. They're run by a friend of Harry's uncle, Hugo Ambrose."

"All very admirable." He took another step closer. "But you haven't answered my question. We've already established that you don't need to be *in* love to *make* love. Do you think fucking someone who's in love with you will feel different?"

"I'm not sure."

He was in front of her now, and his proximity made her breath come a little faster. The delicious scent of him, dark and tempting, made it hard to think.

"I'm trying to understand the logic here," he continued softly. "Would a man who loves you be gentle? Or rough? Or a combination of both?"

His eyes roamed over her face in the dim light, resting lightly on each of her features as if cataloguing each one. "He'd obviously desire you so much that he'd be desperate for you, yes? But he'd *also* take the time to pleasure you before he saw to his own needs. Do I have that right?"

"Well, yes, I suppose . . ."

Daisy frowned. She wasn't sure of anything anymore. What he was saying made sense, but then *he'd* been both rough and desperate, gentle and selfless, when they'd been together at the inn. And *he* didn't love her. He was simply an accomplished lover.

"It's . . . complicated," she muttered.

His lips curled in a look that was half amused, half resigned. "It is indeed. I hope you're not telling me it's all down to some mystical feminine instinct. Because if that's the case, what hope does a man have?"

Daisy glared up at him. Why was he so determined to have a deep, meaningful conversation on the essence of love right here, in the corridor, at midnight? There were other, far more enjoyable, things they could be doing instead.

"Can't this discussion wait until morning?"

His eyes darkened. "Am I keeping you from your tryst with the leftover crème brûlée? Or is there something else you'd rather be doing?"

Daisy stepped forward so her breasts brushed his chest. "You are the most aggravating man, Lucien Vaughan."

"You're not the first person to make that observation."

She grabbed the lapels of his dressing gown. "Just so you know, we are *not* engaged. I haven't agreed to marry you."

"Understood."

"I haven't made my mind up yet."

"You will."

She ignored the ambiguity of that remark. "That said, I have no objection to you giving me another demonstration of what it's like to bed a man who doesn't love me."

"A scientific study?" he growled. "For comparison?"

She licked her lips and his hungry gaze followed the move. "Exactly."

A muscle ticked in his jaw, as if she'd said something to annoy him, but his expression was pure wickedness as he loomed over her. "Oh, sweetheart, I am more than happy to oblige. Your room, or mine?"

Chapter Thirty-Eight

"Mine."

Daisy twisted the doorknob to her room and stepped inside. Lucien followed, closing the door behind him with the faintest click, but instead of gathering her into his arms, he leaned back against the wood and let his gaze rove over her.

She felt his regard like a physical touch. Heat flashed over her skin and her nipples beaded against the silk of her nightgown.

"I'm still intrigued to know what differences you think there might be between a man who loves you and a man who only wants your body." His gaze settled on her lips. "Take kissing, for example."

He reached out and caught her wrist, pulling her to him with a faint tug. Daisy went willingly, her heart galloping at the brush of his robe against her chest.

Still loosely holding her wrist with his right hand, he lifted his left and stroked the side of her neck before threading his fingers through her hair at the back of her skull. His pupils were huge, his brown eyes almost black in the dim light.

"I think a man who loved you would kiss with his whole soul. As if you were the most precious thing in the world."

He bent his head and kissed her, so softly it made her shiver. His lips barely grazed hers, nibbling and soothing, dancing so gently that she grew impatient. She pressed closer, but he pulled back, refusing to let her deepen the kiss.

Daisy groaned her frustration against his mouth, caught his lapels, and tugged him to her. His hand tightened in her hair as he increased the pressure, and his tongue finally slid against her own.

The world narrowed to where they touched, the languid swirl of his tongue. She hadn't thought him a man who would enjoy kissing. Their previous kisses had all been hot and hungry. Delicious, but also urgent, a necessary step on the journey, and not a destination in themselves.

He kissed her now as if he had all the time in the world. As if he'd be happy to do this for hours, for days.

He tilted his head, slanting his mouth across hers at a different angle, scattering kisses on the side of her mouth, the tip of her nose, her chin, the center of her top lip.

Daisy felt as if she were floating, drowning in a sea of sensation. She kissed him back, holding nothing back, pouring her whole heart into her response.

His right hand came up to cup her jaw, his thumb stroking her cheek, then her lower lip, pulling it down to slide against the slick inner lining, and everything inside her turned molten.

This wasn't a fast-burning flame, it was a slow, deliberate kindling, and when he finally pulled back, they were both slightly breathless. His eyes, so close to hers, seemed to glow with an inner fire.

"The problem with this little experiment of yours, Daisy, is that you're not going to find any difference between me and a man who's desperately in love with you."

Daisy's brain was pleasantly foggy, her body tingling with anticipation. Did he mean that he was such a good lover that he'd be able to feign the actions of a man in love? She wasn't sure she cared about the experiment anymore. She just wanted to keep kissing him.

"Not enough of a comparison," she mumbled. Her breathing was choppy, as if she'd run a race. "Need more."

He made a deep, frustrated sound in his chest, half amusement, half irritation, and she almost laughed at the way she could affect him.

"More? I'll give you more."

He lifted her in one quick move, and she wrapped her legs around his hips, her arms sliding around his neck for stability. Her robe slid open at the front and her nightgown rose up so her hot center pressed against his robe. Her pulse leapt at the press of his iron-hard cock through the fabric, and his hands cupped her bottom as she wriggled against him.

He strode to the bed and followed her down onto the soft mattress. His hands roved over her, the silk providing a tantalizing barrier that allowed the heat of him to seep through but denied the ultimate satisfaction of skin-on-skin contact.

"This color is much better than pink," he breathed. His fingers slid from her hip to the dip of her waist, shaping her curves like a potter molding a vase on a wheel. He traversed the bumps of her ribs, bunching the silk into ripples, then traced her collarbone. He gave her a gentle bite on the side of her neck.

Daisy squirmed against him, desperate for more. As he raised himself on his arms above her, relieving her of some of his weight, his robe fell open to reveal the gorgeous expanse of his chest, and she brought her hands up to touch him with a smile of delight.

He really was the most magnificent specimen. His skin was hot, and the muscles of his abdomen tensed as she smoothed her palms down his taut belly taut and untied the sash at his waist to reveal him in all his naked glory.

She bit her lip. Could she really make him hers? Forever?

She wanted to.

She wrapped her legs around his waist and twisted her body sharply. He toppled sideways, caught unaware, and she rolled on top of him, neatly reversing their positions. It was a move she'd learned from wrestling with her brothers and even though she'd had the element of surprise, he could have countered the move if he'd had the inclination. Instead, he laughed.

She sat up, straddling his thighs, but not touching his cock. He reached up to cup her jaw again and she lifted her chin, baring her throat to him like a cat demanding a stroke, and his eyes flared with desire at the delicate balance of power.

"Daisy," he breathed.

He sounded reverent, almost worshipful, and a shiver passed through her.

Holding his gaze, she straightened her spine, and his hand slid down to her sternum, between her breasts, then down over the soft plain of her belly. When he tried to move his hand lower, however, she shook her head.

"Not yet. It's your turn."

She shuffled backward, down his legs, and wrapped her fingers around his shaft.

He almost shot off the bed. His chin tipped up as he

arched his back, and his hand clenched on the front of her thigh.

"Bloody Hell!" he gasped. "You don't have to—I'm already—"

"You're ready when I say you're ready," she teased.

His eyes narrowed and Daisy bit back a laugh. It would do him good to have a taste of his own medicine.

She stroked him, gently, loving the feel of him in her hand. He was big, and hot, bigger than Tom had been, and she savored the velvet-soft skin over rigid muscle.

"Vixen," he breathed, his chest expanding with a deep inhale. "Keep that up, and there won't be any more experimenting."

She sent him a cocky smile and bent to press a kiss to the silken tip, then laved him with her tongue, and he let out a groan, curving up on the bed to prop himself up on one arm. She took him into her mouth, and he hissed out a breath as his hips jerked involuntarily.

"Daisy. God, that's . . . fuck. Perfect. So perfect."

He cupped the back of her head, threading his fingers through her curls, and she swirled her tongue over him as if she were licking crème brûlée from a spoon. She moved up and down, taking as much of him as she could, loving the way his big body twitched and tensed under her gentle ministrations.

She released him with a final gentle kiss, and the slightly dazed look in his eyes gave her a shot of pure feminine delight. This man might make others quake in their boots, but here, now, he was hers.

She bent again, about to repeat the torture, but his fingers tightened and he shook his head.

"That's quite enough of that."

Chapter Thirty-Nine

Quick as a flash, he caught her shoulders and rolled her back over, and she laughed at the rough way he handled her. He didn't touch her as if she were made of porcelain, liable to break at any moment, and she appreciated it more than if he'd showered her with empty compliments.

She had no hope of actually overpowering him in a physical contest, but she loved the way he treated her as an equal, as a worthy opponent.

He wrestled both of her arms above her head, pressing them down into the covers, then threaded his fingers through hers so they were intertwined. Her heart gave an erratic little thump.

"Back to your research," he panted, and she bit her lips against a smile as his thighs bracketed hers, preventing her from opening her legs.

He leaned down and caught her gaze. "I think a man who loved you would want to catalogue every freckle on your face." He pressed a kiss to her nose, then her cheeks. "He'd make a mental map of them, so he could see them whenever he closed his eyes. He'd try to make shapes in them, the way the ancients did with the constellations."

He kissed the freckle at the outermost corner of her eye, and a strange lump formed in her throat. He was teasing, mocking her, even, and yet the gesture felt so tender. So sincere.

"I think a man who loved you would stare deeply into your eyes." He did exactly that as he slid between her thighs and his cock teased the entrance to her body. "He'd watch your face as he pushed himself inside you to see if he was pleasing you. Because pleasing you would be his favorite thing to do."

Daisy held his stare as he matched actions to words, tilting her hips as he pressed forward, sucking in a breath at the delicious feeling of fullness. Her chest ached, as if sensations too large to be contained were pushing to get out.

His pupils had expanded so his eyes looked almost black. Their fingers were still entwined, and she curled her hands around his as he held himself motionless within her.

"Now here's where things get a little more complicated," he said, his voice low. "Would a man in love be gentle? Take his time?"

He moved his hips and started to withdraw, only to push back in with devastating slowness. She forced herself not to buck against him in desperation.

"Would he never be so cruel as to tease you? Would only a man who *didn't* love you make you beg?"

Daisy could barely think. Her concentration was centered on the way he was sliding inside her, the way her inner muscles clenched around him, the way heat seemed to pulse where they were joined.

He pressed into her again, hitting that spot inside that made her twitch and tense with the promise of pleasure.

"Or would a man who really loved you know that you

love to be teased?" he growled. "Know that teasing only makes it better. Maybe he'd start slow, then take you harder. Give you exactly what you need."

He increased his tempo, and Daisy bit her lip as her excitement built. She tried to move against him, but with her hands still secured above her head, there was very little she could do. He was in total control, and he seemed to know exactly what she wanted almost before she did.

Faster. Harder.

Yes.

He was still talking.

"I think a man would tell you he loved you with his body, even if he didn't say it with words."

He finally released her hands, and Daisy wrapped her arms around his back, pulling him down to her so their chests were touching. He was a glorious weight, and she slid her palms over his shoulders and ribs, memorizing the bumps and hollows of his muscular frame.

She was beyond anything except sensation now, and she bucked against him as he drove into her, pushing her higher with every brutal thrust. She arched up and pressed a feverish kiss to his shoulder, tasting the salt on his skin as she strained and tumbled headlong into pleasure.

Her body had barely finished throbbing when he pulled out of her with a low curse and spent himself on the inside of her thighs, and she gasped for breath as the room came slowly back into focus.

A man who didn't respect you wouldn't have pulled out. The niggling little voice floated through her head. *He'd care for nothing but his own pleasure.*

Respect wasn't love. He was simply a considerate lover.

Lucien rolled off her to relieve her of his weight, and Daisy stared sightlessly at the ceiling. Her body was utterly sated and all she wanted to do was close her eyes and sleep.

Instead, she slid her arm across to his, where it lay relaxed on the coverlet, and stroked her fingers over the textured scars on his forearm. He didn't pull away, and she glanced up to find him watching her, his gaze hooded, yet alert.

Emboldened, she traced her finger up, over the silky sleeve of his robe and across his shoulder until she encountered the hot skin of his neck. She found the tiny, healing nick she'd given him with her blade, and his pupils darkened as she ran her finger lightly over it.

"Do you think you'll have a scar?"

He caught her hand in his and brought her fingers to his lips. "Another one to add to my collection?" His crooked smile did something peculiar to her insides. "I hope so. It will be my favorite. The only one I enjoyed receiving."

Daisy shook her head, confounded by his ability to go from scorchingly seductive to sweetly teasing in an instant.

He confused her in a way no man had ever done before. The feelings she had for him were so much deeper and more complicated than what she'd felt for Tom. Tom had been an easy, playful tumble in the sunlight. Vaughan was suffocating in pleasure in the dark. A tangle of longing, frustration, and desire. And moments of devastating charm.

The heat from his body was incredibly comforting, and she wanted nothing more than to snuggle up in his arms for the remainder of the night, but just as she was about to suggest that he stay, he gave a languid stretch and pushed himself upright.

"Stay there. I'll get you a washcloth."

She bit back her instinctive protest, and accepted the damp linen he handed her to wipe her thighs.

If they married, he wouldn't have to pull out of her, and her belly clenched at the thought of him finishing inside her. It was an intimacy they'd been denied, and the thought of it made her almost giddy with longing. She wanted to feel him lose himself inside her, completely unrestrained, without having to retain part of his sanity to remember to withdraw.

Such recklessness could result in a child, of course, and while she'd never given much thought to whether she wanted children or not, the possibility of bearing *him* a child didn't feel wrong. Quite the opposite.

But she held her tongue as he pulled his robe back around his body and tied it around his waist.

"I'll leave you now. We've a long journey back to London tomorrow."

Daisy nodded sleepily, but her heart stuttered as he leaned over and brushed her cheek with his thumb, smoothing over the freckles he'd waxed so lyrical about, and she found herself wanting to believe in the fairy tale he'd described.

She wished it had been her face he'd thought of when he'd needed something to take his mind off the pain of his burns. Wished he could love her for longer than a sweaty, passionate tumble between the sheets.

He bent and pressed an almost-chaste kiss to her cheek. "Sleep well, Hamilton."

Chapter Forty

Daisy shared the carriage with Ellie and Tess the following morning while the three men rode, and Perry and Violet occupied the second vehicle. It was a journey the three women had made together on countless occasions, usually filled with a joyous round of lively discussion, and this time was no exception.

"How do I know Justin loves me?"

Tess's brow wrinkled as she considered Daisy's question. "Well, it wasn't obvious at first, I'll admit. He desired me before he actually fell in love with me. But he shows his love in lots of different ways now. Of course, he likes to give me expensive presents, like jewels and dresses and *racehorses*"—she rolled her eyes at that particular absurdity—"but it's the smallest things that mean the most. Like the way he always refuses to let the servants remove my cloak whenever we go to the opera; he likes to do it himself as an excuse to put his arms around me in public."

Ellie grinned. "Harry's the same. He'll always sit nearest the door because he knows I hate a draft. And he'll offer to steal me a fan if I'm hot and have forgotten my own. Not that I'd ever let him, of course."

"Justin stays in my bed on the week I'm having my monthly courses," Tess added. "I know a lot of husbands keep to their own rooms, but he just holds me close, even though he knows we won't be making love. And he's always touching my hand or kissing my hair."

"When we're separated at a ball, or a party," Ellie said, "Harry always manages to catch my eye from across the room. We have these little private jokes, just between us."

Daisy bit her lip. She and Lucien had those.

"I suppose it's not just about offering physical pleasure," Tess continued thoughtfully, "but comfort, and companionship as well. Justin and I have plenty of shared interests, and we like doing things together, but we also have our own separate pursuits, and that's important. We both respect the work the other does, and we find ways to be flexible and understanding if work occasionally has to take precedence."

Daisy sighed. "Vaughan does all those things too. He kept me company when I was ill. And he's always been appreciative of my skills and my work for King and Company."

Ellie adjusted her spectacles. "I admit, it is sometimes hard to distinguish the difference between a man who's merely enjoying your company and a man who's fallen in love with you. Men are terrible at saying what they mean, especially when it comes to matters of the heart. They usually deny they're in love at all until it becomes impossible to ignore."

"They'll call it almost anything else too," Tess chuckled. "They'll convince themselves it's dislike, or jealousy, or even indigestion, rather than admit that they're in love. It's only when they make unusually stupid decisions, or do something completely out of character, that proves they're well and truly smitten."

"Vaughan never does anything stupid," Daisy said miserably. "He's far too self-controlled. And he's such a scoundrel that to do something out of character he'd have to do something ridiculously sweet to prove his love."

Ellie tilted her head. "Like what?"

Daisy shrugged. "I don't know. He's hardly the romantic type. I can't see him proposing in a field of wild-flowers, can you? Or getting down on his knees in the middle of a ballroom to profess his undying love."

Tess chuckled. "You'd think less of him if he did. That's the sort of thing Peregrine would do, and Violet would think it dizzyingly romantic."

"True," Daisy said. "I wouldn't love him if he wasn't a little bit wicked."

Ellie was still looking pensive. "He should still propose some other way, though. It's pretty clear you're going to have to marry him to salvage your reputation, but if he proposed now, when there's no real need, then it would show he isn't just doing it out of duty. It would show he actually wants your hand. And that he's willing to humble himself to get it."

Daisy snorted, remembering the way she'd rejected him at the inn. *The only way I'd accept your hand, Vaughan, is if you put it between my legs.*

She wanted him now. All of him, not just his hand. She wanted him, body and soul. And she wanted him to want her.

Bloody Hell.

The rest of the journey passed quickly, since the weather was fine and dry. When Daisy recognized The Mitre at Barnet, she looked out the window and tried to pinpoint the exact spot she'd encountered Vaughan that fateful night, but the trees and bushes all looked remarkably similar, and she felt a pang of disappointment that she couldn't identify the place. It seemed significant. Not merely as the spot where two men had died, but as the start of their unexpected adventure.

"Do you want us to take you to Dalkeith House?" Tess asked as they rattled toward Knightsbridge. "Or would you rather come back to Wansford House with us?"

Daisy often stayed with Tess and Justin when her father and brothers were out of town.

"I'm not sure my father's at home. If I'm lucky, he'll be off visiting and won't even have noticed I've been missing."

It was a forlorn hope, but there was still the slight chance that none of the gossip about his wayward daughter would have reached his ears.

"I should to go and see Violet's father, first, and explain why I didn't complete my mission," Daisy said.

Ellie nodded. "Peregrine mentioned that he and his uncle were going straight there to talk with Mr. Brand."

"Would you like us to come with you?" Tess asked. "On behalf of King and Company, Harry can be there as 'Mr. King,' too, if you want extra support."

"No. It's all right. I appreciate the offer, but this was my mission. My failure. I'll own up to it directly. I'm just sorry we've lost Brand's five hundred pounds, that's all."

Tess gave a gentle snort. "You won't need to worry about money if you marry Vaughan. Even Justin's in awe of his skill on the stock market. The man could buy you a new knife every day of the year if you wanted one."

"I don't need any more knives," Daisy said despondently. "What I need is a husband who loves me."

Ellie patted her knee. "You'll get one. I'm sure of it. Remember what that hermit said about true love and dark highways?"

Daisy rolled her eyes. "That fact that we put *any* store

in the random scribblings of a man paid to wear a false beard and live in a fake grotto in Vauxhall Gardens just shows how desperate we all were to find husbands a couple of years ago."

"True, but he hasn't been wrong yet," Ellie countered stubbornly. "If your fortune had said something about hot air balloons, or boats, or haunted castles, then it would be different. But you have to admit that it seems more than mere coincidence. It feels like fate. *Destiny*."

Daisy was saved from having to reply as they drew up outside Wansford House. Ellie and Tess both descended to join their husbands on the front steps, while Daisy remained in the carriage.

She hoped Vaughan might accompany her for the final part of the journey, but he chose to keep riding.

At least he hadn't joined Perry and Violet in the other carriage. That would have been the ultimate snub.

Violet and her father lived not far from King & Co., in Bloomsbury, near the British Museum, and Daisy glanced up in awe at the newly built mansion they occupied. The area had undergone a frenzied bout of gentrification over the past few years, as newly rich merchants like Brand constructed their own grand houses to rival those more established ones in Mayfair and St. James's.

Violet was already rushing up the steps, with Perry close behind, when Daisy opened the carriage door, and her heart made a foolish *thump* as Vaughan materialized to help her down. She took his hand, and the feel of his black-gloved fingers steadying hers brought a flush to her face.

Those hands.

Brand himself was waiting for them in a rather grand study. Known to be a ruthlessly competent businessman, he had a broad face and slightly jowly cheeks that gave him the look of a tenacious bulldog.

Despite the affectionate way he was embracing his daughter, there was no mistaking the frigid air of displeasure that emanated from his stocky figure. The corners of his mouth turned down as he disengaged himself from Violet's tentacle-like hug, and Daisy's spirits dropped as he shot an awkwardly loitering Perry a cold glance, then nodded curtly to Vaughan.

"Your Grace, good morning."

"Mr. Brand."

"And Miss Hamilton, I see. Well, what a party this has become." Brand's tone was icy.

He gestured to a group of chairs and settees positioned near a large globe. "Please, have a seat."

Violet tugged Perry down to sit beside her on one of the love seats while Brand settled in a leather-and-mahogany library chair. That left Daisy and Lucien to share a green velvet chaise longue, and Daisy tried not to fidget as his long thigh brushed against her own.

He was definitely doing it on purpose, but the look on his face betrayed nothing but lordly disinterest. He was an excellent dissembler, and she had a sudden thought about what it would be like to work with him on a case for King & Co. He would make a formidable partner.

"So, you're married," Brand said brusquely to Violet.

"I am." She nodded, and there was a trace of defiance in the slight jut of her chin that made her look remarkably like her father. Violet might seem like a fragile little flower, just like her namesake, but beneath her pretty frivolity she apparently had a will of iron. Daisy's opinion of her went up several degrees.

Brand gave an unhappy grunt. "Without my permission."

Violet tossed her golden ringlets and opened her mouth, but Daisy decided to intercede.

"Mr. Brand. Please accept my apologies for failing to complete the task you set me."

He turned to her, and his eyes narrowed. "A failure indeed. I must tell you, Miss Hamilton, that I am most seriously displeased. King and Company came highly recommended to me, but it seems my faith was misplaced."

Daisy felt her cheeks heat at his chastisement. She hated the fact that she'd failed—and that his anger was justified.

"You have forfeited your payment, of course," he said severely. "And if anyone asks me about your firm, I shall caution them against engaging you for anything but the most basic of tasks."

It was hard not to defend herself. Lucien was the one at fault; he'd thwarted her at every turn, but she refused to pin the blame on him.

"Again, I apologize. If there's anything King and Company can do to make amends—"

Violet, apparently reaching the belated realization that her father's indulgence only extended to herself, interrupted her.

"Now, Papa. Don't be mean to Miss. Hamilton. It wasn't her fault. We were too far ahead. She didn't stand a chance of catching us."

Violet was conveniently forgetting just how close it had been, but Daisy wasn't about to correct her. Better for Brand to think he'd set her an impossible task.

"You know what I'm like when I set my heart on something." Violet reached over and took her father's hand. "I'm dreadfully stubborn. Just like you. I couldn't help it."

Brand let out an unhappy huff, as if acknowledging that rather backhanded compliment.

Violet continued. "You told me you were exactly the same way with mother. You said you took one look at her across the sheep-pen at the Harrogate country fair and just *knew* she was the one for you. You didn't stop until you'd made her your wife."

Brand's rugged features softened, just slightly. "That's true enough. It was a love-match between your mother and me." He glanced over at Daisy. "My Susie was taken from us far too soon. She died of a fever when Violet was just ten years old."

"I'm sorry for your loss," Daisy murmured.

"Well, it was the same for myself and Perry," Violet insisted doggedly. "Love at first sight."

Brand scowled. "But to elope, against my wishes—"

Violet squeezed his hand. "I know you've been worried that Perry's a fortune hunter, but that's not true at all. Tell him, Your Grace."

She turned her beseeching blue eyes on Vaughan.

Chapter Forty-One

"It's true," Vaughan said, apparently unperturbed by Brand's ire. "And believe me, Mr. Brand, your concern that my nephew lacks any kind of stable profession is something I have lamented myself, on numerous occasions." He sent Perry a sardonic look. "That said, until I have sons of my own, Perry here is my heir presumptive, and as such he'll benefit from an allowance of a thousand pounds per year now that he is wed."

Brand's expression relaxed a little. "Well, Your Grace, that's extremely generous of you. I must admit that my objection to young Peregrine has nothing to do with him personally, but more an abundance of caution where my precious little girl is concerned."

"Perfectly understandable." Vaughan nodded. "There are scores of unscrupulous 'gentlemen' who would take advantage of an innocent young lady like Violet, especially if she came with the alluring prospect of a sizable dowry."

"Quite so," Brand said. "Peregrine, I understand you father is currently abroad with your mother?"

Perry nodded. "Yes, sir. I believe they're somewhere near Naples at the moment."

"Well then, I suppose I'll have to wait until they return before we negotiate the settlements."

Violet's face broke into a relieved smile as she took this concession as proof of her father's acceptance. "You're not cutting me off?"

"Of course not," Brand said gruffly. "You're my only child. You'll have a dowry of twenty thousand pounds. I'll not have people calling me a miser."

Violet beamed. "Thank you, Papa. I promise we'll manage it extremely well, won't we, Perry?"

Brand snorted in clear disbelief, and Daisy bit back her own smile at his cynicism. Perry and Violet reminded her of the characters Jane and Bingley, in the novel *Pride and Prejudice*—both so amiable that they would doubtless be cheated by their servants and always exceed their income.

Brand turned back to Daisy. "Did anyone see them on the way to Gretna? The last thing I want is unseemly gossip floating about town."

"I don't believe so," Daisy said. Brand seemed to appreciate straight-talking, so she decided to give her unvarnished opinion. "But I'll be completely honest with you, sir. Even if word doesn't get out about their elopement, there will still be talk if you simply announce their marriage. People will ask why they didn't wait the usual three weeks to have the banns read in church, or have a have a big, public wedding."

Brand's expression darkened again. "What do you suggest? You know the ways of the *ton* far better than a cit like myself."

Daisy racked her brains, desperate to salvage something from this disaster.

"Well, you're known to be a doting father, so I think people would believe it if we say you indulged Violet's youthful impatience and agreed to a common license."

"What else?"

"You should have a big celebration, to show everyone that Violet and Perry have your blessing. If there are rumors about the swiftness of the wedding, or any hint that they acted without your permission, such a public display of unity will go a long way to dispelling them."

Violet almost leapt out of her seat. "Oh, yes! A party would be lovely! Say yes, Papa!"

Daisy tried not to groan. The parallels to her own situation were all too obvious, and the irony that Violet's marriage should have remained a secret, while gossip about her own *non*-marriage to Vaughan was apparently all over town, thanks to Letty Richardson, was hard to swallow.

She and Vaughan needed to do something similarly overt and announce either their engagement, or their supposed wedding, but the thought of it made Daisy feel oddly despondent. She'd played hundreds of different roles while undercover for King & Co.: an exhausted servant, a belligerent fishwife, an expensive courtesan. But pretending to be engaged or secretly married to Lucien might just be the hardest of all.

The thought of him gazing into her eyes and pretending to be in love with her, knowing it was only for show, would hurt. She would have to keep reminding herself that he was acting—however convincing he might appear.

"Miss Hamilton."

Daisy blinked as the pressure of Vaughan's knee against her own and Brand's voice jolted her out of her dismal thoughts.

"Yes?"

"I have very little experience in organizing any sort of large party, especially at short notice, and I have no wife to act as hostess. You and your colleagues at King and

Company, however, are accustomed to both hosting and attending such social events. Especially your friend, the Duchess of Wansford."

Brand's expression was decidedly calculating. "Considering your failure to stop the wedding is partly the reason I'm having to host—"

Daisy hid her wince, even as she silently congratulated Brand on his excellent use of both logic and guilt to pressure her into agreeing.

"—perhaps you and your colleagues could organize the ball to announce Violet and Perry's marriage? It will give you, Miss Hamilton, another chance to earn that five hundred pounds, and put King and Company back in my good graces."

"It's not that easy to—"

Brand's mouth pursed as he sensed her hesitation. "Like you, poor Violet doesn't have a mother to help her with such things."

Daisy ground her teeth. Oh, Brand was a master at manipulation. He and Vaughan should compare notes.

"I'll pay for everything, of course," Brand continued. "No expense spared. Whatever you ladies think would be appropriate."

Damn it all. She couldn't refuse an offer like that.

Daisy forced a smile. "Of course we'd be delighted to help. Did you have any preference for the day?"

"As soon as can be arranged," he said, smiling now that he'd got his way. "Would a week from today be possible?"

"It will be a rush, certainly, but anything is possible if you throw enough money at it."

"I want everyone who's anyone to be there," he cautioned. "The whole *ton*. Three dukes, at least. Royal ones, if you can." He glanced over at Vaughan. "We can count on your attendance, Your Grace, of course?"

Lucien sent him a cynical smile, fully aware of the other man's desperate desire to climb the social ladder. "Of course."

"I hear you and your friends are also great favorites of the queen," Brand said silkily, turning back to Daisy. "Didn't she make an appearance at the recent marriage of the Earl and Countess of Cobham?"

It was all Daisy could do not to roll her eyes at his shameless maneuvering. "Indeed, she did, but I couldn't possibly guarantee her attendance at *this* ball, even if she were sent an invitation."

"Nevertheless, an invitation should be sent. Just the chance that Her Majesty might grace us with her presence will add a cachet to the proceedings. I don't suppose the prince regent could be persuaded to come?"

Daisy pressed her knee sharply against Lucien's, silently commanding him to help. This situation was as much his fault as it was hers.

"Unlikely," he said coolly. "His Royal Highness can rarely be prevailed upon to attend social functions due to the precarious state of his health."

Daisy bit back a derisive snort. The entire country knew the prince regent's health would be greatly improved if he didn't spend his days drinking, eating, and whoring himself into a torpid state of dissolution, but that wasn't something one could say in polite company.

Brand grunted, but seemed to recognize the truth of Lucien's words. "Very well. The queen will have to do."

Daisy turned to Violet. "Violet, can you draw up a list of people you want to invite and send it to me by the end of the day?"

"Absolutely. Oh, I can't wait! Can the party have a theme?"

Daisy did her best to hide her dismay. "Of course. What did you have in mind?"

Violet's eyes were practically glowing with excitement. "Well, I've always loved costume parties, ever since I was a little girl. Everyone dressed as shepherds and dairymaids, and harlequins and such. How about something like that?"

"You *could*," Daisy said slowly, "but Veronica Cardew did something like that only a few months ago. You wouldn't want to be thought unoriginal."

Violet looked stricken. "Oh, goodness, no. What do you suggest? I want this to be the absolute best party of the season."

Daisy racked her brains. "How about a romantic theme? Something that hints at a wedding? That will get people talking before they even get there."

Violet clapped her hands. "Yes, I love that!"

"Shakespeare's play *A Midsummer Night's Dream* was originally designed to be performed as a wedding celebration. Why not have that as your theme? The garden here might not be quite big enough to accommodate everyone, but we could fill the ballroom with flowers and trellises and such."

Violet's blue eyes sparkled with enthusiasm. "Yes! I can dress as Titania, Queen of the Fairies, and Perry can be my consort."

She patted Perry's knee and Daisy hid a smile. Perry looked slightly dazed, and she had the feeling he was going to have his work cut out controlling his new wife's enthusiasm. What was that phrase? Marry in haste, repent at leisure. She hoped neither Perry nor Violet would come to regret their impetuosity, but considering how similar they seemed in terms of temperament, it was probably unlikely.

"We should be able to manage that," Daisy said briskly. "Even given the short notice."

Brand nodded, apparently happy now that he'd been appeased, so she stood and held her hand out to him. "Mr. Brand, if you'll excuse me, I'll be off to start organizing things."

Brand shook her hand while Vaughan rose to his feet next to her.

"I'll take my leave too," he said. "Perry, I'll see you back at Cranford House."

Daisy allowed Vaughan to usher her back out into the hallway. His proximity, as ever, made her jittery, and she tried her best to ignore the subtle hint of his cologne that teased her nose.

"Congratulations," he said drily. "You're now in charge of the social event of the season."

Daisy rolled her eyes. "As if I had any choice in the matter. I blame you entirely. If your stupid nephew had just waited until your sister returned from her travels, this would have been *her* problem, not mine."

His deep chuckle made her stomach somersault as he caught her chin and tilted her face up so their eyes met.

"Speaking of weddings, have you made up your mind to attend *ours*, yet, my sweet?"

"I have not," she said mulishly.

His eyes danced at her continued evasion. "Perhaps you could make a decision in time for this party? We should probably avoid one another in public for the next few days if you don't want to set tongues wagging even more than they are already, but we'll both be expected to attend this affair on Saturday. We need to have a plan in place for when we're seen together. The world will be watching."

Daisy pulled her chin from his hand and turned away,

heading toward the front door. "I know that," she said crossly. "I'll have a decision for you on Saturday night."

A servant opened the door, and she made her escape, but Vaughan's taunting voice followed her into her waiting carriage.

"I look forward to it, my love."

Chapter Forty-Two

As desperate as she was to go straight back to Wansford House to tell Tess and Ellie about the party, or to the sanctuary of her office at King & Co., Daisy instructed the carriage driver to take her to Dalkeith House.

The hope that her father would be absent from town, hosting one of his infamously rowdy parties at Hollyfield, their country estate, or attending something similar elsewhere, was dashed when she entered the back hallway and tried to sneak up the stairs to her bedroom unobserved.

"Dorothea!"

Dalkeith's carrying tones stopped her in her tracks on the first stair, and she cursed at the way he always made her feel like a naughty child caught in some scrape, as opposed to an intelligent, self-sufficient woman of twenty-three.

She straightened her spine and headed toward her father's study, and her spirits dropped further when she saw him seated behind the huge mahogany desk, a position he always adopted when he wished to make one of his children feel inferior.

"Hello, Father." She took the mahogany chair on the opposite side, the one that had been deliberately chosen because it was so uncomfortable.

The Duke of Dalkeith was not an unattractive man. A few years over sixty, he kept himself in shape with regular hunting and riding, but his penchant for drink and general debauchery showed in the slightly florid tint to his cheeks and the bags beneath his pale gray eyes.

"I returned from a visit with Lord Ashford in Kent yesterday, and when I went to my club for dinner, I heard a series of interesting rumors."

Daisy kept her face completely impassive. "Oh, really?"

"Rumors concerning *you*, Dorothea, and the Duke of Cranford."

She raised her brows and tried to look surprised. "Hmm?"

Dalkeith tapped his fingers on a pile of papers stacked on the leather desktop. "Rumors of an elopement. A clandestine engagement. Or even a secret marriage conducted at Gretna Green. Would you care to explain?"

Daisy's throat felt tight as she swallowed. "I didn't elope. And I'm neither engaged nor married to—"

Dalkeith shook his head. "Rumors are rarely unfounded. I don't know what you've been up to, and quite frankly, I don't care. I've never meddled in your affairs before now, because unlike your brothers, you've generally been discreet. But now you've been *in*discreet, and I will *not* have you bringing this family into disrepute."

Daisy's temper surged at his hypocrisy. "That's not—"

He wasn't listening. A sneer curved his lips. "You're

just like your mother, after all. Ruled by your passions. She 'followed her heart' too." His tone was scathing.

Daisy ground her teeth, willing herself not to leap to her mother's defense, nor point out his own shortcomings that had contributed to the decision. For all his sins, Dalkeith had still provided her with a roof over her head, food in her belly, an education, and countless other necessities. He'd claimed her as his legitimate daughter, and she'd benefited from that deception for her entire life.

But the fact that a woman's behavior was judged a hundred times more harshly than a man's was bitterly unfair.

"That's not how it is. I'm not in love with—"

"I can only be grateful that you ran off with a duke, instead of a chimneysweep. Or a fencing master." Dalkeith continued as if she hadn't spoken. "Cranford will make you an excellent husband. Better than I'd ever dared to dream for you, if I'm honest. You will marry him as soon as can be arranged."

Daisy's mouth dropped open in shock. "I—"

"He's willing. I received his letter this morning."

Her head was spinning. Letter? When had Lucien written a letter? Had he sent it from Carisbrooke Hall? From Wansford?

It didn't matter.

"And what if I don't want to marry him?" she managed.

"Your wishes are of no consequence. It's too late for regrets. If you merely meant to have an affair with him, you should have been more careful. Now that you've been compromised, nothing less than marriage will do."

His pale eyes roved over her face. "Is there a chance you might be with child?"

Daisy choked back a mortified groan. "No."

"Well, that's something, I suppose. There'll be enough talk, without the next Vaughan making an appearance in less than nine months. I don't suppose you did this on purpose? Started the rumors yourself, to force his hand?"

Angry heat warmed her cheeks. "Of course not! I would never do something so calculating, just to trap a man into marriage."

"You wouldn't be the first woman to do so." Dalkeith shrugged cynically. "Still, you should be grateful that Cranford's coming up to scratch. He said he'd apply to the Archbishop of Canterbury for a special license. You will marry as soon as it is granted."

Daisy's heart felt as though it would punch its way through her ribs.

Dalkeith continued, unaware of her inner turmoil. "In the meantime, you will silence the worst of the rumors by confirming your engagement as soon as possible. And when you are wed, an announcement in *The Times*."

He tapped his knuckles on the desk to signal an end to the discussion. "I'll discuss your marriage portion with Cranford at his leisure. You may go now, Dorothea."

Daisy stood and made her way back out to the corridor on trembling legs. She ascended the stairs, and it was only when she reached the privacy of her bedroom that she allowed her emotions full rein. She threw herself down on her mattress and screamed her frustration into her pillow.

A special license? The presumption of the man! She hadn't agreed to marry him yet.

Daisy hated the sensation of being trapped, of not being mistress of her own destiny. And yet being married to Vaughan was something she desired with her whole heart.

If only his urgency was due to passion, instead of regrettable necessity.

She took a deep breath. Fine. She might not have had any control over the way she'd ended up in this position, but she *could* control what happened from this point on. She would marry him. And she'd take Tess and Ellie's advice, and use every weapon in her arsenal to make Lucien the most loving, most faithful husband in England.

It would be her greatest challenge yet.

Chapter Forty-Three

Daisy, Tess, and Ellie were so busy during the following days that Daisy had little time to fret over Lucien and what he might be up to.

Violet's imagination had run riot, and she'd convinced her father that their Bloomsbury home wasn't big enough for a forest-themed event. Brand had therefore accepted an offer from his friend, the Earl of Mansfield, to host the party at his property, the magnificent Kenwood House, on the northern edge of Hampstead Heath.

This was the perfect compromise: near enough to central London that guests wouldn't need to travel too far, but far enough in the countryside that everyone would feel like they were having an adventure, and with vast gardens and an impressive ballroom to appease Violet's romantic aspirations.

Invitations to the surprise summer ball had been dispatched to over a hundred families, and the majority of them had accepted. It was going to be an absolute crush.

Tess, as the most senior of the three of them, had sent an invitation to Queen Charlotte, but none of them had the least expectation of her attending. Still, as Ellie said, they'd done their duty, so Daisy could rest easy on that score.

It was too late to get any new gowns made up by Madame Lefèvre, or any of the other modistes in town, so all three of them borrowed costumes from the Royal Opera House via Rose, a friend who worked as a seamstress in the dressing rooms backstage.

Since *A Midsummer Night's Dream* was supposedly set in ancient Athens, Tess and Ellie were both going in Greek-style draped dresses, with gold headdresses made of metallic oak leaves. Daisy, however, had chosen something even more dramatic: a costume worn by the soprano who played the Queen of the Night in Mozart's opera *The Magic Flute*.

The fabric had been dyed to look like the evening sky, the color bleeding from a pale twilight blue at the top of the bodice to a deep midnight navy at the hem, and the overskirt of dark net had been embroidered with hundreds of tiny silver stars and seed pearls that made it shimmer. It was a glorious garment, striking and powerful, and it gave Daisy a much-needed boost of confidence.

He'd called her freckles constellations.

She'd give him the whole night sky.

The three women shared a carriage over to Kenwood House on the morning of the ball, and Daisy wondered at how innocuous the green expanse of Hampstead Heath appeared during the daytime, compared to the dangerous place it became at night.

In recognition of its reputation for opportunistic highwaymen, most guests would travel with their own armed outriders, but in truth the risk to them would be fairly negligible. The main road across the heath would be so busy that few thieves would risk it. It was only if they ventured onto one of the less-traveled routes, as Daisy had done that night two weeks ago, that the chances of being accosted would increase.

Daisy spent most of the day helping Tess and Ellie oversee the numerous florists, garden designers, and handymen who had arrived to set up the decorations. Thousands of fresh flowers had been ordered from nurseries around the city, and by early afternoon the ballroom had been transformed into an enchanting summer glade bursting with blooms.

Tables and chairs had been set up beneath a temporary wooden gazebo. The orchestra would be positioned in the flower-bedecked minstrel's gallery, and the kitchen staff was run off their feet producing a delicious array of food for the guests. Daisy eyed the fruit tartlets with a sigh of anticipation.

When it was finally time to get ready, they made use of a bedroom they'd been offered as a dressing room, and a lump of nostalgia caught in Daisy's throat as she realized how long it had been since the three of them had readied themselves for a party together like this.

It had been a regular occurrence a few years ago, all of them giggling about the possibilities of the night ahead. They would lace each other's stays, fix their hair, and add subtle makeup to their faces. Since Tess and Ellie had both married, such silly, inconsequential intimacies had become rarer and rarer, and Daisy hadn't realized quite how much she'd missed them.

She had, of course, told them both about her father's high-handed insistence that she marry Lucien as soon as possible, and Lucien's infuriating presumption of applying for a special license when she hadn't actually agreed to a wedding.

Ellie, reasonable as ever, had tried to point out that Vaughan was simply being efficient in anticipating her response, but Daisy hadn't been so forgiving. He was a man who thought he knew best, and he would ride roughshod over her if she gave him an inch. It was not to be borne.

"So, have you decided what you're going to do?" Tess asked as she tried to pin some of Daisy's wayward curls up onto her head. "Because you know everyone's going to be watching the two of you as soon as he enters the room."

Daisy wrinkled her nose at her reflection in the mirror. "Ugh. I suppose I ought to at least confirm that we're engaged, but I don't want to steal Violet's thunder. Tonight's supposed to be about announcing her wedding to Peregrine."

Ellie sent her a skeptical glance that clearly said she thought Daisy was stalling—which was entirely correct. Her friends knew her so well.

"You're going to be the main topic of conversation whether you like it or not," Tess said succinctly. "So you might as well brace yourself." She sent Daisy's costume an approving glance. "I must say, that dress looks sensational. Vaughan doesn't stand a chance."

Daisy gave a pleased snort, but she knew she looked good. Excitement, and the prospect of crossing swords with Lucien again, had brought a pink glow to her cheeks and a wicked sparkle to her eyes.

"One last thing."

Daisy hitched up her skirts and strapped her favorite blade and its leather holster to the outside of her thigh.

Ellie rolled her eyes in mock horror. "I know the Queen of the Night is famous for giving her daughter a dagger and ordering her to stab her lover, but do you need to be quite so faithful to the script?"

"I feel naked without my knives," Daisy said. "And in this dress, I can only hide the one."

Tess gave the folds of her own gown a final twitch and added an extra gold ring to her slim fingers. "All ready?"

Daisy glimpsed at her own ringless fingers and sighed. Vaughan hadn't even sent her an engagement ring to wear.

"Yes. Let's go."

Chapter Forty-Four

The ball was well underway when Daisy finally caught sight of Justin and Harry arriving together. And then her breath caught as Lucien stepped out from behind them.

The buzz of conversation rose another notch as the other guests registered his presence, and Daisy fought to keep her expression neutral as several faces turned her way to gauge her reaction.

She'd already deflected a couple of extremely pointed questions from both ladies and gentlemen, the less-subtle of whom had asked her outright whether the Duke of Cranford would be attending.

She'd merely replied that he'd accepted his invitation and had declined to comment further. This, of course, had only increased the whispers of those convinced she had something to hide.

Lucien was dressed impeccably in almost the same outfit he'd been wearing the night they'd met on the road. A black satin evening jacket molded faithfully to his impressive shoulders. Black breeches and his signature black gloves added to the imposing figure he cut, the darkness only alleviated by the white of his shirt and cravat.

Daisy watched him scan the room, his height easily allowing him to see over the crowd from his position on the ballroom step, and she stilled as his piercing eyes found her. Her heart gave a jolt of recognition, and she had the bizarre thought that he would be able to find her anywhere, in a crowd of a hundred thousand.

His presence made the whole world that much sharper, more exciting.

He ignored the people who crowded around him clamoring for an introduction and made a beeline toward her, his determination obvious as Justin and Harry fell into step on either side of him.

A group of ladies nearby giggled and whispered behind their fans as they noticed the direction of his purposeful strides, and several of them sighed in admiration at the striking trio.

Justin and Harry both sent lazy smiles to their wives, but Lucien's expression remained stern. He never took his eyes off her, and Daisy was struck with a sudden spike of terror that he was about to do something absolutely uncivilized, like simply pull her into his arms and kiss her, right there in front of everyone.

The dark glimmer in his eyes suggested he might well be considering it, and while *intellectually* she absolutely detested the thought of a man stamping his possession on her in such a primitive display—really, it was only one step removed from a dog relieving itself on a lamppost to mark its territory—a small part of her still fluttered at the thrilling possessiveness of it.

"Brace yourself," Tess whispered wickedly from Daisy's right.

The three men stopped in front of them and bowed in unison. Justin took Tess's hand and pressed a kiss to the back of it.

"Good evening, my love. You look ravishing, as ever."

"Thank you," Tess murmured.

Harry stepped to Ellie's side and gave her waist a fond squeeze. "Hello, trouble. What shall we steal tonight?"

Ellie tapped him fondly on the knuckles with her fan. "Nothing, except a kiss."

He obliged with a kiss to her cheek.

Daisy barely heard their byplay. Lucien's broad chest had blocked out much of the room and the heady fragrance of the roses in the garland behind her mingled with his night-forest scent and made her heart pound. Blood rushed to her cheeks as he extended his black-gloved hand toward her.

"Miss Hamilton. Will you do me the honor of accepting my hand—"

A woman just to the left, clearly eavesdropping, gasped, and Lucien's lips twisted up in dark amusement.

"—for this dance," he finished drily, and Daisy quashed the urge to punch the wicked look from his face.

Oh, he was *loving* this.

She placed her fingers in his.

They matched. Her hands were encased in evening gloves that extended past her elbows, in an inky blue satin so dark they were almost as black as his own.

She sent him a serene smile. "I'd be delighted, Your Grace."

Every eye in the room followed them as they took their positions on the dance floor amongst the other couples, but Daisy's attention was focused on Lucien's hand as it settled at the small of her back, an inch lower than propriety demanded. She placed her left hand on his broad shoulder, and when he raised their joined right hands in readiness for the waltz, she looked up into his handsome face.

"I must admit, *A Midsummer Night's Dream* is the perfect theme for tonight," he said lazily. "Isn't it the one with all the young lovers running around the woods and making themselves ridiculous?"

Daisy bit back a smile. "It is."

"I'm amazed Perry isn't dressed as Bottom, the donkey."

"Oh, hush! He's your own nephew. You shouldn't go around calling him an ass."

He shrugged, and the muscles of his shoulder twitched under her palm. "If the shoe fits."

Violet and Perry were just to their left, also waiting for the music to start. Violet, in a gown of pale peach that would have made Daisy look as if she had jaundice, was the Fairy Queen Titania, complete with a glimmering tiara and tiny net fairy wings emerging from the back of her dress. Perry was equally handsome in a pale blue suit in the style of a French musketeer. They were gazing at each other, so clearly besotted and impervious to the rest of the world, that it made Daisy's heart clench. Had she ever been so starry-eyed? So naively sure that life was a fairy tale?

She didn't think so.

But she curved her lips up to answer Lucien. "It's easy to be cynical, but I think they're sweet. I hope they'll come to appreciate each other fully, when the first rush of infatuation fades."

"You *are* a romantic."

Heat scorched her cheeks at his gently mocking tone and she glanced away, unable to deny it or think of a clever response. Thankfully, the orchestra started playing the first bars of a waltz.

"Everyone's watching us," she muttered as they started to move.

"Of course they are. We make a striking couple."

Such typical arrogance made her look up at him again, and the twinkle in his eye bolstered her fighting spirit.

"That's not why. They're all waiting for a formal announcement. Half of them think we're secretly engaged, the other half think we've already married at Gretna, and *all* of them think I've succumbed to your wicked charms."

"They're all wrong," he said, amused. "It was me who succumbed to *your* wicked charms. You've compromised me shamelessly."

Daisy snorted. "My father wants us to marry as soon as possible."

"He does indeed."

"And he wants us to announce our engagement here, tonight." Her mouth was dry.

"Your father's wishes don't interest me in the slightest. What would *you* like to do? It's still your decision."

"How is it my decision if you've already requested a special license?" she hissed, careful to keep her voice low so they wouldn't be overheard. "My father said that's what you were doing."

His expression betrayed no hint of remorse at her accusing tone. "A special license just allows the couple listed on it to marry somewhere private, without the need for banns to be read. Having it doesn't mean you *have* to marry me. There's no obligation to use it. You can still say no."

Daisy narrowed her eyes at him. "Really?"

"Really. I can throw it on the fire, if you like, and to hell with the thirty pounds it cost me."

Daisy winced. Thirty pounds was more than most ordinary people earned in a year.

His lips curved in a smile at her obvious conflict. "The fact that you're even debating this makes me question you sanity. Stop looking so cross. Anyone would think you don't want to marry me."

Oh, the arrogance of the man!

"I *don't* want to marry you, you dolt. I want to be married to someone who actually likes me. Someone who cares for my opinion. Respects me. Values me."

Loves me.

She didn't say that out loud.

His brows rose. "When have I ever given the impression that I don't value you? Or respect you? Or like you?"

She opened her mouth to give an example, but struggled to think of one. Despite being the most aggravating companion, he'd never made her feel as though he didn't give weight to her thoughts, or considered her a lesser being.

"Perhaps you gleaned my *dis*like of you from the way I refused point-blank to make love with you?" he said drily. "The way I could barely stand to be in the same room as you. The way my cock didn't even twitch in your vicinity."

The heat in his eyes brought a flustered blush to her skin.

"Liking someone isn't the same as desiring them physically," she murmured. "You said it yourself. You don't need to be friends to . . . fornicate."

His lips quirked at her sudden modesty. "True. But don't you think we might be friends now, after all our adventures?"

"We're more like accomplices. Partners in crime. Besides, I don't see why you're so keen to marry me either."

"I would have thought it's obvious. Entertainment. If I marry you, I get someone to aggravate and torment on a daily basis."

His teasing was ridiculous. "You have your family for that. And Finch. And all your servants."

"It's not the same. You're far more amusing."

He guided them into a sweeping turn that made her pulse race, then glanced back down at her, his eyes glowing with devilry.

"You seem to be under the false impression that I'm harboring a crushing sense of guilt. I'm not. I'm not noble. I'm selfish and lazy, which is precisely why I told Perry to elope: to make my life easier. Marrying you will mean I won't have to go to all the bother of seducing other women or keeping a mistress. I'll save a fortune in jewels and furs. Not to mention the relief of not having to worry about contracting the pox."

"And you call *me* romantic," Daisy drawled. "I wonder if this is how Perry convinced Violet to run off with him? With such flowery words."

He grinned at her sarcasm. "The day I model my behavior on Peregrine is the day I take one of my Mantons and shoot myself in the head."

"*I* could be expensive," she threatened. "If I put my mind to it, I bet I could make a serious dent in your fortune."

"You're welcome to try, but for the record, I have an *obscene* amount of money. And the beauty of compound interest means that it just keeps on multiplying. I bet I've made enough to buy you a whole new outfit, and a diamond choker, just while we've been having this conversation."

Daisy rolled her eyes. Really, just because he was rich didn't mean she should cave on her principles. Even if a tiny voice in the back of her head told her to think of all the *good* she could do with his fortune at her disposal. She could set up all kinds of charities to help women in need, the ones who couldn't afford to pay King & Co. to take care of their problems.

"If you're worried that I'll forbid you to work for King and Company, let me put your mind at rest," he said. "I have no objection to it, provided you take reasonable precautions to keep yourself safe."

Daisy raised her brows. "Becoming your duchess will make me a more visible target. Just look what happened at Gretna."

"*Not* becoming my duchess will severely limit your ability to continue doing your job. If you're excluded from the *ton's* drawing rooms, you'll have to concentrate on the lower levels of society, which are generally in the more dangerous parts of town. You'll definitely be safer as my wife."

There was undeniable logic to that. Damn him.

The waltz ended in a triumphant chord and they swirled to a stop. He looked down at her, his expression inscrutable.

"So, what's it to be? Shall I start telling people we're engaged?"

What choice did she have? Marrying Vaughan was the only logical option, but every rebellious, self-protective part of her protested at having to agree when it was such a one-sided emotional commitment.

What was wrong with her? She was going to be his duchess, the envy of every woman in the *ton*. She should be glad she'd been given this chance, grateful that she wouldn't be ruined. But it felt like a hollow victory. He didn't *really* want to marry her. And making him fall in love with her suddenly felt like a gargantuan task, a feat far beyond her ability.

They were still standing in the middle of the dance floor, being watched by a hundred pairs of eyes. A lump formed in her throat, but she swallowed it down.

"Yes. Do it. Tell them we're engaged."

Something like triumph flared in his eyes, and he sent her that dazzling, arrogant smile she knew so well. "Would you like me to do it the boring way, or the scandalous way?"

"What do you mean?"

"Well, the boring way is to just mention it to someone like our host, with plenty of people within earshot, and the news will be around the room in less than five minutes."

"And the scandalous way?"

His eyes darkened. "I kiss you right here in front of everyone, and let them draw their own conclusions."

Daisy's gaze dropped to his lips, and for a terrible moment she actually considered it. But if he kissed her here it would be a sham, a calculated performance, and she didn't want that. If he was going to kiss her, she wanted it to be just for her. Because he wanted to.

He raised his brows in silent challenge, daring her to be outrageous, but she shook her head and for once in her life took the sensible path. "Just tell Lord Mansfield. Word will get around."

If he was disappointed at her choice he didn't show it. He nodded and turned to escort her from the dance floor, but a flurry of excitement by the main doors made them both look up.

Daisy caught a glimpse of Lord Mansfield's shocked expression, and Mr. Brand's cheeks pink with delight, a moment before a footman intoned, "Her Majesty, Queen Charlotte."

Chapter Forty-Five

Daisy's surprise at the Queen's unexpected arrival was echoed by everyone in the room, and a buzz of delighted chatter filled the air.

King George was still immensely popular, despite his regular bouts of illness, and his queen was similarly beloved. Many of her subjects admired her steadfast loyalty to her husband, and her stoic forbearance when it came to her extensive brood of scandal-ridden children.

Her Majesty accepted the deep bows and curtseys from those around her with a benevolent smile. It was impossible to tell whether she'd come in costume or not, since she regularly favored dresses embellished with all manner of gems and ribbons, but Daisy bit back a relieved smile as she watched Mr. Brand almost bend himself in two as he bowed and was introduced by Lord Mansfield.

He could have no complaint about the service provided by King & Co. *now*. The presence of royalty at his party would be the pinnacle of his most fervent hopes and dreams.

Instead of leading Daisy back to Tess and Ellie, Lucien guided her confidently over to the queen, and Daisy sent the older woman a friendly smile before she ducked into a deep curtsey.

"Miss Hamilton!" the queen said warmly. "How good to see you looking so well. And on the arm of such a handsome partner too." She sent Vaughan a pleased glance. "Your Grace."

Lucien bowed, and remained close to Daisy's side as the queen took a few steps away from their host. Two of her ladies engaged the men in conversation, which gave their mistress a moment with Daisy and Lucien alone.

"I have heard," the queen said, snapping open her fan and waving it languidly in front of her face, "the most *interesting* rumors concerning the two of you."

Her brows rose in a perfect arch and her eyes twinkled in a teasing way that belied her advanced age.

Daisy felt her cheeks heat. "Oh, really?"

The queen chuckled. "Oh, yes. Tales of scandalous elopements and even more scandalous engagements." She glanced over at Lucien, who raised his own brows in a playful, innocent expression, but said nothing.

"Knowing how few rumors have any basis in actual fact—and how certain society ladies are prone to exaggeration"—the queen sent a pointed glance over at Letty Richardson and her little flock, who were fluttering about on the opposite side of the room—"I thought it sensible to find out for myself."

She turned her inquisitive gaze back to Lucien. "The Archbishop of Canterbury likes to keep me abreast of all the special licenses he's dispensed. Imagine my surprise when he mentioned that *you*, Your Grace, had requested one."

Lucien's lips twitched as he fought not to laugh at her shameless prying. "That's correct, Your Majesty."

"In which case, should I infer that the rumor of the

two of you being already married at Gretna Green is false, but the one about you being *engaged* to be married is true?"

Lucien spoke up before Daisy could say anything. "Indeed, Your Majesty. Although we have yet to confirm anything publicly."

The queen clapped her hands in delight. "How wonderful!" She sent Daisy a maternal smile and lowered her voice to a throaty whisper. "Your secret is safe with me. Have you set a time and a place for your wedding?"

Daisy shook her head. "We have not. But a big, public affair at St. George's in Hanover Square has never held any appeal for me."

Lucien raised his brows. "I thought all females were supposed to have dreamed of their wedding day in vivid detail? The dress, the flowers, that sort of thing."

"The only thing I've dreamed of in vivid detail is the cake," Daisy said.

And the wedding night.

She could *not* say that in front of the queen.

The queen chuckled indulgently, clearly enjoying their candor. "Well, as long as you have that special license, the right number of witnesses, and someone to marry you, you can do it at any time and place of your choosing."

Lucien smiled, and the queen visibly melted under his wicked, teasing look, despite being old enough to be his mother. She clearly had a soft spot for a handsome rogue.

"Oh, I have everything under control, Your Majesty. Truth be told, I'm tempted to present everyone with a *fait accompli.*"

Daisy glanced up at him, desperate to know what he had planned, but the queen gave another chuckle. "In that case, let me wish you the happiest of unions, in advance."

Lucien swept her another elegant bow and took

Daisy's hand in his. "Thank you, Your Majesty. I look forward to introducing my new duchess to you very soon."

They took their leave, and Lucien guided her back toward the artificial bower where Tess and Ellie were waiting, their eyes wide with speculation.

Daisy's head was spinning. "Did you mean what you said to the queen about presenting everyone with a *fait accompli*?"

Lucien nodded. "As soon as we say we're engaged, we'll be inundated with questions, and I'm in no mood to deal with it tonight. We might as well just marry and announce that instead."

They reached Tess and Ellie. "Thank you for the dance, Miss Hamilton," he said, loud enough for the group of matrons who were hovering nearby to hear. He kissed the back of her hand, and she felt the heat of his lips through the satin of her glove. "Until we meet again."

He left, and Daisy quashed a ridiculous feeling of anticlimax.

"What's happening?" Tess demanded softly. "Has he proposed?"

"Not officially, but he told the queen we're engaged. We'll *have* to get married now."

"Do you want us to start telling people you're engaged?"

"Not tonight. I'm too tired." Daisy was keeping her expression perfectly serene for the benefit of those watching, but the strain of keeping up a carefree façade was making her feel like an automaton. "In fact, I think I'm going to go home."

Ellie glanced at Tess with a look of concern. "It's a little early to call it a night, isn't it? Why don't we just take a walk in the gardens to get some air?"

Daisy shook her head. "No. I need to clear my head."

"In that case, we'll drive back with you. You can't go on your own," Tess said firmly. Ellie nodded.

"Won't your husbands expect you to go home with them?" Daisy asked.

"Harry won't mind. He's been looking forward to fleecing everyone at the card tables all week." Ellie grinned. "Don't worry, I made him swear to play properly, without using any sneaky tactics. He says it's more satisfying if he wins fairly, without cheating."

Daisy laughed. Harry might be the Earl of Cobham, but he'd had a colorful past as a card sharp, pickpocket, and thief in his younger years.

"And Justin's keen to talk with Lord Mansfield about a new shipbuilding enterprise," Tess said. "He won't mind if I leave early."

Daisy slipped out of the ballroom and went to collect her things while Tess and Ellie went to tell the men what they were doing. A footman called for the coach they'd arrived in—one belonging to her father, with the Dalkeith crest on the door—and Daisy had the sudden wish to be getting into a coach with a golden lion painted on the door instead.

Tess and Ellie appeared soon after, and they all climbed inside while their boxes were stowed in the trunk at the rear of the carriage.

"I told Vaughan you were leaving," Tess said. "He was with Justin. He said to tell you he'd see you soon."

Daisy nodded, even as her stomach clenched in anticipation. Lucien wasn't a man who brooked delay. Did he already have the special license? Would she be his wife before the week was out? Would they be married in his house, in that same study where he'd kissed her so long ago?

Heat flashed over her skin. They had passion. Surely she could temper that into love?

The carriage set off with a jerk, and she stared sightlessly out the window as they bounced along the well-lit drive. They were the only ones leaving, despite it being after midnight.

Darkness descended as they left the gatehouse behind and started along the road toward London. A few stars twinkled in the clear sky above, mirroring the silver thread on her skirts, and she pulled off her satin gloves with a sigh.

Tess and Ellie were murmuring between themselves on the opposite bench, and Daisy allowed herself to fall into a pleasant reverie, with no thoughts in her head except watching the dark leaves of the trees as they passed by the window.

A sudden shout from the driver jolted her back to awareness, and she glanced over at Tess in alarm just as three horsemen galloped past the carriage, one on the left side and two on the right.

The carriage lurched to a stop.

"Stand and deliver!"

The bellowed command from outside made Daisy's mouth drop open in disbelief.

Not *again*.

"Oi! Stand aside!" the driver shouted back.

"I'm afraid I can't do that," the brigand said, and Daisy frowned at the hint of laughter in the man's voice. He sounded awfully familiar. Recognition came almost immediately, and she thrust open the carriage door and jumped down before she could think better of it.

Three mounted figures in dark clothing blocked the road, but it was the central one she fixed with a narrow-eyed glare. He was dressed in black, with a caped grea coat and a tricorn hat pulled low over his brow, and in the moonlight all she could see was the tip of his nose, his chin, and the stubborn line of his jaw.

It was more than enough. She'd know him anywhere.

"Lucien Vaughan! What in hell's name are you doing?"

Chapter Forty-Six

The brigand's lips opened to show a flash of white teeth and Daisy's heart began to pound in reckless anticipation.

Lucien—it was definitely him—dismounted from his midnight-black horse with the easy grace she'd come to recognize. He removed his hat and swept her an extravagant bow in the middle of the road.

"Well-met by moonlight, Miss Hamilton."

Daisy put her hands on her hips, and slanted a censorious look at his two fellow highwaymen, Justin and Harry, for their collaboration. Then she turned and glared up at the driver, and received a mocking tip of the hat from a grinning Finch up on the box.

So. A full-blown conspiracy.

"It's *ill* met by moonlight," she countered, just to be perverse. "If we're quoting from *A Midsummer Night's Dream*. And you, sir, are in danger of meeting the sharp end of my knife."

Behind her, she heard both Tess and Ellie giggle as they leaned out of the open carriage door and recognized the shadowy forms of their own husbands. All three men must have gone to the stables almost immediately after Tess told them they were leaving.

Lucien shook his head. "You're very argumentative for someone who's being held up by merciless highwaymen. You're supposed to be terrified. Cooperative. Compliant."

Daisy bit back a smile. "You've chosen the wrong target. I've crossed paths with highwaymen before, and I'm sorry to say it didn't end well for them."

"I'm shaking in my boots," Lucien drawled.

Daisy spread her hands wide, mocking his earlier bow. "My apologies. I'm sure you're a very competent footpad. What are your demands?"

His lips twitched at her pert answer. "The usual, of course. Your money or your life."

Daisy raised her brows, but her heart was beating against her ribs. "I don't have any money, I'm afraid. Not on me, at any rate." She held up her bare hands. "In fact, I don't even have any trinkets. Not even an engagement ring."

His teeth flashed at her pointed reminder. "That is disappointing. Ladies are expected to be dripping with jewels."

He took a step closer, deliciously menacing, and her breath caught as she inhaled his midnight-forest scent. He reached into the pocket of his greatcoat and withdrew a necklace that he held up before her. Icy diamonds and midnight-blue sapphires glittered in the moonlight.

"Perhaps this would do?"

She forced herself not to reach for it, even though it was breathtaking. "I take it back. You're a terrible highwayman. You're supposed to *take* my valuables, not give me yours."

He ignored her sarcasm and reached forward to fasten the ravishing thing around her throat. Daisy suppressed a shiver as his gloved fingers brushed her nape. The stones were cool and heavy against her skin, and she knew it would match her outfit to perfection.

"Much better," he said, stepping back. "But you're still missing something."

He reached into his pocket again and produced a ring, a sapphire surrounded by diamonds. He removed his gloves with his teeth, and Daisy's pulse gave a joyous little leap as he took her hand in his.

He slid the ring onto the fourth finger of her left hand, then tilted her chin up so she met his eyes.

"If you don't have any money, it will have to be your life. With me. By my side. As my wife." His fingers tightened before she could reply. "It has come to my attention that I haven't asked you to marry me."

"That's true," she managed breathlessly.

"You once told me that you'd only accept the proposal of a man who loved you."

"Also true."

"In that case," he said, "I should tell you that your 'experiment' back at Wansford was fatally flawed. If you want to know what it's like to sleep with someone who doesn't love you, you're going to have to find another man. Because I love you, Daisy Hamilton. Body and soul."

His greatcoat billowed around him as he sank to one knee in the road. "Will you marry me?"

Daisy's blood was rushing in her ears, hope and excitement throbbing in her chest, but she still held herself back. As much as she wanted to throw herself into his arms, he deserved complete honesty from her.

She reached out and touched his jaw. "I'm scared." Her voice was barely a whisper. "Scared you'll lose interest in me. Scared you'll stop loving me."

His eyes bored into hers, but a faint exasperated smile

lurked at the corner of his mouth. "Don't you think I'm scared of the same thing?" He took her left hand and laced their fingers together. "Everything's a risk, Daisy. One of us could be hit by a carriage tomorrow. Or get shot by highwaymen. *Not* starting something because you're afraid it might end one day is stupid."

He paused, probably realizing he'd just called the woman he was proposing to *stupid*, and tried a different tack.

"Think of all the things you'd miss out on between now and some unknown future end point if you didn't take a chance." He shook his head. "God, if we all knew how much time we had left, we'd live our lives completely differently. But we don't. We just have to stumble through each day and hope for the best. We have to make plans that might never come to fruition. But we'll do it together, and we'll enjoy whatever time we're given."

He turned his jaw and pressed a kiss to her palm, and her heart melted even more. She'd never imagined she'd see him on his knees before her, nor hear such words from his lips. If she was dreaming, she never wanted to wake up.

"I love you," he said again, his voice low and rough with emotion. "And if you don't love me now—which I can completely understand because I'm a bossy, selfish bastard—then I swear I'll spend the rest of my life trying to *earn* your love. I'll keep asking you, every week for the next fifty or so years. There's no expiry date on a special license."

Elation spread like a warm ball in her chest, and Daisy threw caution to the wind. "You don't need to keep asking me."

"You're saying yes?"

"Yes." She tugged him to his feet and wrapped her

arms around his neck. "I'll marry you. Because I love you too."

Relief and satisfaction flashed in his eyes. He bent down and picked her up so her face was level with his and kissed her, right there in the road.

Daisy closed her eyes and kissed him back with all the passion in her heart.

A cacophony of whistles, cheers, and applause broke them apart and she turned to grin at Tess and Ellie as Lucien lowered her reluctantly to the ground. She'd forgotten they had an audience.

"About bloody time!" Justin drawled, striding forward and clapping Lucien on the shoulder. "Congratulations."

Tess and Ellie leapt down from the coach and launched themselves at Daisy, enfolding her in a euphoric, sweetly scented hug.

"You're getting married!" Tess squealed, for all the world like the ten-year-old hellion who'd fallen out of Daisy's apple tree and not the socially revered duchess known to the *ton*.

"You're going to be a duchess!" Ellie laughed, squeezing Daisy's shoulders in delight. "I knew it!"

Daisy gently disengaged herself from their arms and glanced, blushing, at Lucien. She was almost too embarrassed to look at him, but he reached out, caught her wrist, and dragged her into his side.

"I hope you didn't have your heart set on a long engagement, because I happen to know there's a chapel in the grounds of Kenwood House, a special license signed by the Archbishop of Canterbury in my pocket, and a clergyman by the name of Reverend Morris who is ready and willing to marry us."

Daisy gaped up at him. "You had this all planned?"

His smile was every inch the arrogant scoundrel she

loved. "The chapel, yes. But not galloping after you on horseback like Dick Turpin. Tess and Ellie were supposed to bring you out into the gardens, to me, so I could propose there, but you decided to leave before they got the chance."

Daisy sent an open-mouthed look at her two best friends. "You knew?"

Tess grinned back from where she'd gone to stand by Justin. "We did. Lucien called on us a couple of days ago and asked us to decorate the chapel."

Ellie nodded. "I've made you the most beautiful bouquet of lilies and white roses."

Daisy shook her head in disbelief as Justin said, "Mrs. Ward has sent your favorite lemon cake down from Wansford."

"I suppose I shouldn't be surprised at the impressive levels of subterfuge from all five of you." Daisy sighed. She found Lucien's hand in the folds of his coat and took it. "Let's go."

Lucien's eyes were brimming with dark promise as he tugged her over to his horse. He released her only for as long as it took him to take the saddle, then he reached down and pulled her up to sit in front of him, astride, just as he'd done when he'd rescued her near Gretna.

Her full skirts billowed out on either side of the horse's neck, the little pearls flashing in the moonlight, but the handsome animal was evidently well trained, because it barely moved a muscle.

Daisy's stomach somersaulted as Lucien pulled her back against his chest and wrapped his arms around her. His lips brushed her ear.

"I didn't mean what I said about finding someone who *doesn't* love you to experiment on," he growled. "I won't share you with anyone. You're mine."

Daisy gripped the horse's mane and turned so her lips just brushed the corner of his own. His breath hitched in the most satisfying manner.

"Same goes for you, Your Grace," she whispered. "You're mine. Now and forever. And if you so much as look at another woman, you'll be getting another scar to add to your collection."

"Duly noted," he said, covering her mouth with his. His right hand slid down her thigh as he kissed her, deeply, hungrily, and Daisy smiled inwardly as he found the lump of her holster beneath her skirts. He rocked his hips against her bottom, and she squirmed against his gratifyingly hard erection.

"The fact that you'll be armed at our wedding should *not* make me so hard," he groaned, kissing her again. "But then, everything you do puts me in this state. You, Daisy Hamilton, are a bloody menace."

Someone—Harry—pointedly cleared his throat and Daisy suppressed a groan of her own at the interruption.

"God, you're as bad as Perry and Violet. If you two lovebirds wouldn't mind waiting until *after* the ceremony . . ." Harry grinned.

Finch had expertly turned the carriage in the narrow lane, so Ellie and Tess both climbed back inside.

"Back to the chapel, then," Finch announced to nobody in particular.

Ellie stuck her head out of the carriage window and sent Daisy a gleeful wave. "You know what I've just realized? That hermit at Vauxhall was right!"

"What hermit?" Lucien muttered.

Daisy suppressed a laugh. "Oh, nothing. Just a silly fortune-teller we met at Vauxhall Gardens years ago. He predicted I'd meet my match on a dark highway."

"And so you have," Lucien said. "Twice, in fact."

"Are you disappointed I'm not going to marry you wearing my breeches?" she teased.

His arms tightened around her as he urged the horse to follow the carriage. "I don't care what you wear, as long as you say I do. You're going to make a sensational duchess."

Chapter Forty-Seven

The Times, May 17, 1817.
 Married. At Kenwood Park, in the private chapel of the Earl of Mansfield, by the Rev. George Morris, Lucien William Devereaux Vaughan, 12th Duke of Cranford, and Lady Dorothea Georgiana Hamilton, daughter of the Duke of Dalkeith.

Cranford House, Mayfair.

Daisy glanced up from her seat behind Lucien's desk—the very desk that still made her blush whenever she remembered how she and Lucien had "christened" it the first week she'd come to live with him at Cranford House.

The sight of her husband still made her heart rate increase, especially when he lounged in the doorway in that elegant, slightly menacing way he had, and looked at her with that sleepy, possessive gaze.

He tilted his chin at the letter in her hand. "What's that?"

"A present from my mother. And a letter."

"What does it say?"

Daisy smiled. "Well, I wrote to her about our wedding, of course, and she's delighted. She sends her apologies that she and Lorenzo weren't here for the actual ceremony, but she invites us both to go and visit them in Naples at any time."

"Would you like to go? We can if you like."

Daisy's heart swelled with love. Lucien would give her the moon and the stars if she asked for them.

"It might be nice. I've always wanted to go on a grand tour. All three of my brothers went, at various times, and they all came back expounding on how beautiful and welcoming Italy was. I'm fairly sure they were talking about the women, not the architecture and culture, but I've always fancied going to see it for myself."

"In that case, we'll go. Your wish is my command, Your Grace."

Daisy shook her head with a wry smile. She still couldn't quite believe she was a duchess. Or that she was married to such a wicked, wonderful duke.

He pushed himself off the doorframe and started toward her. Daisy held up the other item she'd received.

"And she sent me this. A beautiful cameo brooch."

Lucien leaned over the desk to look. "Who's the woman?"

"It's Venus, I think. The Roman goddess of love. And that little cherub with a bow is Cupid."

"How romantic. Amorous, even."

"Indeed."

Lucien's lips curved upward and Daisy's skin tingled as his lazy gaze traveled over her face then dipped down, to linger on her breasts. She was wearing a new pale blue dress from Madame Lefèvre and she'd known the enticing cut of the bodice would drive him to distraction.

It was precisely the reason she'd bought it.

From his higher vantage point, he doubtless had an excellent view down her cleavage. And since she was quite as wicked as him—he really was a terrible influence— she deliberately leaned forward to give him a better look. She loved the way he looked at her.

Heat kindled in his gaze.

"What are you thinking?" she asked, trying to sound innocent and not at all like a woman who wanted her husband to do all manner of scandalous things to her.

"I'm thinking about inheritance. Legacies. That sort of thing."

Daisy blinked. She hadn't been expecting *that* response. But then she saw Lucien's eyes crinkle at the corners and his lips curve up and realized he was teasing.

"Oh? In what way?"

"Specifically, I'm thinking about this dukedom. Running it is no small feat."

"That's true," she agreed. "You make it look easy, but it's a tremendous amount of work."

"It is. I can't, in all conscience, let someone as peabrained as Perry become the next Duke of Cranford. I love the boy, but it would be *irresponsible* to let all this thinking and managing fall on him."

Daisy bit back a smile. "Practically a punishment," she agreed.

Lucien's eyes darkened in that hot and hungry way that made her stomach knot in wicked anticipation. His gaze fell to her lips.

"What do you think I should do?"

Daisy was fairly convinced she knew where this discussion was heading. "I'm no expert on inheritance law—you'd have to check with Ellie—but I think the only way to prevent him from succeeding you would be to produce a legitimate male heir of your own."

Lucien's brows quirked. "Hmm. I think you're right. And, since you're the duchess, and therefore the only one able to provide me with said legitimate heir, that would require your assistance." His eyes met hers again. "A joint collaboration, so to speak. Is that something you might consider?"

Daisy rounded the desk to stand in front of him. "Perhaps."

She slid her arms around his waist, but the teasing light faded from his eyes as he looked down at her.

"If you don't want children, Daisy, then we won't. It's your choice. I didn't marry you just to give me heirs." He lifted his hand and stroked her jaw. "I honestly don't care if Perry inherits. He can run the dukedom into the ground. Turn the great park at Carisbrooke Hall into a petting zoo."

Daisy bit back a chuckle. That was precisely the kind of hairbrained thing Perry *would* do. And Violet would probably convince him to dye all the sheep and swans on the estate pink, to match her outfits.

"That would be a shame. I have rather fond memories of Carisbrooke Hall. We should go back there soon. I want to sleep in your bed with you in it, this time."

She went up on tiptoe and pressed a soft kiss against his mouth. "I'd like to have children with you Lucien."

He made a soft growl of pleasure against her lips. "You would?"

She nodded. In truth, this wasn't something they'd ever discussed. On their wedding night, after they'd said their vows in the tiny candle-lit chapel in the grounds of Kenwood House, Daisy had changed into the shirt, breeches, and jacket that Tess had miraculously produced. Justin had gallantly lent her his horse, and Daisy and Lucien had galloped together back across Hampstead Heath and come here, to Cranford House.

Daisy had seen barely a glimpse of the lavish interior before Lucien swept her up into his arms, carried her up the stairs and into his bedroom, and stripped them both of their clothes in a passionate blur of limbs.

His urgency had made Daisy's heart sing with joy, and when he'd finally joined his body with hers, they'd both let out twin groans of relief. He'd taken her to the very peak of pleasure, but when he'd been about to withdraw to spend himself on the sheets, Daisy had vehemently protested.

She'd wrapped her arms and legs around him, stalling his movement.

"Don't leave me," she'd panted, half dazed with pleasure. "Inside. I want to feel you inside me. Finish it. Please, Lucien."

For a moment he'd stilled, as if afraid he'd misheard, and then he'd kissed her with such passion that she'd lost her breath.

"God, Daisy. Yes."

He'd pushed himself deep, finding his rhythm again, and the sound he made when his body released inside her had been music to her ears. She'd held him close through the aftershocks, loving the way his heart pounded against her chest, the way he whispered her name so reverently. She'd felt blissfully complete.

Daisy had assumed that Lucien would see her action for what it was: a willingness to risk becoming pregnant with his child. The thought of bearing him children was not something she viewed with dismay. Far from it. If it was meant to be, she would conceive, and be fiercely glad.

But he'd obviously thought she'd only allowed him to finish inside her because the timing meant she was unlikely to conceive. Plenty of women tried that method of contraception, although it was rather unreliable, from what she'd heard.

Or perhaps he'd thought she'd taken measures to prevent a pregnancy from taking hold? Either way, the fact that he was asking her opinion, instead of merely assuming his "husbandly rights" and forcing her to bear him children, as Dalkeith had done to her mother, made her immensely glad.

Daisy gazed up at him. He still looked serious, worried, and her heart cracked open a little more. He might call himself selfish and overbearing, but in every way that mattered, he was an excellent human being.

"I'd like to have children with you Lucien," she repeated softly. "I'd certainly like to try."

His expression softened as he kissed the tip of her nose, then the freckle on her left cheek. "I'd like that too. And it doesn't matter if none of them are boys. We could have a dozen girls, and I'd love them all, because they'd come from you."

"And you," she reminded him with a smile. "But let's not get ahead of ourselves. There's no guarantee it will even happen. It could take months of trying. Years, even." She gave him a gentle bite on the earlobe and felt him twitch in response "In fact, I think we should start trying right now."

Lucien sent her a mock-scandalized look. "We're due for dinner with Tess and Justin in less than an hour."

"I'm sure they won't mind if we're a few minutes late."

He pressed a kiss to the corner of her mouth. "We'll tell them we were held up by highwaymen."

Daisy chuckled. "In Mayfair?"

He shrugged. "You never know. Stranger things have happened. The crime in this city is getting worse by the day."

"Good news for King and Company. We'll never b
short of work."

"I can't believe you're thinking about business at a tim
like this. I'm clearly losing my touch. Now stop talking
and kiss me."

"Yes, Your Grace. With pleasure."